Spa

Spa

A Novel of Love in the Caribbean

GLYNNIS WALKER WRITING AS

Olivia De Grove

Copyright © 1988 by Olivia De Grove

Cover design by Kat JK Lee

ISBN: 978-1-5040-1399-4

Distributed in 2015 by Open Road Distribution
345 Hudson Street
New York, NY 10014
www.openroadmedia.com

To Anne Brooks,
who knows what's in a name.

Spa

PART ONE

The Guests

CHAPTER 1

Joyce

THE FOG FLOWED OVER THE BRIDGE IN THICK, sulphurous swirls, its vapors so dense that anyone crossing would have thought the observation turret in the middle of the center span was unoccupied. Then, suddenly, a chilling updraft from the river below sent the miasmal mass billowing out over the girders and into the darkness beyond and revealed a woman standing alone against the far railing.

She turned her head from side to side, peering into the darkness, as though she were waiting for someone or something to materialize out of the night.

After a few moments, her gaze fell on a young couple who had joined her on the deck. Sheltering from the night? Looking for a place to neck, more likely, she thought, and half-turned her back to them. But curiosity dragged her eyes sideways, and she continued to observe them.

They were standing close together, holding each other loosely with all the confidence of youthful possession, but another gust of wind made the girl shiver as its icy fingers reached up under the hem of her thin coat.

"Cold?" the boy asked, wrapping his arms more tightly around her.

She nodded and snuggled closer to him, burying her nose in the warmth of his neck. The lone woman turned her attention back to the other end of the bridge. Their cosy twosome suddenly made her feel uncomfortable, an intruder in her own space. She edged away as far as the railing would let her.

A moment later, the girl giggled and put up a hand in mock protest as the boy tried to kiss her. "Not here." She hooked a thumb in the direction of the woman. The boy nodded and, grabbing her hand, pulled the girl back out onto the bridge. They were immediately absorbed into the fog; only the tap-tapping of the girl's high-heeled shoes on the pavement and a sudden burst of shrill laughter gave evidence that they had ever been there at all.

The woman sighed and leaned over the railing, staring down into the mist, trying to see the river below. She could hear it rushing along, anxious to reach the sea, but its churning tide was obscured from view.

All at once, mixed with the sound of the rushing water as it gurgled and slapped against the fenders of the bridge, there was a new sound. She listened harder, trying to pinpoint the source, but the fog made the echo seem to come from more than one direction.

The thump-squeak, thump-squeak of awkward, uneven footsteps grew closer. A familiar dread crept over her. She turned, clutching the railing with one hand to steady herself, and waited.

Like a subway train rolling into a station, the suit of armor came to a halt a foot or two in front of her. With the grating whine of gnashing metal, it raised its left arm and pushed the visor up until it rested on top of the helmet.

A pair of tired brown eyes blinked in the orange glow of the sodium lamps. The woman gasped.

"Harry?"

"Joyce."

"What're you doing here, dressed like that?"

"You tell me."

"I . . . I . . . What's that?"

She was interrupted by the fog-thickened clanging of a bell.

"Big Ben, what else?" said the suit of armor, with a squeaking shrug.

The clock continued its mournful tolling as it marked the full hour. Five times it sounded, then six.

"Big Ben! In New York City?"

The suit of armor and Harry within began to fade like the Canter-ville Ghost . . .

. . . seven times, then eight . . . the clanging changed to a sharp, insis-tent ringing. . . .

Joyce Redmond reached out one arm and punched the digital alarm into silence.

Morning. She lay still for a moment, letting the dream recede, puz-zling over fragments of it as it fled from her rapidly returning con-sciousness. What the hell was all that about?

In a moment, the feelings of dread and surprise that had saturated the dream were gone. All that remained was the memory. She sat up and swung her legs out of the bed.

"These dreams are getting too weird. What was that one supposed to be, Brief Encounter meets Camelot? And what about Harry? Don't I see enough of him all day? Do I have to spend my nights with him, too?" And then she winced at the pun. "No more Chinese take-out from Wong's Delicatessen for me. I swear it."

She continued to mutter to herself as she felt around for her robe, found it at the foot of the bed and pulled it on, while her feet automati-cally sought out her slippers. But before she could get them on, Fredo came into the bedroom and began the morning ritual of persuasive purring which he hoped would culminate in the joyous sound of the can opener being applied with full force to a container of his favorite cat food. She pushed him away, stuffed her feet into the slippers, and started down the hall.

"Get out of the way, Fredo, before I trip over you." He was weav-ing in and out of her legs now, as she made her way groggily into the kitchen and turned on the cold-water tap.

But the sound of running water was not what he had been waiting for, and so he gently reminded her with another bout of purring and rubbing. She filled the coffee pot half-full and turned off the tap.

"I suppose you want to be fed, do you?"

"Meow," replied Fredo, in his best "Morris" voice.

"Alright. Hold on. I guess *I* won't get any peace until *you* get some breakfast."

She went to the cupboard that usually housed his supply of cat food and her supply of coffee and reached inside. Out came the can of Folger's. This was followed by a pause while her hand returned once more to the darkness and, as far as the cat could tell, groped around for the more essential of the cupboard's contents before coming away empty-handed.

"Sorry, cat. You're out of luck. I guess I forgot to pick up some more food for you last night." She shrugged. "That's what you get for moving in with a single woman."

She shut the cupboard door and picked up the Folger's. Fredo remained expectantly looking up at the counter. Joyce put the can of coffee back down.

"O.K. I guess I can't ignore that pitiful look." She picked up a cardboard carton from the counter and looked inside, wrinkling her nose at the sight of the contents. "There's some cold chow mein left over from last night, but I don't recommend it." She moved across to the far side of the kitchen. Fredo followed hopefully.

"I thought cats were supposed to be natural hunters, predators of the night. Why don't you go catch a mouse or something?" But Fredo only looked confused.

"No mice? How about some Tender Vittles, then? I think I've still got a few packs under the sink from when Amy foisted you on me last summer. Remember, before we established that your tastes were a little more gourmet than she had led me to believe?"

Joyce reached under the sink next to the garbage can and a box of odds and ends that had been put there when she moved into the apartment three years ago and were still waiting to be put away—wherever "away" was. She pulled out a red and yellow box marked "Beef Flavor." It still had one foil pack in it, which she tore open and dumped into the dish marked CAT that sat next to the empty margarine container serving as a water bowl.

"There you go. At least you won't be hungry until I get back tonight."

Fredo walked across the kitchen, took one sniff at the moist brown lumps in the dish, flicked the tip of his exquisite orange tail, and left the room with all the ceremonial cat pomp he could muster.

"That's fine. That's just fine. Go hungry, then. It's your choice," she shouted after him. But Fredo kept right on going, ignoring the undignified human outburst, and she pushed the kitchen door shut behind him.

"Look at me. I'm talking to a cat and, worse still, I'm talking to him as though he understands me."

Her mother's voice echoed in the back of her head: "You live alone too long, you go a little strange. What you need is a nice man, children, a life. . . . "

She told her mother's voice to shut up, and went back to the can of Folger's. But, even as she pried open the lid of the coffee can, her nose told her that it was empty. No smell of mocha java wafted upwards. No rattle of freshly roasted beans. Empty. No cat food. No coffee. Joyce vowed one more time that she had to do something about getting her life in order.

Without the excuse of coffee there was no reason not to get ready for work, and Joyce Redmond was a woman who liked to spend no more than fifteen minutes getting ready, no matter what the occasion—less, if possible.

Her usual routine consisted of showering, finding something to wear that didn't need to be ironed that morning, brushing her hair, and grabbing whatever shade of lipstick was nearest to the edge of the vanity. Today was no different.

She showered. Shaved her legs. Thought again about getting them waxed to save time, and then realized that she didn't have the time to book an appointment for waxing. Then she wrapped a big terry bath-sheet around herself and padded back into the bedroom.

Its pink and black color scheme, a leftover from the previous tenant—a Design major who was, by his own admission, "heavily into Deco"—always made her feel that she was going to work in the middle of the night. One of these days she was going to get around to painting it a nice, soft blue. One of these days.

She opened the closet to look for something to wear and, as usual, picked out whatever was easiest to reach. This time it was a grey cashmere dress she had paid a fortune for, five years ago, and which had worn well enough to be worth it. She pulled it over her head, found a pair of pantyhose with only a small run in the right foot, and then bent down to fish out a pair of black patent leather pumps. In two minutes she was dressed. She turned in front of the mirror, decided she looked alright, if not great, and went back to the bathroom to brush her hair and put on some lipstick.

Bending from the waist, she ran the brush through her long chestnut hair five or six times, and then stood up and fluffed it in place. Her hair had always been her best feature. She knew this, because other women always asked her where she got it done and didn't believe her when she said she didn't.

Next she reached for a tube of lipstick, and was just about to apply some, when she noticed an ugly red bulge forming beneath the skin of her lower lip. Right now it hid itself in the corner of her mouth, but by tomorrow it would be a full-fledged cold sore. Yuck! That meant she was run down—what else was new—and probably on her way to her usual spring bout with the flu. She dabbed a little alcohol on the spot, and then followed it with a shade called Raspberry Rhapsody—where did they get these names from?—and made it out the door in fourteen minutes and twenty-eight seconds.

CHAPTER 2

Cathy

CATHY STEWART, Mrs. Michael Stewart, Mommy, slipped quietly out of bed at six-fifteen. She didn't turn on the lights or open the drapes, so that she wouldn't run the risk of waking her husband before seven. By then she would have the coffee made, his breakfast ready, and the children up.

In the early morning dimness she groped around for her jeans and one of Michael's old sweat shirts that she had put on the chair beside the bed the night before. And then, careful not to make any noise, she tip-toed out into the hallway to get dressed.

First she pulled her cotton flannel nightie over her head, and then followed the reverse path with the sweat shirt, which was equally soft and worn and comfortable and hid the bulge occupying the place, where, a few short years ago, her waist had been. Then came the jeans which were neither soft nor comfortable, and which, even though they were size sixteen, did nothing to disguise the rapidly inflating condition of either her rear end or her thighs. She sighed. Everything she owned was tight on her, even the jeans that had taken her through both pregnancies.

She held her breath and sucked in her stomach as she tried to do up the zipper. It wouldn't budge beyond the first half-inch. She tried again. No luck. She exhaled and then inhaled even more. In the end she had to resort to pulling the material on either side together and closing it inch by inch with little zipper victories, until finally the deed was done. She exhaled in relief, hoped that she would not pop the fastener at the top of the zipper, and started down the stairs.

The swish-swish of the denim made her stop halfway down. Her thighs were beating out a symphony of fat as they rubbed together. What had happened to Cathy the model, Cathy the sylph, Cathy the 110 pounds distributed sparingly over a 5'7" frame? Motherhood had happened . . . and peanut butter, and Oreos and candy and boredom and. . . . She refused to finish the thought.

In the kitchen she pulled a container of fresh orange juice out of the refrigerator—Michael insisted he would tolerate no substitutes— and poured his glass and then three smaller ones for the twins and Joey. She thought about pouring one for herself, decided that 100 calories was too much to use up on mere juice, and put the container back in the fridge.

Next she poured cereal into the children's bowls and started to make waffles for Michael, from scratch. With the batter made and the waffle iron heating up, she turned her attention to the coffee. And then finally she made Joey's lunch.

It was his first year of all-day school and lunch was now required. This morning it was tuna salad on whole wheat, an apple, and a Twinkie. There were a couple of spoonfuls of tuna left in the bowl so, rather than throw it out, Cathy ate it before putting the bowl into the dishwasher. Then she licked the remaining Twinkie cream off her fingers. It was now a quarter to seven. She went upstairs to wake the children and Michael.

Swish-swish down the hall. Into the twin's room. Then into Joey's room across the hall and swish-swish back into the master bedroom.

Michael was already awake.

"Good morning, Michael. Sleep well?" She leaned over and kissed him on the forehead. He made as if he were going to pull her into bed and she laughed and resisted, but he had caught her off-balance and she collapsed on top of him. His OOOFFF! was audible. He rolled her off of him and slapped her on the behind.

"How's my Big Mama this morning?"

"Michael, please don't call me that. You know I don't like it." She tried hard to keep the edge out of her voice and rolled over until she hit the far side of the bed and then, denim creaking with the strain, she pushed herself to her feet.

"Sorry, Cathy. I guess I still think of you as pregnant. It's only been a couple of years since the twins were born and. . . ."

"And I weigh more now than I did then."

"I didn't say that, Cath. I didn't mean that I think you're fat, just big. Anyway, what difference does it make? I don't mind you that way."

"But I do." A sudden thump-crash from across the hall caught her attention. "Let's drop the subject, shall we? Breakfast is ready and I can hear Joey destroying the bathroom."

An hour later, Michael had left for the agency, the school bus had picked up Joey and his lunch, and Cathy was sitting in the kitchen looking out at the back yard. Spring was definitely on its way. The crocuses were up a couple of inches, all the snow had melted, and the daffodils along the sheltered side of the house were already tipped with yellow.

She sighed. Spring. Could summer be far behind? And summer meant only one thing. Bathing suits. She slowly sipped her coffee. It took her a long time to drink one cup, now that she took it without either cream or sugar. But black coffee had no calories, and these days the absence of calories was the definitive consideration. Today she was going to start her diet—again.

The twins, who had been busy playing quietly in their playpen, suddenly erupted into baby pandemonium. She put the coffee down.

"Jeffrey, stop that. Don't pull Jennifer's hair." Jeffrey, surprised by his mother's sudden intervention, let go of his fistful of golden curls and watched as Cathy scooped up the still-screaming Jennifer.

"There, there, Jen-Jen. It's alright, Mommy's here, Mommy's here." She rocked the little girl back and forth and the screaming abated as Jennifer nestled against her mother's expansive bosom and her thumb found her mouth. She was satisfied and smug.

But Jeffrey, watching from the playpen, soon realized he was missing out on something. Mother-cuddles were not as frequent as he would have liked, because he had to share them, not only with his sister but with Joey too. His face began to crumple, and five seconds later he let out a wail that could be heard three houses away.

"O.K. O.K., Jeffy, I get your message. A little sibling rivalry going on here." Cathy slipped Jennifer back into the playpen and picked up the alarmingly red-faced Jeffrey. She began her rocking motions again and a big, fat, baby tear slid down his face and onto her sweat shirt. She kissed the top of his silky blond head and held him against her.

But there was to be no peace. Jennifer, finding that her place had been usurped, began her own feminine version of Jeffrey's wail. So Cathy scooped her up in her other arm and sat down again at the breakfast table. She placed them on her lap so that one was sitting on each cushiony thigh—at least they were good for something—and, with an arm round each tiny waist, she stared at the rapidly cooling coffee which was now out of reach.

Later that morning, while the twins were having a nap, Cathy had a good look in the mirror and decided that, fat or no fat, she had to buy something that fit. There was no point in being uncomfortable, and the jeans were seriously becoming that. She already had chafe marks on the backs of her knees and around her waist. So, the only sensible thing to do was to go shopping and find something that fit. Besides, it wasn't forever, only until her diet kicked in. She had weighed herself twice since breakfast, and had already lost half a pound. It was only a matter of time.

Cathy gave herself another five minutes of this pep talk and then went to wake up the twins. She was going shopping.

CHAPTER 3

DESTINY MAGAZINE OCCUPIED the twelfth floor of the Condé Nast building. It shared its prestigious Madison Avenue location with the likes of *Glamour* and *Mademoiselle*, two other women's magazines which Joyce liked to think of, not as The Competition, but more as The Prelude. As far as she was concerned, as soon as girls became women and women became adults, they were supposed to switch from the fashion and beauty rags to something with a little more meat. And *Destiny* was a magazine with meat. It was, as she had only recently observed to Fredo, what *Esquire* would have been, if it had been a woman's magazine. In other words, in the eyes of the magazine-buying public, it fell somewhere between *Ms.* and *Cosmopolitan*

As senior editor, Joyce was listed second on the masthead, right beneath the executive managing editor, Harry Kraft. But though her title may have looked impressive and was some kind of solace to her mother who at least had *something* to show her friends when they trotted out the latest pictures of the grandchildren, it didn't carry much weight. Harry Kraft was the only boss, the last word, the head honcho, and the reigning point of view. And he controlled his *Destiny* accordingly.

Joyce wasn't too surprised, therefore, to see an URGENT!!!!!! memo taped to her door when she got in. The exclamation points were Harry's little way of letting you know that he really thought it was urgent and that he had not just succumbed to the gratuitous use of an over-used word.

She pulled the taped message off the door and, crumbling it into a small pink paper ball, flipped it into the garbage can beside her desk. Then she opened the bottom drawer which had a lock on it that had been broken ever since she had moved into the office nine years ago, and threw in her purse and her scarf. Next, she picked up the phone and dialed her assistant, Michelle.

"Coffee."

"You're in? Did you know that Harry's been puffing and panting for the last half-hour waiting for you? He's built up a real head of steam. Says he's got to see you right away. It's. . . ."

"I know—URGENT!!!!!! First the coffee, then I'll deal with Harry."

"It's your funeral."

Joyce sat down and opened her appointment book.

Today she had two interviews and a lunch. The first interview was with a woman who was running for Congress, raising five children, and teaching at her local college, and who wanted to talk about how to have it all and still be a good wife, and perhaps garner a few extra votes for her efforts. Joyce had read over her material the night before, became tired just thinking about the woman's "average" day, and decided that the secret to having it all was simple. You gave up sleep.

Next there was lunch at Jake's with a new literary wonder from the Midwest who had made it to the top of the *New York Times* bestseller list by writing about life in his hometown—someplace called Culpepper, Kansas—which had, of course, touched numerous deep chords in everyone who had never visited there or lived in a small town in Kansas. In short, the entire literary intelligentsia.

And, in the afternoon, she had scheduled a two-hour session with a tennis pro who was renowned for both her backhand and her bankbook, and who rarely gave interviews. Joyce felt she had made a real coup on this one, and was already well into planning her piece.

Mixed in with this was the usual day-to-day stuff that went into creating, on schedule, an original and hopefully buyable, 200-page, four-color magazine by the first of every month, no excuses accepted.

In addition, she also had two in-house meetings. One with the art department and one with her own staff to discuss the August issue, even though it was only March. And now Harry and his URGENT!!!!!!

Michelle arrived a few minutes later with a large mug of coffee—no styrofoam cups at *Destiny*—two sugars, one cream, and the message that Harry was aware that Joyce was in and wondered if she knew what the word URGENT!!!!!! meant.

"Tell him I'm just looking it up now."

Michelle started for the door, but Joyce stopped her.

"Michelle, do you ever have weird dreams?"

"Weird dreams? How weird?" asked Michelle cautiously.

"Not really *weird*. Just. . . . Look, last night I had this dream, alright. It was kind of like that old movie, you know, 'Waterloo Bridge'?"

Michelle nodded.

"Well, it was like that, except that there was this suit of armor, and Harry was . . . oh, never mind." It sounded more silly than weird, now that she was trying to tell it to someone else.

"You dreamed about Harry? Must have been a nightmare. Maybe it was something you ate. My mother always says, if you eat cheese before you go to bed, it'll give you nightmares."

"It was Chinese food."

"I guess Chinese could do it, too." Michelle paused by the door. You know, I have this cousin who used to dream about being in the Olympics."

"The Olympics?"

"Hmmm-mmm. She kept having this same dream over and over about winning the 500-metre race, until finally she went to a shrink to find out what it meant."

"What did he say?"

"He said that it was probably her subconscious mind telling her she needed to get more exercise."

"More exercise? What did she do?"

"She joined a fitness club and the dreams stopped, so I guess either the shrink was right, or she was too tired after working out to dream anymore." Michelle shrugged and opened the door. "Don't forget about Harry."

"O.K. O.K. I'm going. But I'm taking my coffee with me." Joyce picked up the white mug with the shocking-pink *Destiny* logo splashed across one side, avoided spilling some on her dress by mere millimetres, and made her way to the corner suite, complete with shower and bar, that was Harry's home away from home—literally.

When she got there, Trixie, his secretary, placed one index finger over her well-proportioned lips, went "SSSSHHHHHH," and motioned in the direction of Harry's inner sanctum. It was evident that Trixie didn't want any pre-emptive interruptions in her eavesdropping. But the "Sshhh" was completely unnecessary. Even if a brass band had been playing in the reception area, Harry's voice would have transcended its music.

"Whaddaya mean you want more money!"

"He's on the phone." She mimicked holding a phone to her ear.

"No kidding." Joyce sat down and sipped her coffee. Harry's voice grew louder. She wondered if his face had started to turn purple yet.

"A vacation! What do you need a vacation from—shopping?"

"It's Maxine." Trixie's voice was just above a whisper, and she nodded as she spoke and raised one eyebrow.

Joyce nodded back. Everybody at *Destiny* knew about Harry and Maxine, thanks in part to Trixie, who felt it was her duty to keep all employees informed of essential company news.

"What's up?"

"The usual, money and Bradley."

"Again?" Bradley was Harry and Maxine's son. Maxine had been holding Bradley over their relationship for years, refusing to divorce until her baby was old enough to understand. Baby was now twenty-two and Maxine still showed no signs of giving up the ghost of their marriage. Joyce had to admit she felt sorry for Harry. He could be a tyrant at times, but he really wasn't a bad guy. There were times when she almost liked him. Times when. . . . Suddenly, the shouting stopped and the phone could be heard being slammed down into its cradle. Joyce counted to herself.

"One . . . two . . . three. . . ."

The door to Harry's office flew open.

"Where the hell have you been? Didn't you get my message? When I say 'URGENT!!!!!!', I mean 'URGENT!!!!!!'"

Harry's face was only red, not purple. It gave him a healthy, outdoor look and Joyce reflected, not for the first time, that, unlike most women, a lot of men got better-looking as they got older. In Harry's case, his weight had finally caught up with his height, making him look even larger and more threatening than when he had hired her, but also more attractive. If you could call a grizzly bear on the rampage attractive. He stood in the doorway clenching and unclenching his fists.

"Good morning. Harry." Joyce stood up. "I understand you wanted to talk to me." Trixie suppressed a smile, and Joyce followed the still-steaming Harry into his office.

"Sit down." He waved an arm in the direction of the chair opposite his desk.

Joyce sat on the couch and crossed her legs. Harry was pacing up and down muttering to himself, running his hand through the thinning top of his hair. Joyce waited for him to get to the point and, while she waited, she flicked the tip of her tongue over the cold sore. It felt like it was getting bigger. Stress, probably.

"How come you always sit on the couch?" Harry stopped pacing and turned to face her. She noticed he was wearing the same suit and the same shirt he had been wearing the day before. If it had been anybody else she would have guessed a one-night stand but, in Harry's case, she knew that it meant he had slept in his office again.

"I like the couch, Harry. It's not so formal. Besides, if I'm going to get hauled over the coals for something, I'd rather be comfortable."

"Who said anything about hauling you over the coals? You done something I should know about but don't?" Harry sat down behind his desk and lit up a cigarette.

"No. But I counted the exclamation points after your URGENT. Six means it's something big, right?"

"Cute, Joycee, very cute. But, as it happens, this time you're right. Except it's not about something you've done. It's about something you're going to do. I got a story for you that I want done ASAP. It's got to go to bed with the May issue. I can hold the space, but I need the story researched and written in two weeks. Understand?

"I understand. I've got that piece on the tennis player skedded for the May issue. It'll be a squeeze, but I only got the go-ahead for the interview yesterday. It's tight, but I can do it.

"Cut it."

"Cut it! What for? She's news, Harry. Everybody's been after an exclusive with her."

"What's news about some dyke tennis player who couldn't even get to Wimbledon last year? She's history. Besides, spring is self-improvement time. Everybody wants to get themselves straightened out. That's why I want this piece in the May issue."

"What piece? Aren't you going to tell me what it's about before I tell you it's impossible?"

"Don't be smartass. If I thought it was impossible, I wouldn't ask you. But because I am asking you and not somebody else means I know you can do it."

"Thanks for the vote of confidence, Harry. Now, how about telling me just what it is that you think I can do."

"You know what a spa is?"

"A spa? Of course I know what a spa is. It's one of those ritzy places that rich, bored women go to, to lose weight and look younger. If that's what you're thinking of for a story, Harry, forget it. It's been done, lots of times . . . La Costa, The Golden Door, Main Chance. Besides. . . ."

The telephone rang. Harry grabbed the receiver. "Yeah? . . . Who is it? . . . Mrs. Kraft? My sister-in-law? . . . Maxine! Tell her I don't want to talk to her, and if she calls again tell her I died or tell her whatever you like. Just keep her off my phone." He slammed the receiver down again. Joyce wondered how many telephones he went through in a year. They didn't make them like they used to.

"Not the way I'm gonna do it, or rather the way you're gonna do it." He picked up the thread of his idea without missing a beat. "What I want you to do is go and stay at this new spa they just opened in the Caribbean and write me a real gut-wrenching, in-depth, investigative piece about the women who go there. You know the kind of stuff I like. Get right down to the nitty gritty. Why are they there? What do they think it's gonna do for them? Are they hiding from something? Afraid of something? Do they really think it can stop them from getting old? You know, get into the psychology of it. I want a piece that tells me all the details of their desperate struggle to ward off old age. The tyranny of the beauty industry feeding off the paranoia of an aging society. That kind of thing. You get my drift?

"Yes, Harry, I get it, and I don't like it one damned bit. This is something for Paula to do. She's the fashion and beauty editor. This is her territory, not mine. Or get Naomi. You can treat it as a food piece."

He shook his head. "Naomi is still on maternity leave."

Joyce searched for another angle, any other angle. She really didn't want to get caught up in this piece of fluff. It offended her impression of herself as a serious journalist. "But Harry, I covered Geneva, remember? I was in the Philippines getting the goods on Imelda Marcos just before Ferdy got the boot. I interviewed Margaret Thatcher—for six hours! This spa thing is too light-weight for me, Harry. It's not my style at all. . . . And I've got to tell you I think you're reaching. A spa is a spa. You exercise. You eat veggies for a week, lose six pounds, come home and revert to your old self again. Big deal. . . ." She shrugged, palms up, to show the meagreness of the idea. "Besides, I've got a full calendar for the next six weeks. I can't go anywhere."

"You did a terrific job on that Thatcher piece, and your exposé of Imelda Marcos as the real power was great. But. . . ." He was trying the old schmooze play, and they both knew it.

"That's why I want you on this, Joyce. You are the only one on this goddamn magazine that really writes. You know what I mean? I don't want all that cutesy-pie shit about what goes in the facial masks and how many times you have to do situps before you get a tight ass. I want the real stuff. I want to 'feel' it." He put five or six extra e's into the word "feel." "The human element, Joyce, that's the key. It's people, Joyce, their fears, their joys. That's what makes *Destiny* what it is. Anyway, who knows, you might run into a few celebs, get a little inside dirt. . . ."

"You fake. So that's it. . . ."

Harry ignored her, and continued. "Oh, and I think it would be better if the other guests didn't know you were writing about this. So make up something else about what you do. You know, tell them you've got a husband who's got money. Whatever you like; just make it sound convincing." He opened his desk drawer and pulled out a sheet of paper.

"Here's your itinerary. And a cheque to cover your expenses. Don't go wild on the spending, Joyce. Remember, you're not the wealthy. You're just there to write about the wealthy."

Joyce took the paper and glanced over it. Her hands were trembling. Where did he get off sending her on this hare brained assignment? The "human element," my ass. He didn't want to know about the human element; he just wanted some gossipy *National Enquirer* piece to boost his circulation and keep the advertisers happy. Whatever happened to journalistic integrity? Well, he could just get somebody else. She was going to tell him a thing or two, and then. . . .

"Your flight leaves next Saturday morning at nine." He handed her the tickets. "B.W.I.A. direct to Barbados. You can catch an island hopper to St. Christophe from there."

Joyce took the tickets. "St. Christophe?"

"It's an island. The spa is the only thing on the island. That's why they call it 'The Spa at St. Christophe.'" He said it with exaggerated patience. "I expect to see you two weeks from today with the completed story."

Harry got up and came around from behind the desk and looped a fatherly arm around her shoulders. "You'll enjoy yourself. Think of it as a working vacation, that's all. You look like you could use a tune-up. Got a little cold sore there, I see." He smiled. His anger had receded. He looked pleased with himself.

"Thanks, Harry. Your concern overwhelms me." She ran her tongue over the offending spot one more time.

"You know I always have your best interests at heart, Joyce."

"What can I say?"

"How about 'goodbye'? I've got another meeting, five minutes ago."

He walked her toward the door. She caught a whiff of his cologne. What was that? "Brut"? It seemed appropriate.

Still clutching her tickets and her expense check, she hesitated and turned to face him. If she was going to stand up to him, now was the time. All she had to do was say, "No. I'm not going." It was that simple.

"Well, have a good trip. I know you'll do a great job." And she was back in the waiting room staring at the closing door.

"Harry. Wait."

"Yeah, what is it?"

"I. . . . Goodbye, Harry."

"Goodbye, Joyce."

CHAPTER 4

Cliff

CLIFF EASTMAN WAS WAITING for the telephone to ring. He had been waiting since yesterday afternoon, and it was past the point where he could ignore its smug silence any longer.

Last night and this morning he had passed the time reading from the stack of scripts that forever seemed to be piled by his chair and on his desk. None of them were any good—at least not for him. He had thrown the last one across the room in utter disgust. It was absolute bullshit, and would probably be a big hit.

Now he sat by the pool, a portable phone and a large vodka and tonic on the wicker table beside his chaise lounge. He sipped the drink. Put it down. Stared at the telephone, remembered that a watched pot never boils, or whatever idiotic saying was supposed to explain moments such as this, and then sipped his drink again.

Why didn't Alvin call? Why hadn't he called yesterday? Was it a case of no news is good news? Or, was the news so bad he couldn't bring himself to make the call? What kind of an agent was he, anyway? Didn't he know that Cliff's whole career was hanging in the balance? Cliff knew he had a chance to be box office again if he got this part. Otherwise, it would be a gradual downhill slide until he ended up on some fatuous TV sitcom playing father to some obnoxious ethnic brat who earned more money than he did. . . .

The telephone rang. He grabbed the receiver.

"Hello, Alvin?"

"No, Cliff, it's Marty. Just wanted to know if you were going to come to that little soiree we're throwing for Paul tonight. It's his last night before going back East. You know he got that part in 'Two For The Road'?"

"No, I didn't know."

"Yes. Isn't it exciting? He's replacing Tommy Tune."

"Great." Cliff drained the last of his drink and chewed noisily on a mouthful of ice. Other people's success was not what he needed to hear about right at this moment.

"Well, are you going to come? You know Anne and I would love to see you." He paused. "Amanda's going to be here."

"Who cares." He spit the remaining ice back in the glass.

"I thought you two were an item."

"Yeah, well, as the world turns. Amanda got what she wanted from me—and I don't mean the pleasure of my company. She got that part on "Dynasty," and all of a sudden it's 'So long, been good to know you.' You know what I mean?"

"Sure, Cliff. I know what you mean."

"Still, it's her loss, right?"

"Right, Cliff. Look, about tonight?"

"I'll give it some thought, O.K., Marty? I'm just waiting for a call from Alvin. This could be the big one. I've got to hang around the phone until I hear from him. But, if it gets settled early, I'll probably come over later."

"O.K. Cliff. See you."

"Yeah, see ya, Marty."

Cliff got up and went back into the house—the house that used to belong to Elvis—the house that had cost him pretty well every cent he had earned from "Darkness Before the Dawn." But then Belladgio Road was one of the most prestigious addresses in Bel-Air. And, if nothing else, a star had to be conscious of giving out the right image, especially if he was a fading star. Let them know you were anything but successful and they would eat you alive in this town.

He took a fresh glass out of the kitchen cupboard, threw in a handful of crushed ice from the ice bucket, followed that with a healthy slug of Silent Sam, squeezed half a lime into the mixture, thought about adding some tonic and didn't. Then he went back outside.

The heat was still searing, and the air had taken on the thick murkiness that settles on southern California when the wind doesn't come along to blow the crud over the mountains.

He looked out over the city. It was after three now, and a purple haze had begun to form that would, in a couple more hours, turn into one of L.A.'s famous sunsets—great to look at, but bad for your health. Just like Amanda, he decided, as he sat down on the edge of the lounge chair and then stood up again right away. In his absence the yellow-and-blue-striped pad had become white-hot. He dragged the chair and then the table into the shade, placed a towel over the cushion, and sat down again to wait.

Fifteen minutes later, he couldn't stand it any more. He picked up the phone and dialed Alvin's number.

"Celebrity Management Group. Good afternoon."

"I'd like to speak to Mr. Minter, please. This is Mr. Eastman calling."

"I'm sorry, Mr. Eastman, Mr. Minter is taking a meeting. Would you like to leave a message?"

"Yes, I would. Tell him I called and it's important that I speak to him this afternoon. He can reach me at home."

"I'll tell him as soon as he comes out of the meeting, Mr. Eastman."

Cliff hung up the phone and drummed his fingers on the table. All he could do now was wait. And he hated waiting. It made him feel so helpless. He took another long swallow of the vodka and lay back in the chair, his eyes closed against the smog. His mind was busy plotting.

" . . . If I get this part, I'm going to demand 5 percent of the gross, and I want at least five million. At least. This picture is going to go right through the roof. I can feel it. They'll probably open in at least 400 houses nationwide. And then of course there's the foreign distribution to consider—they love me in France and Germany—and we've got to get it into the theatres in time for the Academy Awards nomination deadline. We're talking Oscar-time, here. . . ."

He must have dozed off, because, when he opened his eyes and looked at his watch, it was four o'clock. Why the hell hadn't Alvin called? He picked up the phone again and dialed CMG.

"Celebrity Management Group. Good afternoon."

"Hello. It's Mr. Eastman again. Is Mr. Minter still in that meeting?"

"No, sir. I'm afraid Mr. Minter has left for the day."

"Left for the day! Didn't you give him my message? Didn't you tell him I *have* to talk to him this afternoon?"

"Yes, sir. I did."

"And he's left for the day?"

"Yes, sir. Would you like to leave another message, Mr. Eastman?"

"No . . . I . . . Yes, I would. Tell Mr. Minter that if he can't return my calls, I can always go to another agency." He slammed down the phone.

"Goddamn agents. When they smell money they're all over you. Go into a little slump and they treat you like the plague."

The ice had melted into the vodka, but Cliff picked up the glass and drank down the warm, diluted mixture in one gulp. Then he got up and went into the house to make another drink.

He had just reached the kitchen when the doorbell rang.

"Miguel, will you get that?" There was no answer. The doorbell rang again.

"Miguelllll. Bloody houseboy's never around when you need him." Cliff went through the kitchen and down the black-and-white-tiled hallway to the front of the house. He reached the door at the same time as Miguel, who came skidding down the other hallway, which led to his room over the garage.

"Been having a little nap again, have we?" Miguel started to protest. "No, Señor Eastman. . . ."

"Forget it. Just remember one thing. I can always tell the Immigration people about your phony 'green card'. Now do *you* want to get the door, or do you want to watch while I get it?"

Miguel, blanching at the mention of Immigration, moved to open the door. On the portico, framed by the bougainvillaea which rioted in purple confusion all around the entrance, stood Alvin, clutching his briefcase.

"Hiya, Cliffy."

"Well, if it isn't my long-lost agent. Come in, Alvin. I take it the news stinks, since you wouldn't answer my calls and now you've come here to plunge the knife into my heart in person."

Alvin Minter stepped into the hallway and Miguel closed the door behind him.

"Cliff, are you drunk?"

"Not yet. But I'm working on it. You want one?" He held up his empty glass.

Alvin shook his head. "No thanks. It's too early for me. Maybe a beer, though. It sure is hot outside."

"Well, enjoy it, Alvin. The weather's the closest you're going to get to hot around here. Isn't that right?"

"Now Cliff, don't get all bitter and twisted on me. It's just. . . ."

"Wait a minute. Let's not discuss my failures in front of the help."

"Miguel, una cerveza, por favor, and fill this up with vodka and a little ice. Don't forget to squeeze the lime."

Miguel took the glass and disappeared in the direction of the kitchen.

"You wanna do this inside or out?"

"In. The smog's making my eyes water."

They went into Cliff's oak-panelled library. It was dark and quiet. A place for retreat.

Cliff lay down on the couch and closed his eyes. The leather was refreshingly cool. Alvin took the matching dark-green leather wing chair. They waited in silence until Miguel had come and gone.

"O.K. Cliff. I guess it's pretty obvious. You didn't get the part."

"Who did?"

Alvin didn't answer. He sipped at his beer. Picked at one of the brass studs on the arm of the chair.

Cliff opened his eyes and sat up. "Look Alvin, I think I'm entitled to know who is going to be replacing me in the hearts and minds of the movie-going public. So tell me, who got the part?"

"You really want to know?"

"I really, really want to know. I really want to know with sugar on it. Do I have to say 'May I' as well?"

"O.K. Cliff. Don't get testy. Pierce Brosnan got the part."

"Pierce Brosnan! Pierce bloody Brosnan got *my* part?" Cliff was standing up now.

"You've got to admit he's right for it. He's a little young, maybe, but they can make him look more mature. A little grey at the temples . . . a few lines around the eyes. . . ."

"A little grey at the temples! A few lines around the eyes! I've got a little grey at the temples. I've got lines around the eyes." He squinched up his eyes to make the point. "I look mature! I am perfect for that part."

"I know, Cliff, I know. I told them that. And Goldman agreed with me. He really did. Said he'd always loved your movies, even when he was a kid. He thought you'd be perfect for the part of Rory. But Glick disagreed, and you know he's the one who really runs the show." Alvin had begun to fidget in his wing chair. Cliff was pacing.

"Glick disagreed, eh? Did he say why? Is it maybe something to do with my personal life he doesn't like? Could it have anything to do with that 'lunch' I had with his cousin's wife? Tell me, O agent mine, what's the real reason I didn't get the part?"

"Cliff, it's nothing to do with you: personal life. Glick doesn't care who or how many, and neither does anybody else in this town. As long as you're box office you can live any way you like, screw anybody you like. It's just that, well, to be frank, your last three pictures only did so-so . . . and. . . ."

"They were good scripts. In fact they were great scripts. But the producers spent no money on production or publicity. What did they expect? It wasn't me who screwed up. It was the goddamn front office."

"True, Cliff, true, but it doesn't look that way to Goldman and Glick. All they see is that Cliff Eastman's last three pictures were flops. Christ, the last one went straight to video. It was never even released in the States."

"It did well in Europe. All my pictures do well in Europe. Did you tell them that?"

"Look, Cliff, it's not just your track record. It's well. . . . How can I put this? Shit, I didn't wanna have to say it, Cliff. I like you too much to wanna hurt you, but. . . ."

"Go ahead, hurt me."

"Glick thinks you're too old for the part." Alvin blurted out the words in an apologetic tumble.

"Too old for the part! Too fucking old for the part?" Cliff's face was turning bright red.

"Blood pressure, Cliffy, blood pressure," warned Alvin.

"Fuck the blood pressure and fuck them. How can I be too old for the goddamn part? Rory is a forty-seven-year-old man who's seen too much of the good life and wants to make a change. *I'm* a forty-seven-year-old man who's seen too much of the good life and wants to make a change. How is that puppy going to play the part like I would have played it? Answer me that." He stopped pacing and willed himself to calm down. Alvin was right. He couldn't afford the luxury of a heart attack.

"I can't answer that, Cliff. This is Hollywood. You know how it is. It doesn't have to make sense, just money. You're still a good actor, Cliff, but you've been around this town too long not to know how the game is played. You know the numbers."

"Sure, Alvin. I know the numbers. Half the movie-going public is under twenty. Two-thirds are under twenty-five."

"That's right, Cliff. They want to see people up there on the screen who are closer to their own age. People they can identify with. Not someone who reminds them of their parents."

"Thanks a lot, Alvin. You really know how to cheer a guy up." Cliff picked up Alvin's glass and saw that it was empty. "You want another beer?"

"No, no thanks. One's my limit. I'm driving. And you should lay off, too. Booze ages you faster than anything."

"Thanks. I'll take that under advisement." He pushed the button on the intercom. "Miguel, get your little brown buns in here with another drink, pronto."

"Cerveza, too, Señor?"

"No. No more bloody cerveza. Mr. Minter is driving, for Christ's sake!"

Cliff went back to the couch and sat on the arm nearest Alvin's chair.

"O.K., Alvin. You're my agent. You tell me. What's the bottom line on this? Where do we go from here?"

"This isn't the only script in town, Cliff."

"Yeah, I know. I've been reading them. Half of them call for kids with braces on their teeth and spots on their faces and the other half are for women who want to live their lives without men. Where does the middle-aged, fading male star find a part?"

Alvin stood up. "Cliff, let me have some time. Go away. Have a vacation. Get yourself straightened out, mentally and physically." He thought about adding "and dry out," but didn't.

"Get out of town for a while, and let me work on a few things. In fact, I've got just the place for you. Irma went there for a couple of weeks. It's this new spa in the Caribbean. She came back looking a hundred percent. You can go there. Get yourself back on track, and nobody will be any the wiser. It's too far for the Hollywood crowd to go, so you're not likely to run into anybody you'd rather not see. And Irma says it's real quiet, hardly anyone there, so you can have a nice rest. How about it?"

"A nice rest." Cliff shook his head. "Who would ever have thought that I would get to the time when a "nice rest" would be the answer? But, what the hell. Do I have a choice?"

The agent's answer was his silence.

"O.K. I'll think about it, Alvin. I'll see. Come on, I'll walk you to the door. I feel a binge coming on."

CHAPTER 5

Belle and Regina

MILDRED MAKEPEACE had one of the toughest jobs in New York City, or at least that's how she saw it. As the secretary cum babysitter cum referee for Belle Taylor and her daughter Regina— yes, *the* Regina Taylor—she approached every working day with the same cautious dread and flooding adrenaline as any soldier going into battle.

The Terrible Taylors, as she had come to refer to them when gossiping with her friends, were about as tranquil as two cats in a sack. When they weren't shouting at each other at the top of their lungs, they were ignoring each other in stony silence. In fact, rarely did a word pass between them that was not taken as an invitation to engage in conflict.

This had not always been the case, though. When Mildred had first come to work for them, the mother had ruled the roost with an iron fist, and the child had been her obedient acolyte. Under Belle's benevolent dictatorship, both the home and the business had run like well-oiled and very profitable machinery. But lately the daughter had begun to try bending the fingers on that fist and the fist had reacted by tightening even further. And so it was that Mildred was the one who invariably had to smooth things over, mend the breaks, and tend the wounded egos.

It was not an easy job, to be sure, and she wouldn't do it for all the money in the world, or so she said, except that working for the Taylors was like living in your very own soap opera. You didn't always like what happened, but you had to stay tuned to see how it all turned out.

And Mildred had been tuning in to this particular soap opera for the last fifteen years. But the truth of it was that, aside from her fascination with their lives, Mildred felt that the Taylors were like family to her, except of course her family was never as rich or as beautiful or as argumentive as this. Still, at sixty, she found that taking care of them provided a real purpose in her life and, even when the fur was flying, she couldn't wait to get to work and was always loath to leave at the end of the day.

Things had been pretty quiet lately, though. Icy quiet. It was only a matter of time, therefore, as far as Mildred was concerned, before something came along that would blow the lid off the mother/daughter relationship one more time.

On this particular afternoon, however, they were out, and Mildred was sitting at her desk in the Taylor's Upper East Side co-op, answering some of the ton of mail which found its way to Regina every year.

She had to admit that it was one of the jobs she liked best. The letters never ceased to fascinate and amaze her, and in some cases make her blush. And so, whenever she decided to tackle a pile, she like to pick a time when both Taylors were out, so she could enjoy them in peace and quiet.

Today, mother and daughter were scheduled for an all-day shoot in front of the Plaza Hotel for a layout of new clothes that would appear in *Seventeen* magazine sometime in the fall. Knowing, therefore, that she still had a good three or four hours before they came home, Mildred put on a pot of her favorite coffee and went to work.

The first half-dozen or so letters belonged to what she like to call "the worshipful" variety. They said things like, "I think you are the most beautiful girl in the world," or "I have every picture of you ever taken," or even "My whole room is plastered with pictures of you but my Mom says I have to take them down."

Next came a couple of instruction seekers. "How did you get your hair that blue-black color?" "What kind of makeup do you use?" "Do you wear tinted contact lenses to make your eyes that purple color?" "Is it true you put lemon juice on your face to keep it so white?" Mildred answered them all briefly and truthfully: "It's natural," "I don't," "No," and "No," and turned her attention back to the pile.

The next envelope was bulky and had some sort of logo on the top left-hand corner, bur it looked hand-typed, so Mildred tore it open.

Inside was a glossy brochure. On the front cover was a picture of waving palms and sun-smitten beaches beneath an intense blue sky streaked by pearly wisps of cirrus clouds.

Mildred was hooked immediately. She opened the brochure and saw that it folded like a map. On each page were pictures of glorious-looking people sunning, swimming, laughing, and playing, all amidst a spectacle of tropical flowers, frothing surf, and soothing sunshine. It looked like they were all having a wonderful time, and Mildred kept turning the pages, ooohing over this picture and ahhhhing over that. Where was this? There was no text to give the secret away until she turned to the back of the last page and there, very simply, it said—The Spa At St. Christophe—Join Us In Paradise. Below, at the bottom of the page, was the phone number.

Mildred sighed and returned the brochure to its envelope. But instead of condemning it to the trash basket under the desk, as she did with most advertising, she slid it into the top drawer. A spa might be just what she had been looking for.

The next envelope she picked up smelled strongly of some cheap, musky aftershave. Mildred sniffed it and pulled a face. She knew the contents before she even slid the letter opener underneath the flap.

"Regina, darling Regina, I love you. I have always loved you. You are the most beautiful woman in the world and I want to marry you and bring you home to my house in Cleveland. . . ."

"Cleveland?" Mildred shook her head. "Cleveland. Do they really think when they write this that. . . .?"

The telephone interrupted her thought and she tossed the letter into the garbage, picking the receiver up on the second ring.

"Taylor residence. Mildred speaking."

"Hello, Mildred. It's Bryan," said a very weary voice. "Look, can you get down here right away? They're at it again and I can't get a word in, let alone stop them. They're scaring the other models and I've only got an hour's worth of good light left."

"Again, eh? Who started it this time?"

"Who cares? I just want to get them away from each other so I can finish this damn shoot. It's supposed to rain tomorrow and I *do* have a deadline to meet."

"Alright, Bryan. Keep your lens cap on. I'll be down as soon as I get off the phone and find a cab."

"Thanks, Mildred. I can always count on you."

"I know. And *I* can always count on them. . . ."

"What did you say?"

"Nothing, Bryan. I'm on my way."

Mildred arrived on the scene about twenty minutes later. It was chaos.

The wardrobe lady was busy picking up the remains of a rack of designer clothing that had been turned over and trampled on. Three of New York's finest were trying, not too successfully, to keep the terminally curious off the set. And a horse pulling one of the Central Park carriages—Mildred couldn't tell if it was part of the shoot or had just wandered into the middle of things—had just heeded the call of nature. This had caused the assistant set director to stop helping the wardrobe lady and begin calling for "A broom, a broom, doesn't anybody have a goddamn broom?"

Near the trailer that served as a changing room, two of the other models were crying and consoling each other in turn. And from inside the trailer the sound of raised voices could be heard. A minute later, the door flew open with such force that it banged against the side of the trailer and Bryan half-fell and half-slid down the four steps that separated it from the ground.

"That's it! That's it! Let's wrap it up. I've had it. Clean up this mess and go home. All of you. I can't work under these conditions." He was walking away from the trailer, waving his arms over his head, his Nikon bouncing from side to side, when he stepped into the pile of manure.

He looked down at the still-steaming substance that had squelched up on either side of his butter-coloured Gucci loafer.

"Horse-shit, how appropriate," he said sarcastically, scraping his shoe on the pavement. Then he kept on walking until Mildred caught up with him.

"Bryan?" She grabbed his arm. "What happened in there?"

"What happened? You want to know what happened? I'll tell you what happened." He stopped walking and turned around to face her. "A Big Mac and fries is what happened."

"What? I don't understand."

Bryan sat down on the edge of the fountain and gave an exaggerated sigh. "I sent a gofer out to get some food for the crew for lunch, so that we wouldn't have to break and maybe risk losing the light." Mildred nodded, urging him on.

"Well, he comes back with McDonald's. That's fine. I mean, it may not be gourmet, but it fills the hole, right?" Mildred shook her head.

"Anyway, everybody else digs in and then Regina comes out of the trailer and goes nuts. Seems Mommie dearest in there has never let her eat junk food. So the kid grabs a Big Mac and packet of fries and starts to eat. That's when Belle comes out of the trailer and. . . . I don't have to tell you the rest. You can read it tomorrow morning on Page Six."

"Oh, Bryan. I'm sorry I didn't get here sooner. I knew I should have come with them today, but I can't babysit all the time."

"That's O.K., Mildred." He patted the back of her liver-spotted hand. "Personally, I don't understand how you can babysit them *any* of the time. Do you get danger pay for this, or what?"

He stood up. "Anyway, I've got to get this lot packed up. We'll just cross our fingers and hope the weatherman was wrong about the forecast. Have a talk with them, O.K.? Just in case there is some sun tomorrow."

"Alright, Bryan. I'll go talk to them. Though God knows what good it's going to do."

Mildred walked toward the trailer, being careful not to step in anything, and, after listening first to see if the battle was still raging, went up the steps and into—dead silence.

Mother and daughter were sitting at opposite ends of the room, eyeing each other like two caged tigers. Belle was puffing furiouly on one of her ubiquitous Camels, but the air was blue with more than smoke.

Mildred looked from one to the other. At nineteen, Regina Taylor was, as they used to say in *her* day, a real looker. The lustrous mane of blue-black hair which Mildred guessed was inherited from Regina's father—whoever he had been—had become even thicker and more wavy as she had grown, while the milk-white skin and deep lavender eyes, which were no doubt a present from her mother's line of Irish forebears, had lost none of their child-like beauty. She had a small, fine nose that tilted slightly at the tip and wide, generous lips, which, though obviously inherited from her mother, looked completely different in her long, oval face. She had grown tall and stayed svelte. She was, in short, everything her mother had planned for her to be, thought Mildred, as the girl regarded her warily from beneath the forest of her lashes.

Mildred gave Regina her best exasperated look and turned her attention to Belle, who was sitting ramrod straight in her chair, ready to take on all comers. She stared Mildred right in the eye, and Mildred stared back.

While her daughter had been growing lovelier over the years, Belle Taylor had been growing tougher. At thirty-eight she was a tall, powerful-looking woman, who had one of those bodies that some might describe as lush and others as overripe. She reminded her secretary of a sort of gone-to-seed Ava Gardner.

But when you got past the fading sensuality, Belle Taylor was all hard edges and steel reinforcement. Mildred credited this to the fact that Belle had never married and had therefore never been subjected to the softening influences of love and wifely compromise. A fact which in itself was not surprising because Belle Taylor also had a mind like a steel trap and, over the years since she had first set the baby Regina on the road to stardom, she had not only developed all the business acumen of a robber baron but the charm, as well.

By the time Regina was fifteen, the mother and daughter team were more than mere millionaires. And, if cracks had begun to develop in their relationship, it was still too soon to tell if they were serious or just the usual railings of a mother and her teenage daughter. Mildred suspected the former, and she had for some time been trying to find a way to pour some cement into those cracks.

"Well, you two have really done it this time."

Regina looked sheepishly up at Mildred, who stood, hands on her ample hips, half-way between them.

"I'm sorry, Mildred. I just wanted a hamburger like everybody else and. . . ."

Belle interrupted. "And I've told you before you can *not* eat that junk. You've got to think of your face. Do you want to get pimples? Do you want to get fat?"

"I just wanted to *get* something to eat, Mother. I was hungry. It's not a crime to be hungry, is it?"

"Then why didn't you eat what I prepared for you?"

"Because I'm sick to death of vegetables and tofu and whatever the hell else is in that plastic container over there."

"Listen here, Regina." Belle took a deep drag on her cigarette. "If it weren't for me taking such good care of you, you wouldn't be one of the highest-paid models in the world. You would be just another sloppy, overweight teenager with spots all over her face."

"And you would have to go out and get a husband instead of bugging me all the time!" Regina clapped a hand over her mouth as soon as she said it, but it was too late.

"So that's the thanks I get, is it? After all I've done for you, all I've sacrificed for you. . . ."

"I think I've more than paid you back for being born, Mother."

Belle stood up. Things were beginning to heat up again. Her face was becoming the same colour as her flaming red hair.

"You sarcastic little bitch!"

Mildred stepped into the fray. "That's enough, Belle. And you, Regina, apologize to your mother this instant."

Regina mumbled a reluctant "I'm sorry."

"You two really take the cake." Mildred shook her head, grey curls bobbing like bubbles. You are so intent on needling each other that you don't see what you're doing."

Belle sat down and started to speak, but Mildred cut her off.

"You pay me to take care of you, and that's just what I'm going to do, before you manage to destroy each other."

Regina started to protest, but Mildred held up her hand. "Sssshush! Now, the way I see it, you two have a lot that needs to be said. You have to get it all out in the open. Not by scrapping like you do, but by honest, serious talking. You need to go somewhere away from the work, away from New York, and settle your differences while you still can. And I think I know just the place. There's this new spa. . . .

CHAPTER 6

WHEN CATHY STEWART HAD DECIDED to go shopping, she headed straight for the local mall. Fortunately, it had both a Saks and a Macy's. But, unfortunately, neither of the ladies' wear buyers of either Saks or Macy's had seen the recent *Vogue* layout and read how fat women could be fashionable too.

After three hours of shopping, the only things that Cathy had found in her size were polyester pantsuits which were designed to cover the offending areas in the least comfortable and most unattractive fabrics.

Maudlin mauves, geriatric greens, and boring beiges had accompanied her into the various change rooms until she felt that there was a giant conspiracy "out there" to force overweight women to wear a uniform which proclaimed, to anybody who cared to look, "I AM A FAT LADY."

Discouraged and tired, she took the twins for an ice-cream cone, thought above having one herself, decided Why the Hell Not! and ordered a triple scoop of pralines and cream at Baskin and Robbins. Then she pushed the twins' stroller out into the middle of the mall and sat licking her compensatory confection by the indoor fountain.

Suddenly Jennifer started to shriek, and Cathy looked down to see Jeffrey mashing "raspberry ripple" down the back of her neck.

"Oh, Jeffy." She took a Handi-wipe out of her purse and cleaned up Jennifer's neck and Jeffrey's hands and then finally her own hands, and looked up in time to see two teenage girls on the other side of the fountain giggling. They stopped as soon as they saw her looking, which of course made Cathy think they were giggling at her—the poor fat lady with the bratty children. She sighed. Would she like to be that age again? That size? Wouldn't she.

"Come on, you two. Before you do anything else, I'm taking you home. I've had enough *fun* for one day."

She pushed the double stroller back through to the other end of the mall and headed straight for the car.

After the twins had been put down for their nap and before Joey was due home from school, Cathy went into Michael's den looking for something to read. Normally she would have steered a wide berth around her husband's inner sanctum, because Michael didn't like anybody "messing with his things," as she had explained to the children when they wanted to know why this room alone was off-limits. But she had finished the latest Kathleen Woodiwiss, didn't feel like turning on the game shows or the soaps, and Michael usually kept a good supply of magazines on hand to see how some of his agency's ads were doing.

She went straight to the magazine rack by the desk and pulled out a few of the most recent issues, perfunctorily discarding both *Road and Track* and *GQ*. Next came *Destiny* and *Cosmopolitan*, but the sexy young girls on their covers only made her feel more depressed about the day's shopping, and she put them aside.

Family Circle and *Homemaker* were next, but they joined the reject pile too. She didn't need to read them, she *was* them.

Toward the bottom of the pile she found the latest issue of *Town and Country*. On the cover was an attractive youngish woman, dressed in what was obviously a very expensive green satin ballgown, leaning against the pillars of an old plantation house veranda. The caption on the bottom left corner of the cover read, "Mrs. Beauregard Simpson Chase enjoys a breath of air on the veranda of her antebellum home in Atlanta."

"I'll bet she does," said Cathy out loud, and took the magazine back to the family room.

Half an hour later, having digested the lives of Mrs. Beauregard Simpson Chase and the beautiful people of Atlanta, and having found out how the sudden burst of interest in polo was driving the price of a string of ponies almost out of sight, she reached the back of the book. She always read the ads, just in case there was anything she could talk to Michael about, though most of them were usually in black and white and not very interesting.

But a sudden splash of color on page 236 caught her eye. Palm trees and beaches were the backdrop for a beautiful blond girl in a bright orange maillot. She was beckoning. "Join Me in Paradise," read the banner. "Sexist," muttered Cathy to herself, but she read the copy anyway.

"The Spa at St. Christophe can give you the answer you've been looking for. Rest, rejuvenate, lose weight, tone your body. Whatever you need, we can provide it. Join us—in Paradise."

Cathy looked at the picture of the beckoning girl again. A spa. Why not? It might be just enough to get her started in the right direction. So she dog-eared the corner of the page the ad was on, and decided to talk to Michael about it right after dinner.

Michael got home just after seven, earlier than usual. She heard him coming down the hallway and into the kitchen as she stood stirring a pot on the stove. He was whistling—something about everything coming up roses. He came up behind her, reached his arms almost all the way around her waist and kissed the back of her neck.

"How's my Bi . . . How's my Cathy?"

"Just fine, Michael."

"Kids upstairs?"

"I put the twins down already, and Joey's in his room watching reruns."

"Good. We can eat in peace. You want a drink before dinner?"

"No thanks."

Michael went into the bar off the family room, came back a few moments later with a gin and tonic and leaned against the counter next to the stove.

"Guess what?"

"Whatever it is, it must be good news. You're early and you were whistling." She continued to stir, so that the cheese sauce wouldn't get too thick.

"You're right." He turned her around to face him. "Michael Stewart has done it again." He paused until she looked up, a film of steam covering her rounded cheeks. "I got the Buckminister account."

"Really? That's great. What's the Buckminister account?" She turned back to the stove and took the pot off the burner.

"You know. It's the one I've been after for the last year. They're the people who own those vacation time-sharing places all over the world, and I'm going to handle their advertising—exclusively. You know what that means?"

"No, what?" She reached into the oven and the wall of heat hit her right in the face. She pulled out the casserole dish, set it on top of the stove, and closed the door.

"It means, Cath, that we are going places. Exotic places. All over the world. Hawaii, Tahiti, Mexico. No more long, dreary winters. No sir. Your mother can look after the kids and we are going to have fun. It's going to be warm tropical nights, sun-washed beaches. . . ."

"Bathing suits." She was draining the broccoli water into the sink.

"What did you say?"

"I said, 'Dinner's ready.'" She turned around and set the dish of broccoli on the table and poured the thick, creamy cheese sauce over it.

"Mmmmmm, smells great. I'm starving."

"Me, too." She sighed, and started ladling out the casserole.

After dinner, Michael went into the den and Cathy checked on the children and then cleared the table. She put the dishes in the dishwasher, scraped the last of the chocolate icing off the cake plate with her finger and then, armed with a fresh gin and tonic for Michael, she joined him in the den and placed the drink beside him.

"Michael?"

"Hmmmm?" He did not raise his head or lower the newspaper, but she plowed on anyway.

"Michael, I've been thinking."

"Hmmmmm?" He turned the page and continued to read.

"Michael, I'm trying to talk to you!"

Reluctantly, he lowered the paper.

"Yes, Cathy, I can see that. And I am *trying* to read. This is the only quiet time I get all day to read the newspaper. Now, what is it?"

She brought out the copy of *Town and Country* and, opening it to the page with the ad for the spa, placed it on his lap.

"Read the ad."

Michael adjusted his gaze downward and scanned the contents.

"You want to buy a Shar pei?"

"Not that ad. The one about the spa."

"Cathy, I don't have to read it. It's my account. I know what it says. What I don't know, is why you are so interested."

"I want to go there. To the spa. Michael, I've got to lose some weight and I need a little boost to get me going."

He closed the magazine with a sigh.

"Cathy, Cathy, Cathy," he said shaking his head. "You are a wife and a mother. Your place is here, looking after your family, being my wife, not at some glamorous jet-set spa."

"But Michael. . . ."

"There's nothing else to discuss. You're not going, and that's it. I told you this morning, I don't mind a few extra pounds on you. That's all you have to worry about. I understand what happens to a woman's body when she has children. You can't expect to look the same as you did when you were eighteen." He picked up the paper, signaling the end of the discussion.

"Michael, I. . . ."

"Enough said, Cathy. That is my final decision. Now run along and let me read my paper." He smiled benignly.

Cathy picked up the magazine and turned to go. She caught another glimpse of the girl in the orange maillot. I could look like that again, or close to it. I know I could, she thought to herself.

"Michael?"

"Yessss, Cathy?" He hissed the "yes" through clenched teeth, from behind the newspaper.

"Michael, I've never been demanding. I've never said anything to stop you from doing something you thought was important, but now I want to do something that is important to me and I don't think it's fair of you to try and stop me." She was amazed at her own bravado. It was the first time in their marriage that she had ever stood up to him after he had made a "final" decision.

"Cathy, if you went to the spa you would only be setting yourself up for a disappointment. You might lose a few pounds, but you would only gain it all back. You know what you're like. I'm only trying to protect you from yourself."

"No, I wouldn't, Michael." She saw a glimmer of light at the end of the tunnel. "Please let me go. I know I can do it. And it won't be any inconvenience to you. Mother will come in and look after the children and cook your dinner."

He thought for a moment. "Well. . . ."

"Please. Michael, please?"

"Wellll. Oh, alright. What the hell. They're so far behind on the billing I can probably comp it, anyway," he said with benevolent largesse.

"Oh thank you, Michael! I know it will be the beginning of a whole new me."

"Don't get your hopes up, Cathy. Leopards can't change their spots, and you can't turn back the clock. But far be it from me to stand in your way. Go ahead, get it out of your system. But remember, when it doesn't work, that I told you so."

CHAPTER 7

AFTER ALVIN LEFT, Cliff retraced his earlier steps back down the hallway and into the kitchen, picked up the vodka, the ice, and a couple of limes, and then went back to the study.

He sat there staring through the french windows, watching as the sky turned to mauve and then magenta and orange as the sunset proved to be as spectacular as the smog had promised.

He was thinking, going over his life, looking for places where he might have made a wrong turn, things he could have done differently so that he wouldn't have ended up where he was. He had tried to get drunk, but the vodka had only made him reflective. Fortunately, though, it was easier to reflect on the past than to try and deal with the future.

The sky turned slowly to indigo and then to black. The lights at the foot of the canyons came on like so many earthbound stars. After a time, he flipped on the television set. The famous face of a local interviewer filled the screen. Deep tan. Wall-to-wall teeth. He was nodding enthusiastically, apparently interested in what his guest was saying, but Cliff knew from his own experience on the same show that "Teeth" was watching the cameras and the floor director and pacing himself between the commercial breaks. He couldn't care less what his guest was saying. His mind was elsewhere.

A commercial came on, and Cliff wondered briefly if the loyal viewers knew that "Teeth" was keeping a young actress in a house up in Coldwater Canyon. He wondered if Mrs. Teeth knew either, or cared.

The logo of the show came back on the screen and faded to a shot of the set. The next guest came out and took a seat on the couch. It was Nadine Balfour. He had always liked her. Had in fact done a couple of pictures with her, and the chemistry between them on the screen had sent all the gossip-mongers into a tizzy of expectation that they were having a fling. They both thought that was hilarious, and played the lover angle to the hilt whenever they were in public. Not many people knew, even now, that Rose, Nadine's secretary for more than twenty years, was the real love interest in her life.

Nadine was looking pretty good. She didn't look like a woman who was almost fifty. Same age as him. But then, she looked after herself . . . didn't abuse the booze . . . didn't fuck around. What was she saying now? He turned the volume up.

". . . . Well, thank you, Larry; you're looking pretty marvelous yourself."

"You look terrific, Nadine, no wonder you've just landed the lead role on that new evening soap—'Palmer Cove.' Why don't you tell our audience what your secret is. How do you stay so young?"

"No secret, Larry, I'm just lucky, I guess. Good genes."

"And pretty good in jeans too." The audience tittered and Larry Carter flashed a full frontal view of his teeth at Camera One. Nadine smiled graciously, before continuing.

"But actually I do have this teeny weeny little secret. I go to a spa at least four times a year. You know, just to rest and rejuvenate. Get all the toxins out of the old system. I find it works wonders."

"If you're an example, I'll say it does, Nadine. . . ."

Cliff flicked the OFF button. "Works wonders, does it? Well, kid, if I can look as good as you, why the hell not?"

He dialed Alvin's number at home. The agent answered on the third ring.

"Alvin?"

"Cliff? Do you have any idea what time it is?"

"It's only ten past twelve, Alvin. Did I wake you?"

"Yes, you did. Are you drunk?"

"No, Alvin, I'm not drunk. I've been thinking about what you said."

"What did I say?"

"About the spa, remember, the one in the Caribbean?"

"Oh yeah. What about it?" Alvin yawned into the phone.

"I'm going to go. Get back in shape. I bet if I get all the toxins out of my system, I can pass for forty, maybe even thirty-eight."

"Taxes? What taxes?" Alvin was less than half awake.

"Toxins, Alvin, toxins. Aren't you listening to me?"

"Sure, sure I'm with you, Cliffy. Great idea. Do you good. Call me when you get back."

"Alvin. Don't hang up. I need the name, Alvin. The name."

"Oh yeah. Right. Hang on a sec."

Cliff heard him put the phone down on the bedside table.

"Irma. Irma. Wake up."

"Huh. Oh, Alvin, not again."

"Forget it, Irma. Cliff's on the phone. He wants to know the name of that spa you went to in the Caribbean."

"Spa? Alvin, it's the middle of the night. Go away."

"Just tell me the name of it and you can go back to sleep."

Cliff heard Irma mumble something unintelligible and then Alvin picked up the receiver again.

"Cliff? You there?"

"Where else?"

"Got a pen handy?"

"Got it, Alvin."

"O.K. It's called 'The Spa at St. Christophe.'"

"'The Spa at St. Christophe.' Thanks, Alvin. See you when I get back."

CHAPTER 8

Maxine

THE SMELL OF FRYING ONIONS, mixed with the more tantalizing scents of garlic and hot cinnamon, had just wafted under the bathroom door. Bradley inhaled deeply. Even with his face slathered with Aramis-scented shaving cream, he could smell his mother's cooking, and his mouth watered at the promise of it.

He sighed as he dragged the Track II down one side of his chin and up the other. He hated to miss one of Maxine's dinners again, but at the age of twenty-two he had discovered that there were more important things in life than food. They were called "Janie." So he finished shaving, ran the razor under the cold water tap to rinse out the "whisker buds," as Janic called them, and patted a little cologne on his face. And then, taking one last look in the mirror, he made his way down the hall and into the kitchen to tell his mother he was going out *again* tonight.

Maxine was stirring the béchamel sauce in a pot on the stove, and a spicy meat mixture lay steaming in a casserole dish on the counter beside her.

"Hi, Ma." Bradley scooped up a spoonful of the meat and put it in his mouth. Maxine just kept stirring.

"Don't tell me . . . you're going out again."

"Mmmmmm, hot." He mumbled, tossing the beef mixture from one side of his mouth to the other. She frowned. "But good, very good. How did you know I was going out?"

"You smell like a florist." She cracked two eggs, beat the whites and, turning back to the stove, folded the whites into the sauce, and then continued stirring.

"I've got a date with Janie." Bradley shook his head. "Ma, how come you're always cooking?"

"It's a Jewish mother's therapy. I get nervous—I cook. I have a fight with your father—I cook. My son tells me he prefers the company of some shiksa to his own mother—I cook."

Bradley ignored the reference to Janie. It was just his mother's way of needling him. "But Ma, nobody's gonna eat it?"

She stopped stirring and turned off the element under the pot. "You think maybe I should take Valium instead?"

"No, Ma. I didn't mean that. It's just that most of the time you're the only one who's home for dinner." Bradley knew he was treading on thin ice now, and he stepped carefully around mentioning his father's regular absences from the dinner table.

"So, you don't think a mother has to eat too?"

"Of course you have to eat. What I meant was, you go to so much bother. Cooking all these fancy dishes. What's the point?"

"You never asked me what the point was when you used to eat at home."

Bradley held up his hands. "O.K. Ma. O.K. I take it back." He took another spoonful of the meat mixture. He felt guilty about leaving his mother alone so much, but what could he do? It was not his job to take Harry's place.

But she slapped the back of his knuckles with a wooden spoon. "Doesn't this girl of yours ever feed you?"

"Sure Ma. We'll grab some Mexican or something later."

"Mexican! You know the first thing those peasants do when they cross the border in Texas? They stop eating Mexican. And now my own son, who should know better, tells me he wants to eat what the peasants won't eat."

"Come on, Ma. . . ." Bradley slipped back into an adolescent whine."

Maxine noted this with some satisfaction. Her son wasn't as grown up as he liked to think, after all.

"I used to cook for your father two, three times a week before we were married. That's how he knew I would make him a good wife."

"Ma, I told you, Janie's not into domestic stuff. She's a business-woman. She likes to eat out."

"Eat out? Eat out. The whole world is eating out. Even your father doesn't come home for dinner any more."

Bradley shifted his weight to the other foot. "Dad doesn't come home period, Ma." Talking about his father made him uncomfortable, but, since his mother had brought the subject up, he thought maybe she wanted to talk about the situation, and so he gave her the intro. "Is he still sleeping at the office?"

But Maxine just nodded and poured the sauce over the meat and then put the dish in to bake.

"What can I say. The man chooses to live like a gypsy. I sent a packet of clean shirts over there for him this morning. Otherwise, he'll start to smell like a gypsy, too."

Bradley came over and stood beside her. "Ma, why don't you two get a divorce? What's the point?"

"There you go again with 'What's the point?' Why does everything have to have a point?"

"But Ma, you're not happy. He's not happy. . . ."

"Happy? Happy? That's all you young people think about is being happy. What makes you think marriage is supposed to make you happy?" She wiped her hands on a dishtowel.

"Well, it's not supposed to make you unhappy, is it?"

"Look, Mr. Knowitall, if you know so much about marriage, why don't you marry that girl you spend so much time with?"

"Janie and I aren't ready for that kind of commitment yet, Ma."

"Not ready yet?" Maxine sniffed in disdain. "When I was your age, we didn't have time to get ready to make a commitment. We made it. That was it. Believe me, you think about marriage too long, you're never ready."

"Jumping into something before you're ready is not the answer. Look where it's gotten you. You're miserable. Get a divorce, Ma. Start a new life. You'll see. It'll be so much better."

"What? Are you getting a commission from that divorce lawyer who lives downstairs?" She moved him aside and put the pot and the spatula into the sink to soak.

"Don't make jokes, Ma. I mean it. I don't like to see you like this."

Maxine turned to face him and put her hands on his shoulders. "Bradley my son, you don't understand. You're young. You have your looks—especially now you got rid of those blue stripes in your hair. You have your whole life ahead of you. I'm forty-five. Things are starting to slide. When I married your father I had a shape like zucchini. Now I look more like an eggplant. At this rate, my whole body is going to be down around my ankles by the time I'm fifty. I'm not exactly Loni Anderson, if you know what I mean. If I divorce your father, I'm going to be alone."

"If you're worried about being lonely, Ma. . . ."

"Lonely? Who's lonely? I've got a microwave." She gestured at the contents of the kitchen. "I've got a Cuisinart. I've got a convection oven with a built-in salamander. How can I be lonely? I'm not worried about being lonely. But I don't want to be alone."

"You could find someone else. . . ."

Maxine made a noise that sounded like "pissssssh" and waved him aside.

"Ma, Ma, you've never looked better. Believe me." He picked up the lid of a saucepan and held it so she could see herself. "You look great. You know, some women look better when they get older. Look at Joan Collins."

Maxine looked at her reflection. "I look like a frightened blowfish." She pushed the lid away.

"That's because it's a convex surface. . . ."

"Look, I know you're trying to make me feel better." She patted him on the hand. "You're a good boy, Bradley, a good son, but you just don't understand. I'm your father's wife. Mrs. Harry Kraft is who

I am. It's also what I do. If I divorce your father, I'll be unemployed." She kissed him on the cheek. "And you wouldn't want your mother to be unemployed, would you? Now go. You're probably already late for what'shername."

He hesitated. "You sure you'll be alright?"

"What's gonna happen? I'm gonna get mugged in the living room? Go. Go eat out. Take some Alka-seltzer with you." She smiled and pushed him toward the kitchen door.

Grateful to be let off the hook, Bradley left the kitchen and went down the hall to the front door.

A minute later, Maxine heard the door close and then went back to check on the moussaka. The top was browning nicely, and she stuck a fork in, to see how it was coming along.

"Ten more minutes," she said to the empty kitchen, and began to prepare a tray for herself.

After she had served herself a modest slice of the moussaka, she took the tray into the living room and sat down in the chair nearest the television set. The remote control was on the table beside it, and she switched on Channel Four to catch the last half-hour of "Live at Five" while she waited for the NBC News to come on.

Then, while she ate her dinner and listened to the local news, she picked up the TV guide to see who she would be spending her evening with.

There wasn't much on until 8 p.m., when Robin Leach was going to have some starlet whose name Maxine didn't recognize show him around her favorite getaway, a spa in the Caribbean.

She wasn't particularly fond of "Lifestyles of the Rich and Famous." The truth was that Robin Leach got on her nerves. But the only other choice was the movie of the week, and Maxine thought if she saw one more story about a divorced middle-aged woman who was a) crushed by her loneliness, b) destroyed by her dependence on prescription drugs, or c) bravely fighting a strange and crippling disease, she would give in to the ravages of the menopause and go stark, raving mad.

Besides, she was curious about seeing the spa. Without telling either her husband or her son, Maxine was planning a little getaway of her own. It was the first time she had ever done anything like that, and she was scared stiff at her own bravado. But she felt a need to do something to shake up her life. Either that, or she would soon start cooking lunches as well as dinners.

CHAPTER 9

JOYCE WAS PACKING—OR TRYING TO. Through a process of random selection and distribution, she had managed in a few short hours to transfer every piece of clothing in her closet to a heap on the middle of her bed. The suitcase, however, still remained empty on the floor beside it.

What did you wear to a spa? A bathing suit. She pulled one out of the pile and then threw it back. It was faded and the elastic was gone, so it sagged everywhere it should have snugged.

What else? Not much, she decided. A least most of the time. But what did you wear in between "not much" and a bathing suit? She sighed, turfing Fredo off the pile of clothes.

"Do I sleep on *your* things?"

A knock on the door saved the cat from having to come up with an answer

"Now what?" Joyce padded barefoot down the tiny hallway. She was in no mood for visitors. It's probably somebody who wants a contribution for saving some endangered species I've never heard of, she decided, as she approached the door.

"I'll be an endangered species if I don't get that plane in the morning," she said to her reflection in the hall mirror, as she ran a hand through her hair and tugged at the frayed neck of the Go Mets Go sweatshirt she wore over her jeans.

The sweatshirt was a leftover from a summer sojourn with one of the team's PR men, who had assured her, among other things, that even though it did say "Made in Bangladesh" on the label, it was both machine-washable and -dryable. Unfortunately, the washing hadn't worked out any better than the relationship. Some men, it seemed, found it necessary to lie about more than cleaning.

The banging on the door was repeated.

"Just a minute." She moved across to the door, conscious, once again, that she should have had a peephole installed.

"Who is it?"

"Murbldurf."

"What? I can't hear you."

"Murbledurf!" It was louder, but no more distinct.

"Oh, what the hell!" She began flipping the three locks that served as her barrier against the outside world. "This had better be important," she said, wrenching open the front door.

There stood Harry, looking somewhat rumpled and out of focus, balancing a large pizza box in one hand, carrying a bottle of wine in the other, and holding a brown manila folder in his mouth.

"Harry! What're you doing here?"

And it was at that moment she realized that Harry was one of the few people she had ever met who could convey sarcasm even better with their eyes.

"Oh, right. Here, let me take that." She took the manila folder from Harry's mouth, noting that his teeth prints were well-etched into the paper.

"Thanks!" He breathed a sigh of relief. "I thought you might want to have a look at that before you go."

"Oh? And what about the pizza and the wine? Are they for the octogenarian next door or the two guys across the hall?"

"I thought you might want something to eat while you're looking. I know I do. I'm starving." He pushed past her and headed for the kitchen.

"Why don't you come in?" She followed him down the hall. "Look, Harry, I'm really busy. I haven't even packed yet. I. . . ."

"Have you eaten?"

"Well no, but. . . ."

"So eat." He slapped the pizza box down on the table, opened it, tore off a slice and crammed half of it into his mouth. "You got a corkscrew?" he asked, through the food.

"A corkscrew? Ah. . . ." She had to think for a minute where she had last seen the corkscrew, and then remembered it was in the bathroom. She had used it to pry the stopper out of the bathtub drain.

"You always keep your corkscrew in the bathroom?"

"No, not *always*." And she disappeared down the hallway.

Harry went to the fridge and pried two ice cubes out of the tray which wouldn't budge from its frozen nest, and then pushed the door shut with his shoulder.

Joyce returned a moment later and offered him the corkscrew. He waved it aside, still holding the ice. "The wine's for you. I'm having scotch."

"Oh you are, are you?" Say what you like about Harry, he never bothered with the formalities. She moved across to the other side of the kitchen and reached for a tumbler from the cabinet above the sink and then retrieved the scotch bottle, which was almost full, from the one next to it.

"You want water?"

"Just the hard kind." He plopped the two cubes into the glass she was holding and sat down. "Come on Joycee, your dinner's getting cold."

She glared at him and placed the bottle on the table in front of him. "Help yourself." Scotch and pizza. Bleeck!

"Have I got instincts, Joycee, or have I got instincts?" He poured a healthy splash of scotch over the ice, checked the level in the glass, and then added another splash.

"I don't know, Harry, it depends on what kind of instincts you're talking about." She sat down and poured some of the wine into a wine glass and helped herself to the pizza.

"Do I know a story or do I?" Harry's smile was extended by a wide band of tomato sauce that curled up from each side of his mouth. He pushed the file across the table. "Check it out. Read it. I told you this spa piece is gonna be great."

Joyce opened the file, but before she could read the first line, he began to tell her about its contents.

"I thought I'd help you out a little, so I got Research to do a run-down on the guy who owns the place. Thought it would save you some time and might make a nice little sidebar to the piece. You know, like that one you did on Denis Thatcher as the man behind the woman?"

"Thanks, Harry, but I could have had my department do that. You didn't have to bother."

"Bother. No bother. I got you into this, Joycee and, well, I thought, what the hell, the girl's a real trouper, so why not give her a hand. More pizza?" He passed the box toward her, but Joyce waved it away. Harry shrugged, helped himself to the last piece and threw the box on the floor.

Then he continued, "But you know what I found out?"

Joyce shook her head. She was listening with only half her brain. The other half—the skeptical side—was wondering what Harry was doing here, complete with food and beverage. He had never come over uninvited before. He could have told her this much over the phone. And, besides, she suspected that he had already had more than a nodding acquaintance with his favorite beverage today.

"Not a whole heck of a lot," Harry continued, pouring more scotch into the glass. "You got any more ice?"

With a sigh Joyce got up and went over to the refrigerator. But as she opened the door, Fredo exploded out into the kitchen from the shelf above the crisper and skittered underneath the sink.

"What the . . . ?"

"Sorry. He must have jumped in when I went to get the ice while you were in the bathroom."

Joyce gave Harry a look that said "A likely story," and then proceeded to pry two more cubes from their frozen prison.

"There's your ice. Now, can we please get on with this."

"Well, this guy Voight—he's the doctor who owns the place— seems to have sprung ready-made onto the planet about two or three years back."

"What do you mean, 'ready made'?"

"The man has no past. He does not exist. He's a cipher."

"That's not possible, Harry. He's a doctor. He must have a medical degree from somewhere, a social insurance number, something."

Harry shook his head and took a long pull on the scotch. "Research checked it out. He's supposed to have graduated from that medical school. You know the one the Russians tried to take over when we invaded that island in the Caribbean. What's it called?"

"You mean Grenada. That's St. George's, and it was the Cubans—more or less."

"Cubans, Russians, what's the difference?" Harry belched. "'Scuse me. Anyway, that's the one. And, there's no record of anybody by that name ever going *to*, never mind graduating *from* that medical school. And I had Research check with the A.M.A. and they have no record of anyone by that name as a member, either."

"So? Clerical errors. Computer screw-ups. It doesn't mean anything. Besides, maybe he went to school somewhere else. In Europe, maybe."

"Then why does he put it out that he went to St. John's?"

"St. George's. And I don't know why. But what difference does it make *where* he went to school? Maybe it's a local thing. You know, because of the spa being in the Islands."

"No way. There's a story there, Joyce, I can smell it."

"All I can smell is pepperoni." She got up from the table and pushed away Fredo, who had recovered enough from his ordeal to venture out to check the box for anchovies, picked up the carton, and put it next to the garbage.

But Harry was like a bloodhound on the trail of a mountain lion. No matter how stacked the odds, he wouldn't give up on the chase. "Just ask yourself this, Joyce. How does a guy with no past suddenly turn up with enough money to not only buy an island but to build a ritzy-schmitzy spa on it. Huh?"

"Maybe he won the lottery. Who knows?"

"Or maybe he's got friends in low places. You know what I mean?"

"Maybe. . . ." He always did know how to get at her.

"Anyway, do me a favor, will you, and just check it out. You're going to be there, anyway. What can it hurt? You wanted hard news, maybe this is it. Maybe the guy's some kind of a crook." Harry drained his scotch and reached for the bottle, but Joyce got there before him, and, screwing the cap on, put it back in the cupboard.

"O.K. I'll see what I can find out. But don't get your hopes up. There could be a hundred reasons for what you found out."

She paused by the sink, thinking, hands stuffed into the pockets of her jeans. But after a moment, her mind segued away from the graft, corruption, and money-laundering and she was suddenly conscious of how alone they were in the tiny kitchen. Just the two of them. Late at night. . . .

What was the real reason for Harry's visit, anyway? Whatever it was, she didn't want to know. Did she? He was her boss, that was all. Wasn't it? There was no reason to complicate what had become over the years a good working relationship that sometimes bordered on friendship. Was there?

She answered all the unspoken questions at once. "You have to leave. I still have to pack, and it's already after midnight."

Harry reluctantly got up from his chair. "No coffee?"

"No coffee. I mean I don't have any coffee." Joyce herded him down the hall toward the front door.

"You want to talk for a while?"

"Harry, we just talked. It's late. Go home." She opened the door.

"I can't go home. Maxine'll be there." He turned around until he was facing her. "Joyce, I don't know what to say to her anymore. I haven't been home for days. I've been sleeping in the office."

"I know." She suddenly felt a wave of sympathy for this man who could control a big magazine so easily but who was laid out for the count by his own marriage. She reached up and put a comforting hand on his shoulder. "It'll all work out, Harry. You'll see." She wanted to say more, but what more was there to say?

"Yeah, sure." He lumbered unsteadily through the door. "'Night, Joyce."

"G'night, Harry." She watched as he made his way to the elevator, weaving slightly as he reached out to push the "Down" button, and then she shut the door.

PART TWO

The Island

CHAPTER 10

AS THE DC 10 CIRCLED GRANTLEY ADAMS AIRPORT, one thought was supreme in Joyce Redmond's mind. Pantyhose. Specifically, Hanes Everyday Control Top with the cotton-lined gusset and whatever had possessed her to wear these synthetic sausage casings to travel in.

She was irritable and uncomfortable after the five-hour flight— the last four hours of which had been without air conditioning, for some reason known only to the aircraft manufacturer and possibly the F.A.A.

But worse than the physical discomfort was the opportunity this condition had afforded her mother's voice to echo the prophecy that, because of the pantyhose, the circulation to every cell below her waist had probably been cut off by now. And, since a prophecy is nothing without a warning, the voice continued with the admonition, "Your Aunt Ruth wore pantyhose and you know what happened to her? Varicose veins. No wonder she never found a nice man to settle down with. Who wants to marry a woman with legs like Gorgonzola?"

Caveat gestor, reflected Joyce, as the plane touched down and she pulled her bag out from under the seat in front of her.

There had been few passengers on the plane, and most of them were sitting toward the back, so she was first out the door. Cautiously, she descended the rickety steps that connected the cabin to the runway, clutching the handrail to keep her balance and wondering what kind of a place would have an airport that made its passengers hike halfway across the airfield to get to the terminal. Images of "Casablanca" rose to mind, but she cast them aside.

As she pushed her way through the wall of tropical heat that rose like a circumfusion from the concrete, she anticipated the frigid rush of processed air that would be waiting for her inside the terminal—the signal that she had not departed from the civilized world after all, but had merely taken a small detour.

But, as she shouldered her way through the swinging doors of the old, one-story, pink-stucco building, she was bathed instead in a viscous mass of warm "soup" that smelled vaguely of old, damp basements and something else she preferred not to examine. She wrinkled her nose and started taking short, shallow breaths in an effort to draw as little of the foul stuff into her lungs as possible.

Joyce looked around for the baggage carousel, which wasn't really a carousel at all, but rather a semicircular conveyor belt of undetermined vintage that came in on one side of the terminal and exited about fifty feet further along the same wall. By dodging around some slower-moving passengers, she reached it just in time to intercept her one bag before the belt carried it out of sight behind thick rubber curtains and into luggage limbo.

She put the suitcase down, pulled her ticket out of her purse, and studied the small print. Her connecting flight to the island of St. Christophe left from Gate 7. She looked up, and her eyes wandered over the inside of the terminal. "Gate 7" was painted in big, black letters about halfway down the building, and she headed resignedly in that direction. She had an hour to wait before boarding the plane. A long, hot hour.

As she lugged her suitcase along, she wondered briefly where Harry was, about now. Probably in some cool, dark bar having a cold beer before deciding what to have for lunch. And then, after lunch, a casual stroll back down Madison Avenue to do a little work in the peace and quiet of the weekend-empty offices. Sometimes life just wasn't fair.

But speaking of bars. . . . She was passing the terminal bar and glanced inside. It was dark but not noticeably cooler than the rest of the building. And, like airport bars everywhere, it had a plastic rec-room decor which someone must have once decided would be soothing and familiar to the passenger who needed a little liquid comfort while he waited for his next plane.

For a moment she toyed with the idea of going inside anyway. But airport bars were always so depressing, and she was already miserable enough. Besides, there was only one other person in the room—a man, and that might mean having to strike up a conversation, something which she was not in the mood for at the moment.

He was sitting at the bar, his back half-turned to the door, in front of a large, colorful poster that advertised one of the local varieties of rum. Joyce couldn't see his face very well in the gloom, but he was expensively dressed in a casual sort of way, and he had great shoulders. She imagined he was one of those good-looking playboys who populated the islands with their charm and kept the local distillers in business. She decided to keep going.

At Gate 7 there was no one to check her ticket, so she pushed through the double-glass doors and into the oasis of cool air that she had so recently ceased to hope for. Sighing with pleasure, she put the suitcase down and lifted her heavy mane of hair to let the cool air play on the back of her neck. Then she glanced around the empty room, and, picking up the bag once more, took a seat by the long window that looked out over the single runway.

In spite of the fact that the glass was encrusted with the skeletons of a million dusty raindrops, the window afforded her an opportunity to savor the view, or at least what passed for a view.

As far as she could tell, Barbados seemed to consist, no matter in which direction you looked, of rows and rows of palm trees swaying off into infinity, punctuated here and there with eddies of airborne sand, stirred up, she supposed, by the constant presence of the trade winds.

It was not at all what she had envisioned for a tropical paradise.

And so, as usual when she was in a funk, she turned her mind to work. Unlike men and geography, work was something she knew she could always count on. She reached into her bag and pulled out the file which still had a discernible impression of Harry's teeth marks in one corner, and soon became engrossed in the short history of the mysterious Hans Voight.

CHAPTER 11

MARIETTE FLUNG HERSELF INTO THE TUB chair across from the desk, adjusting her fall of white-blond hair until it lay in a perfect pale cloud around her shoulders. She was wearing a pair of tight cotton shorts and a T-shirt that molded itself to her upper body like a second skin. On anyone else the outfit would have suggested the possibility of a recent residency on Hollywood Boulevard but, for some reason, on her it only served to emphasize the perfection of her seventeen years.

The doctor looked up from the file he was reading. "I hope you don't plan to go to the airport dressed like that."

"Why, do you think it would scare them away?" Mariette squirmed provocatively and stretched out a pair of long, tanned legs.

"Only the women." The doctor noted with some regret the lithe young body that was so invitingly displayed in front of him, and closed the file. In another time, another place, he might have been tempted to take advantage of the situation. But he had other things on his mind right now, and besides, Mariette was not just another yielding, yearning girl. He looked up. "And how many have we got this time?"

"Six."

"Six? That's all?"

Mariette nodded. "Six, but two of them are comps, so it's really only four, if you're talking about paying guests."

"Four!" The doctor flipped on his calculator. "Let's see: four guests at $3,000 a head. . . . His fingers raced over the buttons. "Better put another 20 percent on all the items in the boutique and the gift shop, and tell all but the essential staff they can have the week off—without pay."

"Again?"

"There's no point in having them around, if there's nothing for them to do. They only clutter up the place." He changed the subject. "Who are the comps?"

"One of them is that writer from New York. You know, from *Destiny* magazine. She'd like to remain anonymous. So she doesn't spook the other guests, I suppose." The doctor nodded. "And the other one is the wife of the president of the company who handles our advertising."

"Michael Stewart's wife, eh? Well, maybe comping her will help keep the agency wolves from the door for a few more weeks. As for the writer, if she gives us a good write-up, it can't hurt, so we'll go along with her little charade. *Destiny* is one of the big ones. But keep an eye on her. I don't want her to find out what's going on here."

He got up and came around the desk. Mariette looked up expectantly. He ran his index finger along the side of her face. "You know, you get more lovely every day."

Mariette captured his hand and kissed it. "I'm glad I decided to come with you. You're the only one who's ever been nice to me."

"I know, baby. I know." He patted her face and walked over to the window that looked out across the pool area and paused for a moment before continuing. "I have something to tell you."

The serious tone of his voice alarmed her. But, before she could say anything, he went back to the desk and, opening the top drawer, fished out a letter and handed it to her. "Read this."

Mariette took the envelope. The paper was heavy, expensive-looking. On the cream-coloured flap, just above the watermark, was a coat of arms, embossed in red and gold. Her hand trembled as she slid out the folded sheet of paper. She didn't even have to read it. She already knew who it was from. Daniella. And that could mean only one thing. Trouble.

The doctor watched her as she read, eyes lowered, brow knitted. As she neared the end of the letter, he saw the color begin to rise in her cheeks, giving a ruddy glow to the tan. When she had finished she looked up, her blue eyes flashing with furry.

"That bitch!"

"My sentiments exactly."

"What are you going to do about it?"

"I've been thinking about the options. . . ."

"Well, why don't you tell 'the baroness' to go fuck herself."

He laughed. It was a cold and bitter sound that was completely lacking in humor. "It's more likely to be the other way around, don't you think?"

"How long have we got?"

"I don't know. A few weeks. A couple of months. Not long."

Mariette shivered and hugged herself. "Do you think she'll come here herself?"

"Probably. Daniella always likes to be there for the kill. I remember once in Africa. We were on safari and. . . ."

The girl clamped her hands over her ears. "I don't want to hear about it."

"You're letting your jealousy get the better of you."

"I am not. And anyway, why did you have to deal with her in the first place? You know what she's like. All she ever thinks about is money, money, money." Her voice was getting higher.

"I didn't have much choice. It's a cold world out there, Mariette. You have to *have* something to get something, and Daniella was the only one who was buying what I had."

The girl gave him a caustic look. "I think you're disgusting."

"I thought you loved me."

"I do, but I still think you're disgusting."

"Be that as it may, we are going to have to work quickly if we are going to salvage this situation." He moved back toward the desk. "I've been giving it some thought, and I think fate may have handed us a way out."

"What do you mean?"

He flipped open the file to the page that held the guest list. "Two of our guests this week are going to be Belle Taylor and her daughter Regina."

"So?"

He turned to face her again. "Well, I think they can be very useful."

Mariette was frowning. "I don't understand. Useful how?" But then suddenly the furrows in her brow disappeared and he could see the knowledge jump into her eyes. "You mean you're going to . . . ?"

He nodded slowly. "Exactly. I've done a little research on the Ms. Taylors, and I think that the mother will fill the bill very nicely indeed. In fact I might go so far as to say that the timing of their arrival couldn't be better."

He smiled at her now, and she felt a surge of affection for him. He had always managed to take care of both of them and she trusted that he would again. She smiled back.

"What's that old saying? It takes one to know one? Well, forgive the paraphrasing, but it takes one to beat one, too. Only this one is going to be on our side."

Mariette stood up. "What can I do?"

"You can keep the daughter busy."

"But how?"

"You're a resourceful girl, Mariette. You'll figure something out." He looked at his watch. "And now you'd better get going. They'll be arriving at the airport soon."

"O.K. But there's no point taking the bus, just for the six of them. I think I'll take the Rolls and give them the royal treatment."

"That's my girl." He sat down and opened up another folder and started to scribble some figures in the margin of the page.

"Am I?"

He looked up. "What?"

"Your girl."

"Always were. Always will be."

CHAPTER 12

AFTER ABOUT HALF AN HOUR, Joyce closed the folder and stuffed it back into her bag. Harry had been right; the man was a cipher. But everyone had to have a past, everyone. The arrival of two women in the departure lounge interrupted any further thoughts about the doctor, and she turned her attention to them.

The older one was the more heavily built of the two. Joyce searched for a word to describe her and came up with "buxom." She was wearing a brightly coloured magenta sundress splashed with huge orange flowers, the front of which was cut to show off her well-developed chest.

"Sit over there, baby." The woman said plonking herself down into a seat at the other end of the row by the window. She let out a grateful sigh. "My feet are killing me."

Behind her, her face partly hidden by a large straw sunhat, followed a tall, willowy girl wearing a long-sleeved shirt and long pants of some light cotton material.

She sat in the direction the woman had indicated, but left one seat in between them. As she removed her hat, a cascade of blue-black hair was released from its confinement, and she bent over and shook it out and then tossed her head back until the hair fell like a heavy veil over her shoulders and down her back. Then she leaned forward, placed her elbows on her knees and her hands under her chin, and sighed loudly.

Joyce was able to see her face now, and visions of last month's *Vogue* cover floated before her eyes. Regina Taylor. There was no mistaking that face, or that hair. And, since everybody knew she never went anywhere without her mother, the other woman must be the redoubtable Belle.

Joyce perked up a little bit. This could prove interesting. She had been hearing for years all about the Taylor empire that Belle had created. You couldn't open a copy of *Forbes* or *Entrepreneur* without some piece about one of Belle's latest coups hitting you right in the face. She had even thought of doing a story on the Taylors at one time, but abandoned that idea when the mother let it be known, in no uncertain terms, that she was not interested.

But maybe now would be a good chance to try again, thought Joyce, taking a good, long, sideways look at Belle. So this was the woman that everybody said had more balls than any two men on Wall Street. From the looks of her, Joyce thought they were probably right. Doing an interview with her wasn't going to be any picnic.

Mother and daughter were whispering to each other now, and Joyce leaned a little closer. Eavesdropping was, after all, part of her business.

". . . . I don't care, Mother. I'm not going to spend the whole week covered up like a piece of precious porcelain. I want to go outside. I want to get a tan. I want. . . ."

Then the mother shook her head and said something that Joyce couldn't quite make out. The girl gave an exaggerated sigh, got up and flounced over to the far corner of the room, where she took up residence in another chair and stretched her seemingly endless legs across the aisle.

The mother took out a pack of Camels, lit one, and inhaled deeply. Joyce waited for her to cough. But she didn't. In fact, she didn't even exhale.

Evidently, the rumors about a rift between the world's most famous model and her mother were true. Well, even if she couldn't get the interview, these two would make an interesting addition to her spa piece. Harry would just love it. He. . . .

Visions of Harry were interrupted by the arrival of a rather bulky young woman dressed in a pale mauve pantsuit, who looked nervously around the departure lounge before taking a seat exactly halfway between Joyce and Belle Taylor. She had a dark semi-circle flowering under each arm, and Joyce thought that it was probably attributable to more than just the heat. The new arrival had the look of a mouse who suddenly finds itself in the same room with two cats.

After she settled herself into the chair, the young woman's eyes darted briefly around the room as if she could only relax once she had a better look at who else was present. When, for the first time, they landed on the magnificent Regina, Joyce saw a flicker of recognition which was then quickly replaced by something else, something that looked a lot like envy mixed with shame.

The large woman shifted in her seat. The molded plastic chair was obviously uncomfortable because of her size, and Joyce found herself feeling sorry for the new arrival. Being fat had to be no fun, especially when it was so hot. What was it, she wondered, that kept the mauve mouse from losing the weight? She looked like she could be a very pretty girl, minus fifty or sixty pounds.

As Joyce was considering this question, the new arrival hefted her bulging straw bag onto what was left of her lap and then rummaged around inside of it for a few seconds before emerging with her prize— a slightly melted Oh Henry bar. She quickly tore off the wrapping and then consumed the candy in two large bites. Licking the sticky remains from her finger tips, she sighed and then settled back to wait.

Well, that answered the "what" question, thought Joyce. Now, how about the "why"? She decided that this seemed like as good a place as any other to get started on the spa story, and was just about to move over and begin a conversation with the mouse, when she noticed that the man from the bar had just walked in.

In daylight, he was even better looking. He was, she also realized with a little rush of excitement, none other than Cliff Eastman, romantic idol of millions and hunk extraordinaire.

Unconsciously, she sat up a little straighter, smoothed her skirt over her knees, glad now that the pantyhose were covering her winter-white legs, and ran the tip of her tongue reassuringly over the last remnants of her coldsore.

He looked around the room, then, when his eyes landed on her, she found herself giving him her best "I-wore-braces-for-five-years-for-this" smile, and, without thinking, moved her suitcase away from the seat across from her. He smiled back and, sauntering over, lowered himself with casual grace into the seat. He knew that she knew who he was, and she knew that he knew. Nobody else seemed to be bothered.

Belle Taylor was frantically puffing on her third Camel, having viciously ground the butt of each of its predecessors on the tiled floor with the toe of her shoe before lighting up again. Her daughter was sulking in the corner, crossing and uncrossing her legs in a kind of stationary version of pacing. And the "mouse" was frantically searching in her bag for another chocolate tranquilizer. Joyce was busy deciding that she like the way Eastman's eyes crinkled up at the corners. It was a room full of activity.

"Going to St. Christophe?" His voice was deeper than his tan, with a resonance which was proof that years of proper breathing had conspired to produce this moment of perfect intonation.

A breathless "Yes," was all she could manage. "Pull yourself together, Redmond," her professional self demanded silently, but the rest of her selves excused the reaction by pointing out that, just because she was an editor and a journalist and worked for a big New York magazine, didn't mean she was immune to the same feelings as any other woman when confronted with a man who had the heartthrob of two generations. A man who wore no socks with his loafers!

And now as she looked at him sitting across from her, all she could think of was the last scene in "Neverending Love," when he had taken Felicity Fox into his arms and kissed her deeply before sweeping her off her feet, carrying her into their little cottage and kicking the door shut with his foot. Every woman in America had wanted a little of what went on behind that closed door. And at sixteen so had she. But she thought she had managed to grow out of that desire—until now.

"So am I." He was speaking again. "Get a little rest. Work on the tan. Eat the right food for a change. Got to keep the old machine in good repair." He patted himself on his incredibly flat stomach.

Was he kidding? He was the best-looking man she had ever seen. No spa in the world could improve on what Mother Nature had already done for him. Maybe he looked a little rough around the edges—eyes a little bloodshot—skin perhaps a trifle dull beneath the tan. . . . She thought back to the way he had sat hunched over his drink in the bar. Perhaps that was his problem. But, even so, he was still the most gorgeous man she had ever laid eyes on.

She smiled. "Me too." How was that for great conversation, not to mention stretching the truth? Anybody with half a brain could see that no spa in the world could make any difference to what Mother Nature had done for her, either.

The next moment, the "mouse" suddenly realized who he was and dropped her straw bag with a thunk on the tiled floor.

"It's you!" She wagged a chubby finger at him, all her insecurities for the moment forgotten. He winked at Joyce and looked playfully over his shoulder to see who was behind him. The other two women were also paying attention now.

"No, *you*! You're Cliff Eastman. I saw you on my VHS just last week in . . . oh what was the movie? I know. 'Murder in Venice.' You were just wonderful, Mr. Eastman," she cooed.

"Video, you say?" He looked bored. "Well, thank you anyway, Miss. . . ."

"Mrs. . . . Mrs. Cathy Stewart. I just think you are the greatest. Really the greatest! Wait until I tell Michael that I met *you*. In person."

"Michael?"

"My husband. He's in advertising."

"Advertising. How nice." Now he sounded bored, too.

But while he appeared to be giving his attention to his palpitating fan, Joyce noticed that his eyes had just landed and paused on the fabulous Regina for the third time. A look of recognition passed over his face. Did that look mean he recognized her as Regina Taylor, or was it just a case of beauty comprehending the presence of its own kind? In either case, she found herself considering for just a moment what it would be like to be on the receiving end of a look like that. Sometimes she wished she didn't notice so much. Any minute now he would get up and go over there and. . . .

A commotion outside the double doors refocused everybody's attention. A rather small woman with a lot of luggage and even more jewellery was arguing with the Barbados Air employee who had just arrived to check the tickets.

"But Ma'am, I told you that only two bags can go. Only two. There is room for no more. You have six. I cannot possibly let you take six bags."

"Oh dear! What am I supposed to do with them, then? Leave them here? Leave them to get stolen while I'm gone? I paid for my ticket and I already told you I will pay extra for the luggage if necessary, but I must take them with me. I must." She looked around as though searching for someone to help her.

The ticket taker shook his head very slowly from side to side.

"It is not a question of money for the bags, Ma'am. It is a question of room. It is a very small plane. There is no room for all your luggage. That is why we make the rule of two bags per person. That is all the room we have."

"I see, oh dear. Well, in that case, can't you send the other bags over on the next plane? That would seem to be a reasonable solution. Surely you should be able to manage that."

"I suppose we could do that, Ma'am. I will arrange to send your bags over on the next plane. It will arrive on Tuesday."

"Tuesday! Oh, but today is only Saturday. When I said the next plane I meant in an hour or two, not a day or two." Her voice drifted off and she looked around her once more.

Again the ticket taker slowly shook his head from side to side.

"She's going about it all the wrong way." Cliff stood up and went to the door.

"Excuse me, but it seems that we might be ale to sort something out for the lady." He spoke directly to the ticket taker. "I know that I only have one bag and that one of the ladies on this flight seems to have only one bag, so perhaps we could then accommodate at least two more of this lady's bags, since we will now have more space." He smiled his best movie-star smile."

I don't know." The ticket taker scratched his head. Joyce thought he was stalling. Probably waiting to see something green and folded before making up his mind.

"Well, let's just try, shall we?"

"Alright, then, we can try. When the plane is ready I will have somebody take the lady's bags out and I will try to fit them in somewhere, but I don't know. . . ."

"Thanks. I am sure the lady will appreciate it." He turned to the tiny woman beside him. "It's all in how you put it, really. And I suggest you put it in his hand, if you know what I mean."

"Thank you so much. I don't know what I would have done without your help. I simply don't handle these things very well. My husband has always been the one to make these kind of arrangements and I. . . ." She waved her hand as though to indicate that without her husband she was quite helpless. Her diamond ring flashed prisms on the ceiling.

He inclined his head slightly. Watching from her vantage point inside the departure lounge, Joyce wondered for a moment if he were going to kiss the woman's hand. It seemed a natural conclusion to this scene of gallantry, but he left it at the nod and came back into the room and resumed his seat.

"That was nice of you."

"Got to keep up the image."

"Which one of your movies was that scene from?"

He smiled. "You're pretty sharp, aren't you. It was 'Return of the Captain from Castile,' I think. One of the early ones, anyway. As I recall, they wanted a 'young' Tyrone Power to play the Spanish count who saved the sweet young thing from a fate worse than death. It's a pity I couldn't have saved us both from the script while I was at it. It was pretty awful."

"You're right, I remember it. But you were a real swashbuckler."

"Wasn't I, though. It's a shame that by then all the swashes had already been buckled. Those kind of films were out of style. I think the only place it ever played was on the Late Show."

"That's where I saw it."

He nodded, but he wasn't smiling.

The tiny woman had taken a seat in the lounge now, surrounded by her luggage. She looked like she was going away for a year, not a couple of weeks.

Joyce thought she looked very elegant, slightly confused, and vaguely familiar. And as always when someone looked vaguely familiar but she couldn't remember who they were, she tried to picture them in context. In this case she thought that maybe she had seen the woman at one of the *Destiny* social affairs, but she couldn't remember which one. That probably meant that she was with one of the other publications in the building, *Glamour*, or *Mademoiselle*, though she looked a little long in the tooth for that crowd.

A minute later the ticket taker appeared, and announced that the plane was ready for boarding and would they all have their tickets ready, please.

After a little shuffling and stretching they lined up obediently by the outer door. The Taylors, who made a big show of not talking to one another, were first in line. Then came the matronly Mrs. Stewart, then Cliff Eastman and herself and, finally, bringing up the rear, the tiny woman and a porter with her luggage. Each handed in their ticket as they passed out into the scorching heat of the Barbadian afternoon.

Joyce paused just outside the departure lounge door to change her tote bag from one shoulder to another. It was beginning to weigh a lot more than when she had packed it this morning. But then she had put her tape recorder and her notebooks in it, along with her toiletries and a couple of paperback books she had been meaning to read when she found the time. She put the suitcase down on the cement and shifted the bag to her other shoulder.

Just as she was bending down to pick up the suitcase again, she heard the ticket taker say to the tiny lady, "Yes, Mrs. Kraft, I will make sure that *all* your luggage is on board."

"Mrs. Kraft!" Joyce, still bent over, turned to look, and the woman, who had started toward the plane, almost fell over her.

"Oh, excuse me." Maxine patted her on the arm as she apologized and then continued on her way to the plane.

"It's Maxine!" said Joyce to no one in particular. "No wonder she looks so familiar. Of all the places in the universe. . . . Oh Harry, why me?"

CHAPTER 13

"THEY'VE GOT TO BE KIDDING?"

"This must be your first time in the islands. What were you expecting, a Lear jet?" Cliff handed Joyce's bag up into the cabin.

"No, but I wasn't expecting one of the Red Baron's rejects, either."

"Better get used to it. This is the only way to get where we're going." He hopped into the cabin and reached down to give her a hand. As he touched her fingers he looked deep into her eyes, and a little charge of electricity ran up her arm. Under different circumstances it would have been a moment to remember. As it was, she simply shook her head.

"I can't. I can't fly in that thing. It looks like the only way it could get off the ground is if it ran out of island."

"You're close. But don't worry. It only flies at about two thousand feet, so if things don't work out, we don't have far to fall."

"You're overwhelming me with security."

"Come on. You flew in here on a plane."

"Exactly. And I'd like to fly out the same way."

But he extended his hand again and she reluctantly took it and hauled herself into the dim interior of the plane.

After her eyes adjusted to the gloom, Joyce looked around. Cigarette burns were everywhere, including the ceiling. Ashtrays were obviously considered an unnecessary luxury. Old, stained life vests were stuffed matter-of-factly under each seat. She wondered briefly which ship they had come from, and then decided she'd rather not know. Then something else caught her attention and she looked up. Thin shafts of light filtered down from above her head.

"I can see the sky through the cracks in the ceiling."

"Don't think about it. Here, sit by the window. The view will take your mind off things." Cliff helped her into one of the seats. It looked like it had been stolen from the front of a '58 Chevy. And no sooner was she settled in, than Cliff dumped a large makeup case on her lap.

"The porter wasn't far off. There is no bloody room in this plane. Do you mind having this one on your lap? Everybody else has volunteered to have a piece of Mrs. Kraft's luggage. I'll put the big piece on my seat and then I can go and sit up front with the pilot."

At the mention of his name, the pilot, who was wearing a leather helmet and goggles, probably, Joyce decided, in honor of the historic significance of his craft, turned around and flashed a brilliant smile punctuated by one gold incisor.

"You folks all ready to go?"

The folks nodded in unison, feeling no doubt that at this point they had little choice, and Cliff climbed over into the co-pilot's seat.

The ground crew-cum-propellor-turner slammed the door shut and returned to his station at the front of the plane, ready to fling the propellers into action when he got the signal.

The pilot turned on the ignition and, after a series of coughs and splutters, the variegated thrum of the ancient motor vibrated through the entire fuselage.

"Now I know how a milk shake feels," Joyce said out loud, and found she was clutching Maxine's makeup case as though it alone could calm her reverberant universe. As she looked around the murky interior, she noted with grim satisfaction that the others were also hanging on more tightly than necessary to their various pieces of luggage, and the plane hadn't even started to taxi yet.

"One minute to blast off." The pilot let out a Geoffrey Holder-type laugh, banged on the window of the cockpit, and the "ground crew" kicked a hunk of wood out from under the tires.

The plane began to roll down the runway with a curious thunking rhythm. Joyce thought that maybe one of the tires was flat. Could they still take off? More important, could they still land? She tightened her grip on Maxine's bag.

A few moments later, however, the plane gave a jolt and then a thump and they were airborne. Joyce looked around. Everyone seemed mildly surprised to still be alive.

The pilot turned in his seat.

"Be about twenty minutes to St. Christophe. Just sit back and enjoy the view."

Joyce wondered if he meant the one through the cracks in the ceiling or the one through the grimy little windows. She looked out the one window on her side which was level with her seat.

Not more than fifteen hundred feet below them was the turquoise blue of the Caribbean, so clear that you could see the darker blue of the submerged islands intermingled with the strange shapes of the coral reefs glowing a deep emerald green. And each little island, some nothing more than a pile of rocks protruding from the sea, was bordered with a crescent of white sand, creating hundreds of tiny perfect beaches. All in all it *was* a beautiful sight. . . . The plane gave a sudden shudder as the pilot banked to the left. . . . But not one worth dying for.

Joyce turned her attention back to the other passengers. Up front, Cliff was saying something to the pilot who nodded and gave a massive, glinting grin. Maxine was holding her purse and gripping the arm of her seat with the same hand. Only her white knuckles gave away the truth concealed by her carefully composed face. The Taylors were sitting across from each other, sullen-faced and steely-eyed. And Cathy was sharing the bench from the '58 Chevy with Joyce.

"Are you nervous?" Cathy's voice was only slightly above a whisper.

Joyce shook her head. "Petrified" was the word. But why waste what might be her last few moments discussing her fear of flying in this airborne egg crate?

"No, I'm not nervous. I'm sure it's perfectly safe. These small planes look in worse shape than they really are. They wouldn't let them fly if there was really any danger." Joyce thought that invoking the power of the omnipotent "they" would at least make her companion feel better. Cathy looked as though she were the sort of person who still believed that the "theys" of the world did everything in the best interest of those in their care. It worked. She relaxed visibly.

"You're right, of course." She sighed with relief. "My name's Cathy Stewart." She freed a plump hand from the strap of her purse, and Joyce shook it.

"Joyce, Joyce . . . uh. . . . Allan." Joyce suddenly realized that she had given no thought to the new identity she was going to need for the duration of her stay. And it was more important than ever, now Maxine was along for the ride.

"I saw you talking to Cliff Eastman back in the departure lounge. Isn't he dreamy?" She gave a big sigh. Joyce decided then that when Mrs. Stewart was younger she had probably "gone steady" or, even worse, "been pinned."

"Dreamy."

"I guess I did go a little overboard, back there. Michael's always saying that I don't think before I act. But it was just the shock, I guess. You know it's not every day you get to meet a real live movie star. . . ." Her voice trailed off and she began searching in her purse for something. A moment later she came up with a bag of potato chips. She offered some to Joyce.

"Want some?"

"No thanks."

Cathy shrugged and then proceeded to help herself. "Salt and vinegar's my favorite." Joyce nodded and watched as her seatmate devoured the bag of chips two or three at a time, crunching happily. In another minute they were gone.

"Are you married?" Cathy spoke through the last of the chips.

"Married? Ah . . . yes, of course I'm married." As she spoke Joyce placed her right hand over her left so that her ring finger was hidden.

"Children?"

"Children? Ah, no. No children." Faking a husband was one thing, thought Joyce, but trying to conjure up non-existent children was beyond her. "How about you?"

"I have three children. Two-year-old twins, a boy and a girl, and another boy who is five. And I'm married, of course." Cathy giggled self-consciously. "My husband, Michael, is in advertising. What does your husband do?"

"Alan? uh . . ."

"Your husband's first name is Alan and your last name is Allan? Does that mean his name is Alan Allan?"

"I guess it does. I mean . . . yes, it does. His parents had quite the sense of humor." Joyce laughed to show she appreciated the joke, and made a mental note that to be a good liar you first had to have a good memory.

"What does he do?"

"Do? Uh . . . he's . . . in chips." She clutched at the first thing that came to mind. Besides, it sounded like the kind of hi-tech area that the inquisitive Mrs. Stewart would know next to nothing about and would therefore not wish to discuss any further.

"Potato?"

"No. Silicon. As in computers?"

"Oh." Cathy sounded disappointed.

"My husband is in the magazine business." It was Maxine. "He's the executive managing editor of *Destiny* magazine. You must have heard of it. It's very big. Two and a half million readers. His name is Harry Kraft. I'm Maxine. She leaned forward from her seat across the isle. "Nice to meet you both."

"Hi. My name's Cathy Stewart and this is Joyce Allan." Joyce nodded, searching Maxine's face for any flicker of recognition, but when she saw none she relaxed a little, and leaned her forehead against the cool of the window glass. The air in the plane was turning stale. Belle had been smoking up a storm. How much longer before they landed?

The tone of the engine changed abruptly and Joyce was immediately alert again. They were slowing down. She hoped it was on purpose, and looked below for some sign of land. Thankfully, coming up in front of them was the white crescent of a beach followed by some flat green scrub and next, what looked to be a very short landing strip which they were approaching much too quickly.

Everybody had stopped talking now, sensing the descent, waiting for the bump that would indicate a successful landing. But it turned out to be more like a rattling thud, as though the plane had just dropped out of the sky and hit the tarmac like the crate it was.

They taxied the full length of the runway before stopping. Then the pilot turned around.

"This is it. Last stop. Everybody out."

Cliff climbed back into the cabin, while the pilot jumped down and came around to open the cabin door. The luggage was handed out first and then each of the women received a helping hand to disembark. There were no steps, and it was a good two feet to the ground.

Joyce noticed that Cliff gave Regina the now-familiar deep-eyed look as he took her hand to help her down, and the girl blinked at him like a frightened fawn. Joyce turned away, vaguely disappointed, and looked down the length of the airfield. The place seemed uninhabited. There were no buildings, no people, and no cars. What were they supposed to do now—walk?

But suddenly a cloud of dust at the far end of the runway alerted them all to the approach of their transportation.

In a few seconds, the speeding car drew abreast of the small plane, the dust settling perversely on its smooth white body and its dark-blue-tinted glass. It was the longest Rolls-Royce Joyce had ever seen. Moreover, from its flying lady hood ornament to its matching white wheel covers and shining chrome bumpers, it was also the ritziest car she had ever seen. From the ridiculous to the sublime, she thought, turning her back on the plane. At least things were looking up.

On the side of the driver's door was the logo of the spa, two sets of waves, one above the other, navy and turquoise, and then the name of the spa underneath. The door opened and the chauffeur, a blond-on-blond girl of about seventeen dressed in a uniform that was the precise blue of her eyes, got out.

"Hello, everybody. My name is Mariette. Welcome to St. Christophe."

CHAPTER 14

JOYCE HAD BEEN RIGHT ABOUT HARRY. While she had been sweating it out at the airport in Barbados, he was taking a leisurely walk up Madison Avenue on his way to a quiet lunch.

It was a glorious day. The kind that happens in New York only in early spring. The sky was clear. The sun was warm. And a gentle, inspiring breeze was blowing off the East River, ruffling the yellow-green buds that managed to return to the trees year after year in spite of the pollution. It was a day made for forgetting the dreary, sopping skies of winter and ignoring the sizzling, stinking inevitabilities of July and August. A day that hadn't yet been forced to make up its mind.

Harry stopped and looked in a window near 49th Street. On display were men's clothing and shoes. He looked down at his own worn loafers that were so ancient it was difficult, now, to determine what color they had been when new. He really needed to get another pair, but somehow he just couldn't be bothered. He decided he had probably reached that age that he always remembered his old man as being. The age when one ceases to be a man and becomes instead a father figure, one who is disposed to select comfort over style and ends up shuffling around in worn slippers and a warm vest, mumbling about The War.

The thought made him shudder; he was after all, only forty-nine. Too young to declare himself a candidate for the sidelines of life. But next year he would be fifty and then what? God. He never thought he would ever be fifty.

Turning the corner at 50th Street, he walked toward the Helmsley Palace. He shivered. The wind was a little more biting, out of the sun, and he was only wearing a suit jacket. Maybe the need for a warm vest was closer than he imagined. He had never felt the cold when he was twenty-five. But that, he reminded himself, was almost a half a lifetime ago.

When he reached the entrance of the hotel, he noticed that the doorman was still wearing his burgundy-and-gold winter uniform and that he was sweating slightly inside his greatcoat. Evidently the queen had not yet declared spring at the palace.

Harry pushed through the heavy brass revolving doors and into the posh and incredibly neat interior. It was, he reflected, one of the few hotels in New York that could pass the white-glove test that his mother had inflicted so often on Maxine at the beginning of their marriage. Poor Maxine. She had tried so hard to keep one step ahead of Sophie, and it had never worked.

Sophie knew more about dirt than any woman he had ever known. She was like a bloodhound sniffing out a ferret. Every time she came over to their tiny apartment on East 71st, she went about her task with a single-mindedness only someone who believes in the inherent evil and corruption of dirt can envision. And Maxine had never once passed muster.

He thought now, with the wisdom of distance, that it was probably his mother's way of putting his wife in her place, and perhaps of instilling in her a sense of what wives were supposed to be all about. But, at the time, a bout with her ever-critical mother-in-law had seemed like the end of the world, and Maxine usually ended up in a flood of tears and reproaches the minute Sophie left.

The funny thing was, that over the years since they got married, Maxine had slowly been evolving, until one morning Harry woke up and found that through some quirk of fate he was now sleeping with his mother. Maxine had become Sophie, and Harry was now his own son. Or at least that's the way she made him feel. Kind of too old and too young at the same time. He went into Harry's Bar—no relation to Hemingway or himself—and took a seat on one of the semi-circular brown leather banquettes under the window. There were only a few other people sitting at the bar. The lunch-time crowd had long since departed for a shopping spree on Fifth Avenue or a ride around the park. He was glad. He liked it like this. Nice and quiet. Maybe forty-nine wasn't so young after all.

The waitress came over and offered him a menu, but he waved it aside and gave her his order. He always had the same thing, the chicken club and two Lowenbrau, because "Harry's" was one of the few places in New York where they put real chicken in the club sandwich, not that pressed-out plastic stuff that comes in a roll and tastes like chicken-flavored putty. He also liked the idea that they made the sandwiches right at the bar where you could see what they were putting in, just in case. And besides, along with the sandwich, they served those little, red-hot peppers that were a welcome relief from the ubiquitous dills that dressed up every other "club" in town.

The waitress returned with the first Lowenbrau, and poured it in front of him into a tall frosted Pilsner glass. She smiled as she placed it on the little coaster on the table.

"Your lunch won't be long."

"That's O.K. I'm not in a hurry." He smiled back. She was a young girl about Bradley's age. She had long, long legs and a small heart-shaped face and she wore a ring on the third finger of her left hand. Married already? He shook his head. As she walked away, he noticed for the first time that she had hair like Joyce's. Thick and kind of reddish-brown, bouncing about on the top of her shoulders.

Joyce had been a good sport to take that spa story. Not that he had given her much choice, but he needed it done and she was the best by far to do it. They had to boost their circulation soon. The last few issues had been a little too highbrow, and sales had fallen off. What they needed now was something a little spicy, something the average woman could relate to and at the same time be informed by. And now with this new angle about the guy who owned the place becoming a possibility, he knew he had definitely made the right decision sending Joyce. She would do a good job.

Besides, he thought, taking a long sip of the cold beer, she looked like she could use a rest. She was getting that pinched-in look about her face that said she was under too much stress. Maybe he had been working her too hard.

He was just wondering if she was mad at him for inviting himself to dinner the previous evening, when the waitress arrived with his club sandwich, some mayonnaise, and a small bowl of coleslaw on the side. She smiled. Freckles danced across the bridge of her nose.

"Would you like your other beer now?"

"In a few minutes, O.K.?"

She went back to the bar and stood leaning on the rail talking to the bartender. She really did remind him a lot of Joyce. Perhaps it was her air of confidence. Her I-can-handle-it demeanor. Perhaps it was those long, long legs. Joyce had long legs. They made her almost as tall as him. Well, not almost, maybe, but standing next to her was a lot different from standing next to Maxine. Maxine was so short he sometimes felt he had to lean over in order to have a conversation with her.

He spread some mayo liberally on one quarter of the sandwich, appreciating, for perhaps the hundredth time, the thick slices of chicken that invariably escaped out both sides of the bread, and took a bite. He chewed for a minute and then took a small bite of the red pepper. It was so hot it made his eyes water. Just the way he liked it.

Joyce and Maxine. Now there were two opposite ends of a continuum, and yet there wasn't all that much difference in their ages. Maxine was forty-five. Joyce had to be in her late thirties. And yet they were as different as night and day. Joyce was all work, ambition, and get-the-hell-out-of-my-way, and Maxine was all soft and motherly with those big brown eyes that said please-let-me-take-care-of-you. He had found that quality so appealing when they first met. It made him want to take care of her for the rest of their lives. So what had happened?

He scooped up a forkful of the slaw and the waitress topped up his glass with the second beer. He bet she took care of herself just fine.

Probably had one of those "equal" relationships that were all the rage these days. What would it be like to be married to a woman who wasn't dependent on you for everything? Someone who could be counted on occasionally to be leaned on, rather than always the other way around. Things had changed so much in the twenty-five years he had been married to Maxine. No wonder he felt totally out of it sometimes. It was like the world had passed him by and left him with the burden of a marriage that he no longer fit.

He thought about his shoes again, comfort versus style. And realized that neither word applied any longer to his marriage. Soon, he would have to do something about it.

Slathering the remainder of the mayo on the last quarter of the sandwich, he popped half of it into his mouth before adding the last of the hot pepper, and chewed contentedly.

I wonder why Joyce never got married, he thought to himself, taking a sip of beer and washing down the last of the sandwich. She was alright in the looks department, more than alright really, and yet she lived in that funny little apartment with somebody else's demented cat. Didn't she ever want to have kids? He tried to picture Joyce with kids. It didn't work.

He picked up a crumb of bacon from his plate. Lunch had been just right. It would probably be the only thing he ate today, since he had already decided to sleep in his office again tonight rather than going home to Maxine and face another bout of crying or, even worse, pretending that nothing was wrong.

The waitress brought the check and he threw his American Express card onto the tray. When she came back, he made sure to leave her a nice tip. After all, she was a working girl, like Joyce.

He pushed his way through the doors and back out onto 50th Street. The doorman tipped his hat. The wind had dropped. It felt like it might be getting warmer.

On his way back to the office he decided to call Bradley and take the kid out to lunch during the week. Maybe sound him out about what was going on with Maxine before he broached the subject of divorce, himself.

CHAPTER 15

A "FLOWER FENCE" OF BARBADOS PRIDE lined the half-mile-long approach to the spa with a mass of brilliant yellow blossoms, punctuated here and there along the way with a jolt of pink or red from a cluster of hibiscus bushes. And, towering above both, a double row of royal palms rode the breeze in perfect unison, drawing the eye to its ultimate destination.

At the end of the drive, the Rolls passed beneath an archway and into the cobbled courtyard that marked the entrance to the spa and the end of the outside world.

It was an idyllic location, to say the least.

Mariette came round and opened the doors for her passengers, and then stepped aside so they could get the full effect of the place as they got out of the car.

On the terrace, in front of the main house, a blue-tiled fountain splashed cheerfully as a statue of the nude Venus spilled an endless stream of water from the jug she carried on her shoulder into the reflecting pool below. And twisting thickly over the ivory stucco walls, vines of red frangipani tangled in an aromatic knot with white jasmine, as they wound their way up and over onto the tiled roof. Meanwhile, hidden in the cool thicket of their branches, nesting doves and tiny island thrushes provided the only competition for the music of the fountain.

"Someone will put your luggage in your rooms." It was Mariette. "Please go inside. Dr. Voight is waiting for all of you in the drawing room."

"Oh, isn't it all simply perfect!" Cathy took a deep breath. "and the air. It smells like perfume."

"So does the mezzanine at Bloomingdale's." Joyce got out of the car and stretched. Perfection always made her leery.

"It reminds me a lot of the place where Harry and I had our honeymoon in Bermuda," offered Maxine to no one in particular.

Great, thought Joyce. A reprise of Harry's honeymoon was just what she needed. But Maxine had already turned her attention to counting her luggage.

Joyce made her way up the wide tiled steps and in through the double oak doors which looked as though they had once adorned an abbey or at least the *casa grande* of an old Spanish family. Whoever financed this place must have been loaded. No wonder they weren't shy about asking three grand a week for the pleasure of your company.

Inside, she blinked her eyes in the unaccustomed dimness. It was dark in the hallway, after the brilliance of the late afternoon sun, and cool, although not with the coolness one expects from air-conditioning, more like the kind that comes from thick old walls and smooth, tiled floors. The kind that reeks of expensive antiquity.

Above the foyer, a heavy iron chandelier with eight enormous sconces hung suspended by a single, thick-linked chain from the second floor ceiling. To the right, a wide oak staircase rose half a flight before turning and completing its ascent at the second floor gallery. And, set in the stucco wall, a large stained glass window, infused with tropical light, shed its jewels across the floor.

Joyce craned her neck to study the glass. It looked very old, the colors too rich and deep to be of recent manufacture.

"Lovely." Cliff had come to stand behind her.

His breath was warm on the back of her neck. She shivered involuntarily and turned around.

"It is beautiful, isn't it?"

"I wasn't talking about the window," he said, his voice husky with implication.

She felt the color begin to rise in her face but, before she could think of an off-handedly casual but worldly response, Cathy and Maxine came through the front doors, followed by the Taylors. Then a maid appeared and directed them through the doors to the left. The doctor was waiting.

"Ach. Guten Tag! I see you have all arrived in one piece." This was followed by a little chuckle. "Some of the guests are a little overwhelmed by our local airline. But I can see that none of you were in the least concerned."

Dr. Voight was a large, powerfully built man, and he smiled a broad, encompassing smile that showed off his whiter-than-white teeth. Joyce decided that he was good-looking in a sort of dark, heroic, Wagnerian way.

"I am Dr. Hans Voight, the director and, I am pleased to say, the owner, of the spa." He spoke with an accent which was German or possibly Austrian. After introducing himself, he began to greet them individually by name. Joyce, who was at the end of the line, realized that he had done his homework rather too well for her convenience, and so she introduced herself before he could say her name out loud.

A slight frown crinkled his enormous brow and then he smiled and winked. "Of course, Mrs. *Allan*. We are so pleased you could come."

That had been easier than she had expected. Harry must have tipped him off for the need to keep her identity a secret when he made the arrangements for her to be here. And the good doctor naturally went along with the idea. Anything for a little free publicity, no doubt.

"Please, everyone, sit down. I will order some refreshments and then we will have our little orientation meeting before you go to your rooms to unpack."

He rang a small silver bell and the maid reappeared.

"Six cocktails, please, Gertrude."

While they waited for the "cocktails," Joyce had a good look round the room. It was expensively furnished in a sort of eclectic European style. A Louis XV chair here, a Regency desk there, a Chinois screen on one wall. Very comfortable, yet extremely elegant. Like the doctor himself, it had a well-lived-in but well-kept look about it.

She tried to decide how old he was. It was hard to tell. He had the glowing look of good health and youthful vitality that were no doubt a necessary prerequisite in this business. In fact, just looking at him made her feel consumptive. But finally, unable to pin a more definite age on him, she settled for somewhere between forty and forty-five. She might have guessed even younger except for his eyes, which said that he had been around for at least a century, possibly two.

The cocktails arrived momentarily and were duly passed around on a silver tray.

Joyce sipped hers tentatively, prepared not to like it but finding it rather refreshing, if a little sweet.

"What is this?" Her mother had always said you should never take a drink from a stranger, just in case he had slipped some LSD into it. Not that Dr. Voight looked like an escapee from the acid farm, but old habits die hard.

"Ach, that is my special recipe. Pineapple juice, a little bitters, some mineral water, and something special that is my little secret. You will find it very cleansing for the stomach. A good way to start your stay at the spa, to rid your system of the impurities of the outside world."

As if on cue, Belle Taylor put her drink down and took out a cigarette. Dr. Voight looked as though someone had just drawn a gun and demanded his money or his life.

"*Mrs. Taylor*, please! Was ist das? What do you think you are doing?"

Unabashed, she lit the Camel, took a deep drag, and sat back in her chair before meeting the doctor eye to eye.

"Look, doctor, let's get something straight, up front. I did not come here to 'rid myself of the impurities of the outside world.' If anything, they are the only thing that keeps me going, so don't expect me to give up my cigarettes. I'll go along with the exercizing thing and the facials and all that crap. I'll even put up with the bean sprouts and the tofu, or whatever passes for food around here, but I will *not* give up these." She held up the pack of Camels. "So don't waste your time trying to reform me. O.K.?"

"You are obviously a very determined woman, Mrs. Taylor."

Belle blew out a cloud of smoke and raised a plucked eyebrow. "You can say that again."

"But at least permit me to point out that smoking *is* bad for your health."

"You said the key word, doctor. *My* health. My business."

"I am afraid that while you are here, your health is also *my* business." His voice took on a tone of intimacy then. "Perhaps we could discuss a little hypnotherapy for your problem, later on?"

Belle narrowed her eyes and flicked a long ash from the end of the Camel. "It's possible."

The doctor smiled just for her. "You'll be surprised at how much better you'll feel."

"I don't like surprises."

"I can assure you that you won't feel a thing, if that is what you're worried about."

Belle fixed the doctor with her eyes. "I don't think I have any concerns in that area."

Joyce felt a surge of animal magnetism pass between the two of them. It reminded her of the time she had seen two lions at the zoo about to celebrate the rites of spring. You couldn't tell if they were enjoying it, but they sure did a lot of growling and roaring before they got down to business. She was relieved when Dr. Voight cleared his throat and the tension from the air at the same time.

He moved in front of the fireplace which was more decorative than functional and which, with its huge Venetian mirror, provided a good backdrop for his orientation speech.

"I know that every one of you has come to The Spa at St. Christophe for a different reason. Each of you wants something from your stay and we will endeavor to give you whatever you need. We provide a very personal service here." And here Joyce saw his eyes flicker over toward Belle. "So if there is anything you want, you have only to ask.

"As you may not know, if this is your first time at a spa, there are two separate approaches to the idea of what I like to call "spaing." The European and the North American. The European spa ethic is based on rest and relaxation. The idea is to come to the spa and retreat from the cares and troubles of the everyday world for a period of time, so that you may go back to the outside world feeling not only physically but mentally refreshed.

"The American concept is a little different. The emphasis is more on the body than the mind. Fitness and diet are very important, and the guest activity-level is usually very high. You can imagine the sort of thing I mean. Up early for a brisk hike, hours of swimming and aerobics, lots of general running about. . . ." He paused and looked around.

"Sounds just like work to me." It was Regina.

"Ah, the beautiful Miss Taylor has a point. Too much work, too little play, makes for a very dull life." He tut-tutted and shook his head. "But, at St. Christophe, I like to think that we combine both of these concepts. We want you to enjoy your stay."

His "one of the gang" approach did not impress Joyce, who had already decided that, for whatever reason, he seemed to be trying too hard. Whoever he was, her instincts told her that he had the word "phony" stamped all over him.

"Our guests are encouraged to do as much or as little as they like." He was talking again. "You may decide to take a full program of exercise and diet, or just be lazy and enjoy the sun and the peace and quiet. It is up to you. The only thing we insist upon here is that you eat the dietetic meals we provide. I can assure you that our chef, Adolpho, is a gourmet—no bean sprouts and tofu as Mrs. Taylor has suggested. You will be pleasantly surprised at just how delicious spa food can be. By eating the meals we provide for you, you can be sure that you will feel a hundred percent better and perhaps even a little thinner, by the time you leave here, even if you do nothing more than lift a newspaper."

Joyce noticed that Cathy Stewart was smiling. "Thinner" was the word she had been waiting to hear. The doctor had evidently hit home with her.

"Tomorrow morning each of you will have an individual counselling session and a medical, so that we may decide what program will best suit you during your stay. Now, before I have someone show you to your rooms, are there any questions?

"None? Very well, then, I will see you all for dinner." He displayed his teeth again, and rang the bell. The maid appeared a moment later.

"Please show our guests to their rooms, Gertrude." He turned, saying "See you later," and then disappeared through the doors that led to the patio.

Joyce drained the last of her "cocktail," and picked up her purse. Thank god it wasn't going to be one of those regimented health farms that doubles as a boot camp. At least now she would have the time and the opportunity to get to know her fellow guests well enough to do her job. And, who knows, she might even enjoy a little "spa-ing" while she was at it.

Gertrude showed each of them to their "rooms," although the term underestimated the reality. Each of the guest rooms was actually a suite, consisting of a bedroom and a small sitting room and bathroom done in a blend of European antiques and plantation chic which gave them a timeless air of casual comfort.

Each bathroom contained a marble tub and separate shower and a complete array of things like toothpaste, shampoo, soap, hand-cream etc. etc., as well as a turquoise terry robe and a pair of matching terry slippers embroidered with the double waves of the spa logo.

But, when Joyce finally closed the door on her suite, she was interested less in the amenities and luxuries than in basking in the peace and quiet of an empty room. It had been a hectic and tiring day, and already her mind was busy working on the article. Examining and discarding angles. Summing up her impressions of the spa and the other guests. Anything to keep from thinking about the way she had felt when Cliff Eastman had come up behind her in the hallway and said, "Lovely." It had been so corny. But so effective.

She kicked off her shoes and undid her dress, letting it fall to the floor. Then she squirmed her way out of the clinging pantyhose which stuck to her legs like so many polyester leeches, and lay down on the white and blue duvet of the double bed. The soft, clean cotton felt good against her sticky skin. The curtains were drawn against the afternoon light. The room was cool. She closed her eyes.

Visions of a young Harry and Maxine on their honeymoon drifted at the edge of her mind. She tried to picture them in bed together—

big, blustering Harry and tiny, timid Maxine—bodies twisting in passion on the tangled sheets. But even her imagination couldn't manage that. Harry and Maxine faded from the picture and were replaced in the tangle of sheets with two other figures. The man's face became clearer. It was Cliff. But before the woman's face came into focus, Joyce was fast asleep.

CHAPTER 16

WHEN JOYCE WOKE UP, she could tell it was getting late, because the sun no longer shed a thin, bright line beneath the curtains. She turned over. The digital radio clock beside the bed said 6:31. There was half an hour before they were expected to gather in the drawing room for pre-dinner cocktails. She decided to have a shower and wash her hair.

In the rose-colored marble shower stall, jets of hot water sprayed out from several different levels and angles, and she let them play for a while on the muscles of her legs and back, soothing and relaxing away the tensions of travel. After a few minutes, she ducked her head under one of the higher jets, poured spa shampoo into the palms of her hands, and massaged it vigorously through her hair. In the soft island water it soon lathered into thick, creamy bubbles that smelled heavily of coconut.

After rinsing off, Joyce stepped out onto the fluffy white carpet and, pulling on the turquoise robe, tied the belt tightly around her waist. Then, reaching for one of the luxuriously thick, matching towels from the rail next to the sink, she wrapped her hair in it, turban style, before padding out onto the small balcony that led off the sitting room. She was feeling much better.

It was a beautiful evening. The sun was low, dipping down into the far edge of the Caribbean, its slanted rays staining the wispy clouds lavender and fuschia against the deeping ultramarine of the evening sky. Everything was very still. The birds had stopped their singing and gone to nest for the night. Even the rows of royal palms that lined the drive had ceased their swaying and stood like silent, dark sentinels against the sunset. It was a night made for romance, she thought to herself. If, of course, you were into that sort of thing.

With a sigh, she turned back to face the sea, her mind on the other Venus down on the terrace. St. Christophe was certainly a fitting place for the goddess of love and beauty. Might even make a good title shot for the article. Kind of a "fountain of youth" angle. She took one more look at the escaping sun and went back inside to dry her hair.

That was the trouble with being a journalist. You could never just accept things and enjoy them for what they were. Everything had to have an angle, she thought, bending from the waist, and brushing her hair forward before she began to dry it.

It took her quite a while with such a heavy mane, especially as her tiny travel dryer with the dual voltage attachment seemed to blow with all the power of a confirmed asthmatic. But, when she had finished, she stood upright and tossed the hair back from her face and it foamed around her shoulders like a sun-struck chestnut wave. She looked in the mirror, pleased with what she saw. It was the first time in a long time she had stopped to really notice how she looked.

Then, as usual, she stroked on lipstick quickly, but tonight she added a swipe of peach blusher and a touch of navy blue mascara as well, finishing off with a healthy spray of Galanos. She rarely wore perfume or mascara but, for some reason, tonight she felt like looking her best.

Next she dressed in a pair of taupe linen trousers and matching silk-knit sweater. It was an outfit she had bought on a whim at Bonwit's. Hardly appropriate for her lifestyle, it was too delicate and far too expensive, even though she had bought it on sale. But it made her look like a very well-to-do Westchester matron—somebody who could actually afford to spend three thousand dollars for a week of Spartan self-indulgence—so, she had decided to bring it along.

Finished dressing, she slipped into a pair of canvas espadrilles and tucked her room key into the pocket of the trousers. On the way out the door, she caught sight of herself in the full-length mirror—provided, no doubt, to either intimidate or congratulate, depending on one's success during the week. She looked as good as she felt. Harry would hardly recognize this casual but elegant and unharried woman. She wondered what Cliff would think.

Cocktails were a brief affair for her, since, by the time she reached the drawing room, the maid was just striking the brass gong on the sideboard to indicate that dinner was about to be served.

They all drifted into the dining room, which was furnished in much the same style as the drawing room. A long rosewood table with a border of intricate marquetry shone to a high gleam, and was surrounded by eight matching chairs with pale green silk seats. On the green-and-ivory striped silk-covered wall behind the head chair was a large hunting print showing several horses, a pack of dogs, and one frightened fox cavorting across an English field. Slightly out of place, perhaps, but positively reeking of old world charm. On either side of the painting and behind each chair, wall sconces with dark green lampshades fringed in gold provided a glow of subdued and very flattering light.

Dr. Voight sat at the head of the table with Belle on his right and Regina on his left, and directed the others to sit wherever they pleased. Maxine took the chair next to Belle and Cliff sat next to Joyce who was sitting beside Regina. Cathy, who arrived flushed and out of breath just as everyone was seated, naturally took a seat on Cliff's other side.

The doctor tapped on his crystal water glass to get their attention.

"Guten Abend, ladies and gentlemen, tonight we are using the small private dining room because there are only a few of us and it is much more, shall we say, intimate." He glanced briefly at Belle. "Beside your napkins you will find a small printed menu. On it are the two selections for dinner this evening. You may choose either the A menu or the B menu for your meal, but you may not choose from both, as the caloric content has been carefully calculated for each menu." He smiled benevolently, "Now please enjoy your dinner," and went back to talking to Belle.

The maid came round and filled each of their water glasses with Perrier, floating a slice of lemon on top and tucking a spring of mint down the side.

Cliff raised his glass to Joyce. "Here's to dietetic juleps." He took a sip and made a face. "Wish I had brought some vodka with me."

The appetizer was served next. Joyce had chosen the B menu, and received a minted cucumber salad. Regina and Cliff had both chosen the A menu and were served a small cup of borscht. Cathy, who seemed to have trouble deciding between starvation and deprivation, eventually chose the B menu after seeing how small the cup of borscht was.

Then came the main course, for Joyce a shrimp curry with chutney and brown rice. And for the others chicken Stroganoff with summer squash. The portions were decidedly smaller than any of them were used to, but, to everyone's surprise, it actually tasted like "real" food.

Joyce ate slowly, chewing each mouthful. She had read somewhere that you eat less if you chew more, and since this was certainly less, she wanted to make the most of it. Cliff ate the chicken but left the squash and pushed his plate away. This delighted Cathy, who had wolfed down her Stroganoff and was busy scraping miniscule bits of chicken and sauce off her plate. She looked around to see if the doctor was watching, and then leaned closer and whispered to Cliff.

"Aren't you going to eat your squash?"

"No. You can have it if you want. I don't like squash very much."

Cathy pulled the plate toward her and in two seconds had cleaned up the squash.

"Just wait until my friends hear that I ate Cliff Eastman's squash." Cathy sat back, momentarily sated.

Joyce suppressed an urge to be sarcastic. She bet there were a ton of women in Hollywood who could boast of an even more intimate connection with him than that.

Dessert followed. Joyce got a pineapple boat with coconut sauce that reminded her rather alarmingly of the shampoo she had used earlier, and the others had strawberries Romanoff. All in all, it was a tasty if slight meal, and Joyce kept the menu cards and tucked them into her pocket, in case she might need them for the article.

Throughout the dinner, Dr. Voight had been busy with Mrs. Taylor, and Regina had been sulkily shoving her food around her plate, much to Cathy's chagrin. Joyce noticed that Maxine had been very quiet. She had hardly said two words, breaking her silence only once to ask Dr. Voight a question about the origin of the recipes for tonight's menu. It was the sort of question people usually ask when they feel they have to make conversation but really have nothing to say. And, although she nodded and smiled occasionally, her eyes seemed dull and far away. Joyce wondered if she was thinking about Harry and, if so, what she was thinking. They certainly seemed like an odd couple.

Her thoughts of Maxine were interrupted by Cliff's leg brushing against hers. She started. And then the color rose in her face as he apologized. What was wrong with her anyway? She was as jumpy as Fredo when the cat down the hall was in season. She waited an appropriate length of time and then, in the guise of changing her position, carefully moved her leg away.

She hadn't felt so nervous around a man since she was sixteen and Biff Collins, her first real crush, had asked her to the sock hop. Beautiful Biff: what had ever happened to him?

CHAPTER 17

AFTER DINNER, everyone but Cliff, who said he was going to get a "little air," which Joyce suspected might just be 80 proof, assembled in the drawing room for conversation and herbal tea or, if something more exciting was desired, Perrier and bitters.

Joyce had gone into a mild case of shock when she found out that coffee was not served before, during, or after any meal, because caffeine triggered the release of insulin, which in turn caused the blood sugar to drop, thus stimulating the appetite, a very definite no-no on an 800-calorie-a-day regime. The same rules also applied to diet soft drinks, which also included too much sodium and therefore caused water retention. So for social sipping, it was either herbal tea, Perrier, or one of the ubiquitous cleansing cocktails, and, of course, water.

Water! Joyce had made a face. Nobody in New York drank water. You never knew where it had been. Coffee and Coke were it, even if it did mean going through life bloated and starving.

So, still craving a capuccino, Joyce curled up on a blue and yellow brocade couch, assuming an air of indifferent nonchalance which to anyone who believed in body language, would have signaled that she was neither indifferent nor nonchalant, but was, instead, watchful and on edge.

She picked up a copy of the *National Geographic* from the coffee table, thumbed through it, and then proceeded to appear deeply engrossed in an article entitled "Animal Husbandry in Uganda—The Scientific Solution?" What she was really doing, though, was waiting for Cliff to come back from wherever he had disappeared to.

And so she sat, gripping the magazine, print blurring into solid columns in front of her eyes, afraid one moment that Cliff would sit next to her, thereby declaring that she had read his signals correctly, and the next moment afraid that he would not. Either way, the magazine made a good prop.

Cathy plopped down beside her on the couch.

"I'm still hungry. How about you?"

Joyce shook her head and continued to let her eyes scan the columns of print. She wished Cathy would go away.

"What are you reading?" The curious Mouse, as Joyce had now privately and permanently christened her, craned her neck to see the title.

Joyce closed the magazine. "Nothing really, just some piece about animal husbandry."

Cathy frowned. Animal husbandry sounded slightly salacious. Besides, she wasn't all that sure what it meant. She decided to change the subject.

"Don't you think that Dr. Voight is paying too much attention to Mrs. Taylor?" She nodded in the direction of the fireplace where the doctor had one massive arm draped along the marble mantel just inches above a set of bared shoulders which sloped down to a flaming red dress that lit up the room like a signal fire.

Belle said something and the doctor leaned forward. Joyce thought again about the lions at the zoo.

"Don't worry, you'll get your turn in the morning."

Her eyes wandered toward the door that led to the hallway and then wandered back.

"Who are you waiting for?" echoed her mother's voice, in a tone that said she not only knew but also disapproved.

"That's different." Cathy was not about to be dissuaded. "He *has* to talk to us in the morning. He's supposed to be the host. He should circulate, not stand there with his nose stuck in Mrs. Taylor's cleavage." She was unable to hide the tone of petulance in her voice. She felt hungry and miserable, missing Michael and the children. And she longed for a frozen Milky Way.

"Can't you see there's something going on between them?" Joyce sighed with exasperation.

"There is?" said Cathy incredulously and stared at them again.

"You'd have to be blind not to see it. He's interested in her as more than a guest, that's for sure. And he probably wants to know what makes her tick before he decides to try and ring her chimes."

" . . . Mother ticks, alright." Regina settled herself at the other end of the couch, drawing her long legs up under her taut little bottom. "Like two sticks of dynamite attached to a Seiko. But he'd better watch out, or she'll have his balls for breakfast."

Cathy turned to the new arrival, glad of a diversion from the thoughts of Milky Ways.

"You're Regina Taylor."

"I know." Regina smoothed a crease out of her white cotton trousers.

"My name's Cathy Stewart. I've seen you on all the magazines."

"Impressive, isn't it? I mean all this beauty in one body." She sucked in her cheeks and crossed her eyes. Joyce laughed. She liked the girl for not taking herself too seriously.

"Don't you like being beautiful?" Cathy was amazed. Looks were nothing to be taken lightly, as far as she was concerned.

"Like it?" Regina shrugged her slim, pale shoulders. "I'm stuck with it. People have always made a fuss about how I look. But I guess I'd have to say that it doesn't exactly thrill me. I mean I don't go around saying, "Hey, look: that's me," on the cover of *Vogue* or *Glamour*. Most of the time I try to ignore it."

"Ignore it! Gosh, I'd give anything to look like you." Cathy leaned closer, her enthusiasm making her brave.

Regina leaned back. "Why don't you give up food? That'd be a good start."

Cathy's face crumbled. Joyce thought she might be going to cry.

"Well that rates a minus five on the sensitivity scale," she said to the girl.

Regina's face tinged with pink. "I'm sorry. It just popped out. I didn't mean it. I guess you could say I'm an unfortunate product of my environment." She nodded toward her mother who was laughing at something the doctor had just said, her breasts quivering with the effort. The doctor seemed mesmerized, watching the heavy gold chain she wore around her neck appear and disappear in the cavernous cleavage.

"Actually, I'm really a very nice person." Regina smiled a warm enveloping smile to demonstrate, and put out a hand for Cathy to shake.

"Friends?"

"O.K. I guess I *am* a little touchy about the weight. It's not your fault I'm fat." Cathy relaxed a little and changed the subject again, in an attempt to include Joyce.

"Joyce's husband works in the Silicon Valley."

"No, that's silicon *chips*. Actually, he works in Newark." Joyce was surprised at how easily the lie came out. She was getting better. "My name's Joyce Allan. Nice to meet you."

"My husband is in the magazine business. . . ." Maxine had joined the group now, sitting in the pale-blue watered-silk wing chair on the other side of the coffee table. She proceeded to give her name, rank, and marital affiliation for the benefit of anyone who had not already heard it.

"Oh, *Destiny*. I almost did a cover for them last month, but Mother said they weren't willing to pay the going rate, so I didn't do it."

"Do you always do everything your mother tells you?" That cover was a sore point with Joyce who, on Harry's bellowed instruction, had had to rush around two days before they went to press to find someone else. Unable to find a face famous enough to replace Regina for their piece on "America's New Elite" at such short notice, she had finally ended up getting a picture of Mayor Koch to go with the article on corruption in the boroughs. It didn't have nearly the same impact and Harry had held her responsible.

"I guess I do. Pretty much, anyway. That's why we came here. I think I hate her, and we're supposed to be taking time out to fix our relationship. Fat chance." Regina glanced guiltily at Cathy. "Sorry about that. Anyway, the only thing she wants is to have her own way all the time. She treats me like I'm still a baby and I'm sick of it. I wish she'd just bug off."

"Such a way to talk about a mother!" Maxine was incredulous. "If I ever thought my Bradley felt that way about me I'd be devastated. He's my life. One day you'll have children of your own. You'll find out." She wagged a warning finger at Regina.

Cathy nodded in agreement. Regina looked at Joyce, who shrugged. It was one of those moments that mark a very clear division between women and mothers.

"How old is your son?" The girl made an attempt to mollify the obviously upset Maxine. Even though she was still young, her instincts told her that she had struck a raw nerve. Mothers certainly were a touchy lot.

"My Bradley is twenty-two, nearly twenty-three."

"And do you still try to run his life for him?"

"A mother's love goes on forever," sniffed Maxine in defense.

"Love? Huh! "Possession" is more like it. I'm almost twenty and I can't even go out on a date unless Mother approves, and even then I have to be home by eleven so I can get a good night's sleep and not look like some kind of a droid in the morning." Regina pouted. "Sometimes I wish I could just be normal. You know, like everyone else?" She looked around the group to see if anybody understood. Her eyes landed on Joyce and begged for her agreement. She sensed, somehow, that this woman probably understood how she felt better than the others.

"Why don't you just tell your mother how you feel?" It seemed such a trite thing to say, but Joyce, who was suddenly distracted by Cliff's arrival, knew she had to say something to appease the begging eyes, and so took the easy way out.

"How I *feel* isn't important. It's only how I look that counts. I'm the center of her little empire, don't you know. That's all she cares about. It's all she's ever cared about."

"Maybe you're not giving her a chance." The platitudes were running thick and heavy now. Cliff, spying the group of women around the couch, nodded at Joyce and headed straight for the french doors that led out onto the patio.

"Look, if this is going to be one of those 'After all she's done for you' speeches, I'm off." Regina went to get up.

"No. It's just that you have your point of view and she has hers. If you want her to see your side of things you have to try and meet her halfway." Joyce thought she'd heard that somewhere before. Anyway, it sounded like pretty good advice.

"That's what Michael always says, whenever we disagree, and then he shows me why he was right: 'I have my point of view and now you have my point of view too.' Isn't that cute?" Cathy started to laugh but, seeing that none of the others thought it was funny, she quickly clamped a pudgy hand over her mouth.

"Oh."

"God. You really are *married* aren't you?" Joyce shook her head in amazement. Michael sounded like a real jerk.

Regina yawned. "Look, why don't all you married ladies talk about your husbands or whatever. I think I'm going to go and raise Mother's eyebrows an inch or two." She unfolded herself from the couch and stood up. "If I get anywhere near an M.A.N. Mother breaks out in hives. I'm not sure whether she's worried that he's after me for my money or my body but, either way, it drives her up the wall." She winked at them conspiratorially and then slowly sashayed across the room and out onto the patio, making sure that Belle noticed her leave.

"There goes a mother's nightmare," said Maxine, nodding at the departing girl. She was thinking about Bradley. Young people today seemed so confident. So independent. So unlike her generation.

"Oh, she's just growing up," interjected Joyce, who was wondering why she found it necessary to defend the girl.

"She's so lucky." Cathy had watched her leave the room with envy. "So graceful, so self-assured."

"Is she? Lucky, I mean. I'd say she has a pretty warped existence for a young girl. Probably lonely as hell."

"Not at the moment," said her mother's voice.

"Lonely? How can she be lonely? She's always going to fancy parties and exciting places. I know I see her in *People* magazine all the time. She has thousands of fans. She met the President!" Cathy practically squeaked the last sentence.

"There's different kinds of loneliness." Maxine sounded like she was talking from experience.

"Maxine's right. It can be very lonely out there, believe me," offered Joyce, much to her own surprise.

"How can you both say that? You're married."

"Well, I . . . um. Actually, I'm getting a divorce." Joyce thought she was getting so good at making things up she should write a book.

"A divorce!" Maxine perked up. "Really? But what will you do when you're on your own?"

"The same things I did when I wasn't on my own. Get up, go to work, eat, sleep. The usual. Life isn't measured in marriage, Maxine." Maxine looked shocked. "I. . . ."

But the doctor joined them before she could reply. "I hope you ladies enjoyed your dinner and are having a pleasant evening." He beamed down from above them like a full moon on a fall night. "As for myself, I am going to retire. My bedtime is ten o'clock precisely. It is necessary to adhere to a strict routine, if one is going to maintain one's youth. We all have to get our ZZZZZZ's." He flashed a smile. "Gute Nacht."

Joyce looked past him and watched as Belle crossed the room. With all the stealth of a lioness stalking her prey, she moved out through the french doors and into the scented darkness.

"Uh-oh," said Joyce, under her breath. "Here we go."

But, in a few moments, mother and daughter came in from the patio and, single file, walked wordlessly across the drawing room and out the door. Joyce wondered what had happened out there and why Cliff hadn't come back inside. Perhaps she should wander outside and. . . .

"God, I'm soooo hungry," Cathy whined for the second time since dinner. "Think I'll go up to my room and forage around in my luggage. There has to be *something* to eat in there." With effort she lumbered off the couch and out the door.

Maxine stretched. "I think I'll go call Bradley. I hope there's no trouble with the phones here. Dialing long distance, I mean." She looked for reassurance to Joyce, who thought for a minute that Maxine was going to ask her to dial the number for her.

"I'm sure you won't have any problem. If you do, you can always get the operator to place the call for you."

"Operators. I'll be lucky to get one that speaks English." And gathering up her purse and her sweater, she left the room.

CHAPTER 18

AS SOON AS MAXINE HAD LEFT, Cliff came in from the patio.

"What were you doing, waiting for everyone to leave?"

"Not everyone." He came over and sat beside Joyce on the couch. She felt a tingle of excitement course down the leg he had brushed against earlier. Get hold of yourself, for God's sake, Joyce, she pleaded silently.

"I was going to sit with you when I came in after dinner, but I just couldn't face an evening of women-talk."

"Neither could I, but unfortunately, when you're a woman, people expect it of you." She changed the subject. "Anyway, I'm sure that things were much more exciting out on the ole patio—especially after Mother arrived."

"You can say that again. I was sure The Lady in Red would be out to see what we were up to. Such a charming woman," he said through gritted teeth.

"And *were you* up to something?" asked Joyce matter-of-factly.

"Oh, I was up to about here." The tone of his voice changed and he edged a little closer on the couch and took her left hand in his. "I thought Dr. Voight called you *Mrs*. Allan, but I don't see any ring." He ran the ball of his thumb over her third finger and she shivered slightly at the touch.

"Pretty perceptive, aren't you?" She moved back, trying to put more space between them; her head was beginning to swim from such close proximity.

"Am I making you nervous?" He looked amused and vaguely sinister at the same time.

"Me and fifty million other women." She tried to pull her hand away, but he tightened his grip. "Look, uh Cliff, uh. . . ."

"You're not married, are you?"

"Does it matter?" She could feel his pulse throbbing through her fingers.

"It never has before."

"I . . . I . . . suppose I might as well confess. You're right, I'm not married, but it seemed that it would be easier if I said I was, in case anyone recognized my real name."

"Ah, a woman of intrigue. Sounds right up my alley." He was stroking the side of her wrist now, with his index finger. "Now, let me see if I can guess who you are." He thought for a second. "Let's see, long tapering fingers, short unpolished nails. . . . "He was running his finger down the inside of each of her fingers. It was a gesture designed to set her pulse racing, and it worked. "I've got it. You are a famous European pianist on the run from her brutish lover?"

"You've been seeing too many movies on the Late Show." She tried to sound blasé, but her voice was shaky.

"I've been seen *in* too many movies on the Late Show."

"What's that supposed to mean?" She tried to pull her hand back, but his grip was firm.

"Nothing, forget it. Now where was I? Oh yes, you were about to tell me who you really are."

"Well, actually . . . I'm a . . . a . . . writer from New York." She tried a laugh, but it came out more like a nervous twitter. "On assignment from her brutish editor. And the long tapering fingers that you won't let go of are for typing, not piano playing." He had her off balance now, and they both knew it.

"Ah, a member of the fourth estate. Then I must watch my

tongue, mustn't I." He slowly ran his tongue over his lower lip and then smiled slightly. The tips of two perfectly pointed incisors glinted hungrily in the lamp light. Joyce watched the performance, mesmerized.

He spoke again. "Which magazine are you with?"

"Uh. . . . *Dentistry* . . . I mean *Destiny*." She felt her face grow red.

"I've heard of it but, and don't take this the wrong way, Joyce . . . ?"

"Redmond."

"Joyce Redmond. I don't think I would have known who you were if you were wearing a name tag and carrying a copy of last month's issue under your arm."

"That's alright." Joyce relaxed a little. They were finally talking about a subject with which she felt comfortable, and he had stopped caressing her fingers. "But the others might have known who I was, especially Maxine."

He looked deeply into her eyes and murmured. "Why especially Maxine?"

She felt herself melting under his gaze. "Uh, Maxine is Harry's wife. Harry is . . . ah my . . . ah. . . ." She was having trouble concentrating. "Harry is my editor. I'm supposed to be here writing an in-depth piece on the real reasons why you have all decided to come to a spa and. . . ."

"And is there something between you and this Harry?"

The question shocked her out of her reverie. "Good Lord, no! The only thing between Harry and me is two spaces on the masthead."

"Is that so?" interjected her mother's voice.

"Then you aren't involved with anyone at the moment?" His other hand was now busy stroking her right shoulder. Up and down. Up and down. It paused briefly as it slid past the curve of her breast.

"Involved . . . I. . . . No. It's difficult with my job. I travel a lot, if you see what I m-mean," she stammered.

He leaned forward then, his breath hot against her cheek. "What I see is a woman who has very beautiful eyes."

Very beautiful eyes! That did it. It was the oldest line in the book. She had already heard it a couple of thousand times, and hearing it again restored her perspective.

"And I see a man who's misinterpreting a little friendly conversation." She placed one hand on his chest and tried to push him away. But he remained solidly in place.

"And I see a woman who knows what she really wants but is afraid to let herself go in case she gets it."

She took a deep breath. "Look, before we go in for another round of "I Spy with My Little Eye," can I just say one thing?"

"Of course. Say away. I'm not going anywhere."

"I am not about to bowled over by your movie-star charm, so stop pouring it on, O.K.? If you want to talk, fine, but stop the great seduction routine or I'm going to bed right now."

He was running his fingers along the back of her neck, tangling them lightly in the soft bounty of her hair.

"That's fine with me. We can skip *the* preliminaries and *get* right down to the action."

"I meant I'm going to bed *alone*."

He let go of her hair. "You really know how to ruin an evening, you know that?" he said flatly. "I was just getting into the mood." Moving his arm from behind her neck, he slumped back against the couch. Then his eyes wandered around the room.

"And speaking of moods, mine could use a little elevating. I wonder if they have any booze around here?"

"I doubt it. But you could always order a 'cocktail' and pretend," said Joyce with a hint of sarcasm. She had never seen a man who could switch it on and off so fast.

"No thanks. I've done enough good for my body for one day. Besides, I'm evidently not that great an actor."

"Oh I don't know about that. . . ." She sought for something to say that would cancel out the change of mood she had so recklessly invoked, but nothing came to mind. She was quiet for a minute.

"Listen, Cliff, I'm sorry if I spoiled things. But I . . . I'm just not the kind of woman who falls for all that seduction stuff. 'You have very beautiful *eyes*.' It's so corny. I mean, how many times have you said that to a woman?"

"I don't keep score, but it might occur to you that in your case I meant it. You *do* have very beautiful eyes."

"Please. I don't like playing these kind of games. . . ."

"I'll bet you're a real fun date, you know that? If a man gives you a compliment on *this* dress, you'd probably ask him why he doesn't like *that* dress. No wonder you're not married."

"That was a low blow." She felt a lump of anger rising in her throat. Who was he to comment on her life? "I'm not married, because I put my career ahead of playing stupid sexist games with men like you."

She stood up and turned to go, but he grabbed her hand.

"Joyce, wait a minute."

She yanked her hand away. "Will you let go of me!"

He let her go. "O.K. O.K. But wait a minute, will you?"

"A minute is sixty seconds, and I'm counting." She folded her arms over her chest.

"You're right. You're right. I shouldn't have made that crack about you not being married. And you're also right about this being a game." He shrugged. "I've played it so often it's like second nature. Sometimes I'm halfway through the thing before I even know I'm doing it. I think I go on automatic pilot or something. It's nothing personal."

"Thank's a lot."

"I didn't mean it that way." He heaved a sigh of exasperation. "You really are touchy, you know that? A little game of "hide the banana" is probably just what you need. Calm you right down."

"You've got a lot of nerve." She balled her hands into fists.

He noted the gesture. "See, what did I tell you? You're tense. Very tense. Joyce, you need to let your hair down."

"My hair *is* down, and your minute is up!" And she turned and started toward the door. But he caught up with her.

"Look, O.K. I can take a hint. Maybe you're not into guys."

"What?" She swung around to face him.

"Gotcha! It always works." He was grinning.

"You . . . you.. . . ." She stumbled to find a word that would express her opinion.

"Snake?" he suggested, still smiling.

"Lower than a snake."

"Lower than a snake?" He looked stricken.

Then Joyce couldn't help herself. The whole business had gotten so ridiculous she burst out laughing. Cliff seized the moment.

"Do you think that you could let someone who is lower than a snake walk you to your door?"

"You really are something, you know that?" said Joyce, smiling and shaking her head.

"I know."

He followed her out into the hall. The moonlight was casting pale shadows through the stained glass window, poor successors to the adamantine glory of the afternoon.

As they were crossing the gallery into the long hall where the guest suites were located, they both heard raised voices coming from room number three.

"I think that's Regina's room," whispered Joyce, straining to catch what the voices were saying without seeming too interested.

"Her mother's probably giving her shit for talking to me."

"Really? I wonder why. Well, here's my door." She stopped outside of number five and fished the key out of her pocket. Then she turned, her heart thumping wildly behind her breast bone.

"Look, Cliff. I'm sorry I called you a snake."

He corrected her. "Lower than a snake."

"Alright, alright. Don't make this any harder than it is. It isn't that I don't find you attractive. It's just that, well, you did come on a little strong tonight. Maybe under different circumstances. . . ."

He placed one hand on the door behind her head.

She looked up into his face. "You never give up, do you?"

"Nope." He ran a finger around the neck of her sweater. "You know, 'under different circumstances' I'd invite myself in, but you look like you've had a rough day. So, I'll take a rain check for tonight."

She tensed. The nerve of the man. She was trying to apologize, and he was telling her she looked tired. Well, she would tell him what he could do with his rain check.

"You're going to have a long wait. The forecast doesn't call for any rain in this area for another six months."

He moved closer and she caught the scent of his cologne. His body was pressing ever so lightly against hers. "That's funny, I could have sworn there was a little drizzle on the way."

She fumbled for the doorknob. "Well, you'd better check it again.

There's absolutely no possibility of any moisture in these parts, believe me."

He sighed resignedly, but a smile was playing at the corners of his mouth. "In that case, I guess I can put down my umbrella." And with that he turned and sauntered down the hall toward his own room.

Slowly, Joyce exhaled the breath she had been holding in, and let herself into her room.

CHAPTER 19

JOYCE SPENT A RESTLESS NIGHT, what there was of it. It seemed like she had just gone to sleep when there was a knock on the door.

"Whosit?" She mumbled into the soft comfort of her feather pillow. She didn't remember ordering room service.

The door opened and a black maid entered, bearing a silver tray covered with a large turquoise linen napkin.

"Time to get up, Mrs. Allan." She placed the tray on the night table and shook Joyce gently by the shoulder.

"Go away, Fredo. It's not time yet." Joyce rolled over, wrapping the covers around her like a cocoon, and sticking her head half under the pillow.

The maid sighed. They were all like this the first morning. She went over and drew the curtain back. A bolt of sunlight struck the bed, hitting Joyce squarely in the face.

"Ugh!" Red rockets went off in front of her eyeballs. Joyce dragged herself awake and sat up.

"Sorry, Ma'am, but sometimes it is the only way. I brought your breakfast." The maid retrieved the tray and, placing it over Joyce's lap, whipped off the turquoise napkin to display the smallest bran muffin

Joyce had ever seen. The word 'thimble' came to mind. Next to it were three slices of papaya and a small pot of what smelled like coffee but which Joyce knew could only be Sanka. There was no butter, no cream, and of course no sugar. Breakfast?

The maid disappeared out into the hall. Maybe she's gone to get the rest of the breakfast, thought Joyce, picking up a piece of the papaya. It had a ripe, earthy sweetness that quenched her morning thirst. She nibbled the bran muffin and poured a half of a cup of the "coffee" into a delicate white china cup.

"The hike starts at half-past six." The maid returned from the hallway, carrying, not food, but a turquoise and white sweat suit. "Everyone is assembling on the main patio beside the pool."

"The hike? What hike?" Joyce had thought about lounging in bed for an hour or so and making some notes for her article.

"Every morning there is a two-mile hike around the island. You will see it in your program when you have consulted with the doctor."

"But if I haven't consulted with the doctor yet, why do I have to go on the hike? I thought this was supposed to be one of those do-your-own-thing spas?"

The maid shrugged. "Every morning there is a two-mile hike around the island." She said it as though it were part of the eleventh Commandment. "Thou shalt not sleep in because. . . ."

"Alright. I'll be there," Joyce assured her. But the maid remained standing in the center of the room.

"I said, I'll be there." The maid shrugged and, having completed her mission, she left. Joyce finished the last of the coffee and got reluctantly out of bed, wondering if you could get jet lag going north and south as well as east and west.

She pulled on the fleece-lined sweat shirt and tugged up the matching pants, tying the string tie firmly around her waist. The suit fit perfectly. It was a size eight. Her size. None of that one-size-fits-all nonsense around here, she thought. The doctor and his staff obviously didn't miss a trick.

Down on the main patio, Regina Taylor was already waiting when Joyce arrived. She looked fresh and lovely, as though she had just had ten hours' sleep. Joyce, who had avoided looking in the mirror, in case she still looked like she had "had a rough day," wished she had at least put on some lipstick.

"Hi." Regina smiled at Joyce.

"Hi. Where's your mother?" Joyce was surprised to see the girl on her own, and she looked around, but Belle was nowhere in sight.

"Mother's not coming. She has some phone calls to make. It's already eleven-thirty in the London office and she wants to catch them before they go to lunch."

She was lying on her back, doing stretching exercises. Clasping each ankle firmly in one hand, she bent it back against the top of her thigh. Joyce tried to do the same thing and got a shooting pain down the back of her leg.

"Ouch!"

"Did that hurt?" Regina was touching the floor with the palms of her hands now, without bending her knees.

"A little."

"Your hamstrings are probably too short. It comes from wearing high heels a lot. Do you wear high heels a lot?" She was doing waist twists now, swinging her elbows all the way around.

"I guess so. To work anyway. Don't you?" Joyce was following suit with the waist twists, and could feel her back creaking under the strain. She decided to sit down and wait for the others before she did something to injure herself.

"No. I only wear high heels when I'm on a shoot. The rest of the time I wear Reeboks. Much better for the legs. More support for the ankle, and the flat shoe stretches the hamstrings." She finished her warm-up and came to sit beside Joyce in one of the chairs by the pool.

"Do you work out often?"

"Never." Joyce felt a pang of guilt. She was always planning to start on one program or another, but there just never seem to be enough time.

"Never!" You *never* work out? Don't you go to Dancercize or anything?"

"Actually the only thing I go to is Workercize." She paused. Regina looked suitably confused. "I go to the office everyday and jump whenever my boss says so." Joyce knew she was being sarcastic. It was a defense mechanism she used when she really didn't have a good enough excuse for not doing something that was good for her.

"Wow! I can't believe it. I go to dance class everyday and Nautilus three times a week and. . . ."

Regina obviously inhabited a world where *not* working out was considered in the same class of mortal sins that having sex before marriage was when Joyce was young. The only difference being that you couldn't get pregnant *not* working out.

Maxine arrived then, looking quite uncomfortable and out of place in her sweats. Kind of like Dr. Ruth in a baseball uniform.

"Such a nice morning. I slept like a baby."

Cathy arrived next, waddling across the patio, trying to pull the sweatshirt down over her hips in an effort to disguise her bulging rear.

"Was that breakfast? I mean: all of it?" She sat down on the cement with a thud. "Aren't we going to get anything else when we come back? I can't last until lunch on that." Thank god she was grumpy, thought Joyce. It was a welcome relief from the too-early cheerfulness of Maxine and Regina.

"Of course you will have something when we return." They all turned their heads. It was the young girl who had chauffeured them from the airport the day before. Only this time she wasn't wearing a uniform, but a tightly molded blue body-suit that clung to every curve and crevice and shimmered expensively in the sunlight. Her brown arms were bare, with the well-defined shape of someone who lifts weights regularly. And her white-blond hair hung down to her shoulders with an almost military straightness. She was the epitome of everything a California girl was supposed to be. And, thought Joyce with a little rush of envy, she had no thighs.

"When we come back, you will all have a nice cup of potassium tea." She said it as though she were offering a Thanksgiving dinner for six. Yummie, thought Joyce. A cup of potassium tea was just what she had been hoping for.

"If everyone is ready now, we can go." They all stood up. Joyce looked around to see where Cliff was. It didn't look like he was coming, but she didn't want to ask Mariette why not, in case her curiosity was construed as showing too much interest, which of course is exactly what it was.

Off they went, single file, with Mariette in the lead, her perfect blue bottom straining muscularly against the shiny fabric of her suit. Regina was next and then Maxine and Joyce. Cathy, naturally, brought up the rear. She had started huffing and puffing with effort before they had even left the patio.

Two miles isn't all that far—when you're walking up Fifth Avenue on your way to have drinks at the Plaza. But two miles on St. Christophe seemed immeasurable. For one thing, Mariette eschewed the only road, the one that led from the spa to the airport, saying that it was too easy. So they clambered about the countryside, over rocks and along beaches at a pace that Joyce was sure the army reserved for training its Green Berets.

By the time they were a mile into the "walk," everyone was sweating except Regina and, of course, Mariette, both of whom seemed to take this early morning torture trail in their stride.

At one point Joyce looked back at Cathy who was steadily dropping behind, her round face beaded with perspiration and redder than an apple in October. She slowed her own pace a little so that Cathy wouldn't feel left behind. Also, she needed to catch her breath and cool down a bit. They didn't call these "sweat suits" for nothing.

"Come on. You can make it." She said encouragingly.

"I've *got* to make it," puffed Cathy in response.

Finally the spa came into sight once more. They shambled gratefully back to the main patio and threw themselves down into chairs or onto the cool cement. Cliff was sitting on a chaise lounge reading a newspaper.

"Morning, ladies. Have a nice walk?"

Joyce glowered at him and gratefully accepted her mug of potassium tea. She was dying of thirst and too tuckered out to talk.

Dr. Voight appeared a few moments later, looking very trim and healthy in a white Lacoste shirt and navy blue trousers.

"What do you think of our island, then? Beautiful, isn't it?"

"It wasn't exactly a nature walk." Joyce had finished her tea.

"So our Mariette has been working you hard, has she? You will appreciate her efforts later in the week." He exchanged a look with Mariette, who had draped her incredible body casually over one of the chairs next to Cliff. A thought flashed through Joyce's mind that there might be more to their relationship than simply doctor and enforcer, in spite of the age difference.

"Mrs. Allan, since we are going to begin our counselling sessions alphabetically, you will please accompany me to my office now."

Joyce stood up. Her legs felt like rubber. She hoped her hamstrings appreciated what she had just done for them. Wobbling a little, she followed the doctor to his office which was opposite the main building, on the other side of the pool.

He closed the door behind her and indicated a pair of bamboo armchairs on either side of a small matching table.

"Sit down, won't you, Miss Redmond."

Joyce gratefully sank into one chair while he took the other. She noticed her notebook and pen on the table.

"I took the liberty of having your notebook brought from your room. I thought we might take this opportunity to discuss a few things about the spa. It will be difficult for me to find excuses to talk to you alone later in the week, and we don't want to give the game away, do we?"

"What about my counselling session?"

"Ach. Yes. I have already taken the liberty of drawing up a program for you myself. It will enable you to sample almost every aspect of the spa, and we hope therefore to write a more accurate, not to mention flattering, story about us."

Joyce nodded. She guessed he spent so much time taking liberties, he couldn't afford to waste any getting to the point. She picked up her notebook and pen.

"O.K., Doctor. Why don't we take it from the top?" She flipped the cover open to a clean page and wrote "Spa interview. Dr. Voight, Sunday," at the top of the page.

"How did you first get involved in the spa business?"

"A very good question. It was several years ago, in Europe, when I first went to a spa, that I realized what a truly *wunderbar* experience it was. You know, spas are a very old institution. They go back to ancient

Greeks and Romans. People have always needed a way to combat the rigors of everyday life. . . ." He droned on for a few more minutes as Joyce rapidly took down his answer.

"It must cost a lot of money to open a spa. Could you comment on that?"

"Yes, it cost a great deal of money to open The Spa at St. Christophe. Almost six million dollars. But of course I bought the island as well, so my guests could have their privacy." He smiled munificently. "Every cent I had has gone into creating this place. . . ." He waved his arm around in a gesture of encompassing possession.

"You mean you financed the spa personally?"

"Yes, as I said, every cent I had."

"Did you come from a wealthy family then, Dr. Voight? I mean, not everybody has six million dollars they can lay their hands on." Joyce didn't believe in beating around the bush. If he was going to try snowing her under, she would give him the opportunity now. Then she would still have the rest of her stay to find out the truth.

"Yes, I was fortunate to be the only son of a very old German family. Shortly after I finished medical school, both my parents were killed in a very tragic plane crash and I, of course, inherited the entire family estate. Later on, when I found this island, I sold the estate to raise the money for the spa."

"I see." Not very original, she thought, and not very likely, either. "And tell me, Doctor, just what motivated you personally to go into the spa business?"

"My dear Miss Redmond, or may I call you Joyce?"

She nodded.

"My dear Joyce, a spa is more than just a business. It is a philosophy, a way of life." He noticed that her pen had stopped scribbling across the page.

"I think you should take this down. It is an important point. Now where was I? Oh yes. Beauty is a quest that has always plagued mankind. Artists, architects, sculptors, have always sought to create physical beauty, to immortalize loveliness with their art. In my own small way I, too, am an artist, an architect of the living body. I cannot create such a wondrous thing, no, that is for powers far greater than I—but, I can preserve it and mold it, until each and every one of my guests has the most beautiful body, both inside and out, that they can possibly achieve." He paused, giving her time to get down every word.

Joyce thought she hadn't been exposed to this much bull since the barbeque she had attended for the governor of Texas last summer. Did he really believe all this bullshit? Did he expect her to believe it? Maybe he did.

Twenty minutes later, the interview was over. As Joyce was leaving, with instructions to send in Maxine, the doctor gave her his hand. She noticed that his palms were sweating. What did he have to be nervous about?

She found Maxine out by the pool with the others. This time they were all dressed in white bathing suits with little blue terry coverups. Regina, taking advantage of her mother's prolonged absence, had left off her coverup and was sunning her length on one of the chaises next to Mariette. Joyce thought that together they looked like a pair of very exotic salt and pepper shakers.

Mariette sat up. "Here is your robe and your swim suit. You can change over there." She pointed to the bath house that peeped out from behind a hedge of hibiscus. Joyce took the suit and the coverup. She could do with a nice dunk in the pool. All that walking had made her feel very hot and sticky.

When she returned, the others, minus Maxine but now including Belle Taylor, were already in the water. Joyce waded in from the shallow end and joined them in the center of the pool. The water was silky warm and felt good against her aching legs. But she had a feeling that they were not getting ready for a leisurely swim.

She was right. Mariette was speaking.

"This is what we call an aerobic pool class. It allows you to do a little more than you can on dry land, and therefore increases the benefit you will get in toning the muscles. We use the resistance of the water to work against the pull of the muscles." She gave a short demonstration.

Suddenly from out of nowhere someone turned on the music and they were assailed by Michael Jackson and "Billie Jean." Mariette went into action, stretching, jumping, leaning this way and that.

Joyce looked around. Nobody was keeping up, although everyone including Cathy was giving it their best try.

As they were resting for a moment while the tape was changed, Cliff walked by wearing a white sweater and a pair of very snug white shorts, a tennis racket clutched lightly in one brown hand. He waved to them. Cathy waved a water-sodden hand back. And why not, thought Joyce, she was the only one who looked better submerged.

Finally it was over. They dragged themselves dripping and puffing out of the water. Joyce staggered over to her coverup and checked her program card. What next? A sea-salt massage. That didn't sound too bad. At least it didn't sound like it required any movement. And she could do with a rest.

What she really wanted to do, of course, was have a look around the doctor's office—this time alone. But that would have to wait until later. He still had to work his way through the other individual counselling sessions first.

CHAPTER 20

BY NOON, Joyce had five ticks on her program itinerary. She was feeling both exhausted and elated, relaxed and raring to go. Now, she decided, was the perfect time to have a little look around the doctor's office. Everybody else would be at lunch—starving for calories after the morning's activities—and he would probably be presiding over the meal as he had done at dinner the night before.

Nonchalantly, she strolled toward the office, having already decided that if anybody interrupted her during her search, she would just say she had forgotten her notebook and come back to get it. She had even had the presence of mind to bring it with her, just in case. And if it turned out that the doctor was still there, she could always pretend that she wanted to ask him a few more questions. It was a simple-enough plan and it even had a nodding acquaintance with the truth. After all, she *was* just doing a little more research for the article.

"You call it research, I call it snooping," warned her mother's voice. "Remember, curiosity killed the cat."

But Joyce shrugged off the little prickle of apprehension that ran up and down her spine, and continued on her way. When she got to the door of the office she listened first to see if there was any sound coming from within. But it seemed quiet—no voices, anyway. And so, bucking up her courage, she knocked firmly on the door and waited. There was no answer. She knocked again, even more firmly this time and, when no response came, she decided it was safe to try the handle.

For a fleeting moment she found herself hoping the door would be locked, and she could at least tell Harry she had tried. But the handle turned easily and, opening the door a few inches, she stuck her head around it and called out.

"Hello. . . . Dr. Voight? Dr. Voight, it's Joyce Redmond, may I come in?"

But her query struck the only human note in an otherwise deserted room.

"So far, so good," she muttered to herself, moving inside and closing the door behind her.

She stood by the door for a few seconds and glanced around the room. Where to start? There were no filing cabinets, so she decided that the desk looked like the best bet and started toward it.

Other people's empty rooms were so different from your own, she reflected, as she tip-toed across the tiled floor. You're always waiting for something to happen. For someone to suddenly appear. Another shiver of apprehension slithered up her spine and she turned around to make sure no one was standing in the doorway watching her play Nancy Drew.

"I'm getting too old to be an investigative reporter," she said out loud.

However, secure in the knowledge that she was quite alone, she examined the desk. It had five drawers. Two deep ones on either side and a shallower one which ran the width of the desk top. She began with the bottom left-hand drawer, reasoning that if she did get interrupted in the middle of her search, she could always say she had dropped something on the floor while looking for her lost notebook.

But her search of the bottom drawers proved somewhat less than exciting. The drawers on both sides of the desk contained nothing but blue bookkeeping ledgers, and the ledgers contained nothing but columns of numbers.

She opened one that was labelled "Accounts Payable—Kitchen" on the outside, just to make sure they were what they said they were, and quickly read down the last column of entry—"Lettuce $525, Mush-rooms $346, Tomatoes $278." She scanned the rest of the column, trying to imagine what $525 worth of lettuce looked like. The only interesting thing here was that all the invoices were marked "30 days past due." Whatever the doctor was up to, it was not paying bills. She closed the book and replaced it in the drawer.

Next she opened the drawer on the right hand side that sat just below the top drawer. Inside were a few files, containing more unpaid bills, mostly for utilities and fuel, some paper clips, tape and . . . something that looked official.

"Bingo," she said, reaching for the letter.

She was just about to open it up when, out of the corner of her eye, she saw what had been lying beneath it. A blue velvet box.

Blue velvet boxes tend to look out of place in desk drawers, and Joyce felt immediately that whatever was in the box might be a lot more interesting than what was in the letter. So she put the letter down and gingerly extracted the box from its corner.

It felt heavy and looked expensive the way that boxes which contain pricey pieces of jewellery usually do. Joyce took a deep breath and snapped open the catch on the lid. Then she took another breath without exhaling the first.

"Wow!"

Lying on a cushion of pale blue silk was the heaviest-looking gold ID bracelet she had ever seen. And on the smooth gold surface which was usually reserved for initials were two set in a one-inch script of pavé diamonds: L.B.

L.B.? She pulled the bracelet out of the box. It was even heavier than it looked. She turned it over. On the reverse side of the band was an inscription. "To Lover Boy from Lady Bug."

"L.B. Lover Boy? Lady Bug? Either way, it's pretty sickening," said Joyce, slipping the bracelet back into its blue silk nest. But, just as she snapped the box shut and was returning it to the drawer, and before she could dwell on the taste or implications of what she had found, the hairs on the back of her neck told her she had company.

Slowly, without turning around, she managed to slip her own notebook into the open top drawer as well. Only then did she let herself look up.

Standing in the center of the room was a little man in a black suit with a white shirt and a black-and-grey striped tie. His black hair was slicked back in a fashion which screamed of the 1920s, and he wore a small, black moustache.

Joyce was so jumpy that her first thought was, My god, its Hitler! But her second was, But he's been dead for forty years. She wasn't sure if that made her feel better or worse.

Seeing that he had her attention, the little man clicked his heels and made a slight bow from the waist. "I am Mittlehoff."

Joyce nodded. "Uh, good morning, I mean . . . afternoon uh . . . I am Joyce. Joyce Redmond . . . uh Allan . . . uh Redmond-Allan." Joyce wasn't sure if she had been caught in the act or not. Who was this? He wasn't one of the guests, that was for sure. And he certainly didn't look like one of the staff, either.

Seeing that his statement had elicited no sign of recognition from the woman behind the desk, he continued: "I am here for the doctor?" His face was polite but expressionless.

"The doctor. Ah yes, well, this is his office."

Mittlehoff glanced around the room.

"But he's not here at the moment." Joyce waved a hand toward the door. "He's out . . . having lunch."

"Lunch?" Mittlehoff looked at his watch. "Ah, lunch. I see. And you are his secretary?" He inclined his head slightly to the right.

"I am . . . uh, I was uh . . . just looking for my notebook." Joyce laughed nervously. "I ah . . . left it here this morning." She laughed again and let her glance drift over the open drawer. "Oh here it is! Right under my nose." She scooped the book out of the drawer and edged toward the door.

"I'll tell the doctor you're here . . . if I see him." She reached the door, flung it open and ran straight into the doctor.

"Miss Redmond, what . . . ?"

"Uh, Dr. Voight! Hello, forgot my notebook. Uh . . . there's a man . . . waiting to see you." She waved the notebook in the general direction of the interior of the office, and then, taking advantage of the doctor's distraction, dashed down the path and didn't slow down until she reached the pool.

Later that afternoon, a small dinghy approached the yacht which had been anchored in a cove just off the north end of St. Christophe since the previous evening.

"Ahoy, the Lady Bug," shouted the man who had identified himself as Mittlehoff, flapping his oars like an inverted turtle as he attempted to bring the dinghy about. "Mittlehoff requesting permission to come aboard."

"Ahoy, already," called a young, blond man of about twenty-five who was wearing nothing but a pair of white shorts and a deep tan, as he scampered down the steps on the side of the yacht to steady the dinghy and help the little man on board.

"You don't have to go through that 'Mutiny on the Bounty' routine every time, Mittlehoff. We know who you are."

The man ignored him and clambered up the steps.

"Where is the baroness?"

"Oh yeah. She said she wanted to see you the minute you came on board. She's in the aft salon." Then he lowered his voice a little and came closer. "You'd better hurry up. She's in one of her moods again."

"The baroness's moods are none of your concern, young man."

"Oh, is that right? Well, that's not what she told me last night." And the young man with the surfer smile laughed as Mittlehoff pursed his pale lips and scuttled off toward the aft salon.

She was lying on the sofa, a vision of well-preserved wealth in a white lace caftan. Her blond hair shimmered around her shoulders, vying for the light with a pair of perfect 18-carat yellow diamonds that dangled from her ears.

"Mittlehoff! Where have you been?" she demanded, the minute he arrived.

"I'm sorry for the delay, Baroness. I . . . I."

"I don't intend to listen to you snivelling all afternoon. There are only two excuses for being late. And since the first one couldn't possibly apply to you, and you don't appear to have been in a train wreck, either, there is no excuse. Is that clear?"

"Yes, Baroness."

"Here, get me another one of these." She waved her glass at him and he came and took it from her.

"Did you do as I told you?"

"Yes, Baroness." He replenished the glass from a pitcher of Bellinis that sat on the bleached-ash bar.

"And what did he say?"

Mittlehoff brought her the glass.

She snapped her fingers. "Napkin, Mittlehoff. Napkin."

Mittlehoff returned with the cocktail napkin.

"Well, don't just stand there quaking in your shoes. Tell me what he said."

"Well, I said what you told me to say. And he said, over his dead body. And then I said that you said that that could be arranged and uh. . . ."

"And then what did he say?"

Mittlehoff turned scarlet to the roots of his slicked-back hair. "I can't re-repeat what he said then."

The baroness sat up. "Stop quivering, man, and tell me what he said!"

Mittlehoff swallowed hard. "He said . . . ah . . . he said . . . 'Tell the old cow to go fuck herself.' I'm sorry, Baroness."

"Oh shut up, Mittlehoff!" She stood up, towering over the little man who shrank visibly at the sight of her, and began to pace the room.

"The old cow, is it? Well this old cow is about to take the bull by the horns. And he isn't going to like it, I can promise you that."

She turned to face him. "I want you to go back to the island, tonight. And this is what I want you to do. . . ."

CHAPTER 21

THE FOLLOWING DAY lunch was served al fresco on the cedar deck that curved around the narrower end of the spa's free-form pool.

Joyce, who had just come from a session where she had been dipped neck to toe in hot wax and left to harden, was feeling understandably a little claustrophobic. She was delighted, therefore, with the idea of eating out in the open. In fact, the more open the better.

In the brilliant tropical sunlight, with a mass of yellow-and-pink striped umbrellas shading the filigreed white iron furniture, the deck looked like a quaint café transplanted from the south of France. It also looked deserted, and Joyce felt a pang of disappointment. She hadn't seen Cliff since the day before yesterday, and in that time had managed to convince herself that because she had turned him down, he was now making an effort to avoid her. This, of course, made her want to see him all the more.

The meals were laid out on beds of slivered ice, according to the menu plan. Since no one seemed to be around to serve, Joyce decided to help herself. She debated for a few minutes, before settling on a raddichio salad with chilled breast of pheasant, goat cheese, and warm, wild mushroom dressing, followed by fresh fruit, and a glass of lemon water. Total, 270 calories.

She carried the tray of food over to a table that looked out across the pool and sat down. No exercise classes were in progress. It was quiet, peaceful. She sat back for a minute, savoring the scene. Her eyes wandered briefly in the direction of the tennis courts, but her ears told her to forget it. There was no thwack-thwack of lobbing tennis balls so, wherever Cliff was, it wasn't there.

She decided to try to turn her mind back to work, and began once more to evaluate and discard the various possibilities to account for what she had seen in the doctor's office.

First of all, there were an awful lot of unpaid bills. That could mean either that someone was slacking off in the accounts payable department or there was some sort of a cash-flow problem, or there was no cash-flow problem but the doctor or whoever was doing something else with the money besides paying the bills. Then, there was that godawful piece of jewellery. Who was Lover Boy? The doctor? And if that was the case, who was Lady Bug? And why did she have such bad taste? And then of course there was the Hitler clone from Central Casting who called himself Mittlehoff. The German Connection? She shook her head. The pieces were not falling into place.

She was halfway through the salad and only slightly further into her list of questions, when Maxine waved on her way to the buffet. Joyce automatically waved back, realizing she was now about to have company. She sighed and chewed on a piece of the raddichio. "The sharp bitterness of the purple leaves made an interesting contrast to the sweet succulence of the pheasant and the fungial fruitiness of the mushroom dressing." Or at least that's the way Naomi would have written it, if she were here. Which she should have been, instead of me, thought Joyce, as she watched Maxine pick her way between the tables.

Harry's wife put her tray down on the opposite side of the table. "So what's the matter? You look a little pale."

"I'm sitting in the shade," replied Joyce, in defense. She was getting a little fed up with people telling her she looked tired and pale.

Maxine nodded. Briefly they inspected each other's food. Maxine had selected cold blueberry soup and a crab quiche with string beans on the side.

"That looks good," said Joyce, for the want of something better to say.

"I've got brooches that are bigger than this," Maxine pointed her fork at the quiche. "But it's only 310 calories. How do they do it? That's not even one of my knishes."

"I know what you mean," replied Joyce. "Mine was only 260. I can get that many calories in a cup of capuccino at home."

Maxine took a spoonful of the soup. "A little too much lemon. You want a taste?"

"No, no thank you." Joyce shook her head to refuse the offered spoon. "Do you like to cook?"

"I'm compulsive. Do you cook?"

Joyce shook her head. "Not if I can avoid it."

"A wife who doesn't cook! What did your husband say?"

"Thank you." Joyce forked up a piece of "fungial fruitiness."

"With me cooking is like breathing. It's second nature. I make everything from scratch," said Maxine, with obvious pride.

Joyce nodded as if she understood, even though her only experience in making anything from scratch was the odd time, usually just before her period when, overcome by a craving for something sweet, she went to the trouble of adding water to a chocolate chip "Snack-n-Cake" mix. It was her idea of baking. You even got to use the box as the baking pan.

"It's a thankless job, let me tell you. My son, God bless him, prefers to eat out these days, and my Harry. . . ." She sighed. "Who knows where he eats anymore?"

I do, thought Joyce.

"So there's usually only me and the NBC Evening News. If it wasn't for Tom Brokaw, I'd be eating alone." She took a bite of the quiche. "So smooth, like velvet. Have a piece."

But Joyce shook her head. "It'll clash with my pheasant."

Maxine nodded, and then paused for a second. "Can I ask you a question?"

"Sure. Go ahead. Ask." Joyce mentally crossed her fingers. Please don't let it be something I don't want to hear.

"The other night you said you were getting a divorce. Remember?"

Joyce swallowed. Feelings of apprehension began welling up inside her on a collision course with the piece of pheasant that was at that same moment on its way down.

Maxine continued. "What I want to know is. . . . How did you know?"

"How did I know what?" Joyce could hardly get the words out because the pheasant was stuck in her esophagus.

"How did you know that your marriage was kaput? And how did you know that divorce was the thing to do?"

Oh boy, thought Joyce, I don't want to deal with this. She obviously wants me to help her make the decision to leave Harry. But breaking up Harry's marriage wasn't part of my assignment. She swallowed again, and the pheasant ran smack into the apprehension. Joyce started to choke.

"Here, have a sip of water. Have two." Maxine jumped up from the table and whacked Joyce so hard on the back that she felt her eyes rattle. But she gratefully accepted the water and took a long sip.

Maxine sat down again. "Better?"

"Much better, thank you," croaked Joyce.

Maxine picked up where she had left off. "Also. . . . You're sure you don't mind talking about this?"

Joyce shook her head and took another sip of water.

"Your husband . . . is he going to support you?" She shrugged. "My mother used to say that it's not that money makes everything good, but no money makes everything bad. Now I know what she meant."

"Look, uh Maxine. I uh. . . ."

But Harry's wife wasn't listening. "Funny how you never think about money when you're going to get married, but when you're thinking about divorce, it comes up all the time."

"I'm sure that Har . . . I mean your husband would never let you go without. I mean he hasn't up to now, has he?" But Joyce was thinking about Harry screaming into the phone that he wasn't going to give Maxine any more money. "After all, he paid for you to come here, didn't he?"

"My Harry? Mr. Cheapskate! Mr. One Pair Of Worn-Out

Shoes!" Maxine looked around to see if anyone was listening, even though no one was there. She leaned closer to Joyce and lowered her voice: "That man pinches his quarters so hard that the American eagle looks like a Thanksgiving turkey. He didn't pay for me to come here. He doesn't even know I am here." She nodded conspiratorially. "I have a little nest-egg that I've been saving up out of the allowance Harry gives me. A few dollars here, a few dollars there. It adds up."

"You mean that you came down here and didn't tell him!"

"What else? If I had told him, I'd still be in New York." She took a sip of Perrier, and thought for a minute before continuing.

"You know, you're the first woman I have met who is getting a divorce."

"Really," said Joyce, who had no idea how to proceed from here. She had no experience in her supposed area of expertise, and Maxine was obviously waiting for her to drop a few pearls of wisdom. She tried to think. What should she do?

"Listen Maxine, I'm really not an expert on the subject, but it seems to me that if you're thinking seriously about getting a divorce, you know, if you're not just going through a phase where you're mad at your husband, then this must be the right time to do something about it. It's your marriage. Only you can know when it's over."

Maxine tried to break off a piece of the quiche crust, but it disintegrated into a pile of crumbs. "No shortening. You need shortening to make good pastry." She pushed the pile of crumbs to the side of the plate. "I think I'll go visit the kitchen later on and tell them about it."

"Good idea. It'll take your mind off things."

"Things. What things?"

"Your divorce?"

"My divorce." Maxine shook her head. "You know, it doesn't sound right. Only yesterday I was saying 'I do' and Harry was breaking the glass. Now I'm thinking about saying 'I don't.' What went wrong?"

"Maxine, believe me, things will get better. Being on your own isn't the worst thing in the world. I know."

Maxine heaved a big sigh. "Maybe you're right. If I could get used to being married to Harry, I can get used to anything. It's just that I've never had to look after myself—financially. Harry may be cheap, but he was always a good provider."

"You know the laws now are very sympathetic to the position of the divorcing woman who has never worked outside the home. I'm sure that Ha . . . I mean your husband, will continue to support you."

"That's just the point. I don't want to have to keep asking Harry for money. To always have to explain *why* I need things. It was bad enough when we were married. If we're going to be divorced . . . well, I want to have money of my own. Do you understand?"

"Of course, I understand completely. But have you thought about what you can do to get it? You know, what kind of job you're qualified for so that you can be independent."

"Qualified? I'm qualified for *bubkess*," admitted Maxine. "I've never worked in my life. No, wait, two Christmases when I was in college I worked at Macy's selling perfume. But I didn't have to support myself on it. And then right after college I married Harry and then Bradley came along. There was never any time for "qualified.""

"Well, what did you study at college?"

"English and Home Economics."

"Home Economics?"

"What can I say? It came in handy."

"Well, do you have any hobbies? Anything you really enjoy doing."

"Cooking and shopping. I used to enjoy sex, but it's a little late to turn that into an occupation. Though I understand that it pays very well."

"Cooking and shopping." Joyce shook her head. "I don't know. You're right, it's not much to take to a prospective employer, but you ran a household for twenty-five years. You brought up a child. You're not exactly without skills. It's just a question of sorting it all out." Terrific, thought Joyce, now I'm a guidance counsellor.

Maxine brightened. "All I have to do is sit down and figure out what I've been doing for the past twenty-five years. Shouldn't be too hard." She paused. "Listen Joyce, thanks for letting me talk."

"That's alright. I'm glad that you feel better, but there's something I think I really ought to tell. . . ."

"My god!" Maxine looked at her watch. "It's twenty-five after two. So late. I'm scheduled for a Norwegian Body Scrub at two-thirty."

"A what?"

"A Norwegian Body Scrub. It's get something to do with seaweed and loofahs. Scrapes away all the dead skin. It's in your brochure." She picked up her tray.

Joyce peeled the last piece of her apple and watched as Maxine hurried out of the cafe. A Norwegian Body Scrub? It sounded painful. She checked her schedule card. There it was, Thursday afternoon right after her herbal wrap. She could hardly wait.

After a few more minutes she got up from the table, took her tray back to the counter, and went back to her room. It was time to call Harry. There were a couple of things she wanted to talk to him about.

First, there was this business about the unpaid bills and the man named Mittlehoff. Also, she didn't buy for one minute the story the doctor had laid on her about financing the spa from a family fortune. Something funny was going on. She could feel it.

The second thing she wanted to mention to Harry was that his wife was talking about getting a divorce.

CHAPTER 22

WHILE JOYCE WAS SITTING IN THE CAFÉ with Maxine, Cliff was in the weight room, toning up his lats, pecs, and glutes with all the enthusiasm of an Olympic hopeful. And when he finished there, he decided that fifteen or twenty minutes in the steam room was in order, to melt away some of the bloat that had collected around all of the above from the amount of vodka he had been consuming lately.

To say the least, this was a significant change in attitude as well as behavior. His stunning good looks had always been something he had taken for granted. Even on those days after the nights when he had been burning the candle at both ends and in the middle too, there had still been enough salivating women around to restore his sense of physical perfection. But the other night, with Joyce, when even though he had turned on the charm full force he had not been successful in turning on the woman, had struck a serious blow to his confidence. Maybe he had been letting himself go a little too long.

Lying naked on one of the smooth marble benches, the steam wafting up around him, he closed his eyes and tried to think of the last time he had gone five days without a drink. He couldn't recall one. Then he tried to think of the last time a woman had turned him down. He couldn't recall one of those, either. Maybe the two were connected.

Twenty minutes later he had had enough of the heat. Sliding down off the bench and wrapping the towel around his waist, sarong-style, he went in search of the masseur. After two sets of tennis, plus the weights and the steam room, he felt that he was due for a little relaxing round on the massage table with someone pummeling the shit out of him.

He padded down the hallway, barefoot, the cold tiles a shock to the soles of his stream-heated feet. The sign on the door read, "Alfred, Masseur," and Cliff pushed the door open and went in.

Alfred—Adonis in a white singlet and slacks—was in the massage room reading a newspaper. Cliff noticed that it was the *Miami Herald* and that Alfred was reading the Employment Opportunities section.

"You busy?"

"The crowd just left."

Cliff hopped up on the table and lay face down. Alfred came over and whipped off the towel, poking a muscle here, a muscle there.

"You're pretty tight today, Mr. Eastman."

"I know. Give me a real good one, just like yesterday. O.K., Al?"

Alfred poured a little rubbing alcohol on his hand. "You got it, Mr. Eastman."

Cliff shivered as the cold liquid touched his shoulders. But Alfred's strong kneading fingers soon started to warm him up, and he began to relax. He was just drifting off into a pleasant drowse when Alfred spoke.

"You ever think of having someone to do this full-time, Mr. Eastman?"

"What?"

"You know, a full-time trainer. I could keep you in terrific shape."

"You mean kind of like 'Bodies by Alfred'?"

"Yeah, sounds good, doesn't it?"

Forty-five minutes later, Cliff tottered back to his room. Every muscle had been kneaded and prodded until his whole body felt limp with relaxation. As Bobby Crystal would say, he felt "maaavellous."

Too bad it didn't last. No sooner had he reached his room and collapsed onto the welcoming softness of the bed, than the telephone rang.

Without getting up, he reached out and picked up the receiver and cradled it under his ear.

"Lo."

"Cliffy baby, how's tricks?"

"Tricks are just fine, Alvin. What's up?" From the exaggerated goodwill in his agent's voice, he could tell that something was definitely in the works. He sat up. The relaxation of Alfred's massage was draining away and being replaced by the tension of possibility.

"Up? Up? I'll tell you what's up, sweetheart. You are. Way up there on the big screen. Have I got a deal for you!"

"A deal eh? Alright, Alvin, stop congratulating yourself for a second and tell me what it is. No, wait. Don't tell me. Goldman and Glick changed their minds about Pierce Brosnan?"

"O.K. I won't tell you that, 'cause they didn't. That's history, Cliff. Forget it. This is bigger. Much bigger. We're talking George Lucas here."

"Alvin, get to the point, will you?" Cliff's heart was beating faster. This could be just what he needed. A new start in a big picture with a world-famous director."

"O.K. O.K. Keep your pants on. Here it is. Lucas has got this great script about this cute but poignant creature from another planet that comes down to earth and. . . ." It sounded like he was reading from a press release.

"I don't do teeny-bopper movies, Alvin. We discussed that already. Besides, that plot's already been done to death. Remember E.T.?" Cliff leaned back against the pillows. The tension of possibility was being replaced by the drag of fatigue.

"No. No. Cliff, wait. This is different. Real different. . . ."

"How different?"

"Well, the kid's a lot older, for one thing, and you get to play the part of the creature . . . it's kind of like 'Bugs Bunny Goes to Ridgemount High.' The kids'll love it. It's a real scream. But deep, very deep." There was no answer from the other end of the line.

"Cliff? Cliff? You still there, Cliff?"

"Yes, Alvin, and the answer is still No. Emphatically, definitely, No."

"You get to die in the end."

"I'd rather die in the beginning."

"Does that mean you'll do it?"

"What do you think?"

"You can have your name above the title. Lucas already agreed."

"No."

"I can get you points on this one, Cliffy. Points."

"No."

"At least think it over. I promised George."

"Alvin, listen to me. There's not enough points in the entire world to get me to play an extraterrestrial rabbit."

"But Cliff."

"Think about it, Alvin. One movie like that and my career as a leading man is over. What's it going to be next, 'Carrot People From Mars,' for Christ's sake?"

"Alright, Cliff, don't get testy with me. You'd better wake up and smell the coffee. Your career as a leading man *is* already over. This is your chance to make some big bucks and keep your name up there. They're willing to go to a million five on this, plus points. I'm not kidding, Cliff, if I were you I would seriously think it over."

"Alvin, you can take this deal and shove it up your. . . ." But the agent had already hung up before Cliff got to the last word.

Slowly, carefully, Cliff replaced the receiver. He felt calm, very calm, almost detached. It was like a scene from one of his movies. He got up and went into the bathroom to splash some cold water on his face. The camera panned in to catch the sight of the water swirling down the drain. Then up to catch the expression of defeat on Cliff's face and then followed him as he turned and went back to lie on the bed. Cut and print it.

CHAPTER 23

JOYCE HAD NO TROUBLE PLACING THE CALL to New York. And, even more surprising, somebody on the *Destiny* switchboard was doing their job with more zeal than usual and she actually got straight through to Trixie.

"Hi, Trixie. It's Joyce. Is Harry in?"

"Hi, Joyce. How's the spa?"

"Healthy. Is he in?"

"Well, he is and he isn't, if you know what I mean. Depends on who's calling. He's in a *foul* mood today, let me tell you. Must be something up with Maxine again."

I'll say, thought Joyce to herself.

"Look, Trixie, I don't have much time, so would you mind seeing if I'm one of the people he's 'in' for."

"Sure. Just a sec, while I put you on hold."

The line went dead, momentarily, and then clicked back into life.

"He says he's always in for you. I'll put you through."

The next second Harry's voice came bellowing over the wires. "Joycee. How's it going?" He seemed exceptionally pleased to hear from her.

"Fine, Harry. Just fine. There's a couple of real biggies down here and. . . ."

"Yeah, who?"

"Oh Regina Taylor and her mother, and believe it or not, Cliff Eastman."

"Hey, that's just great! I told you it'd be a great piece, didn't I? How about you? How are you doing?"

"Oh, pretty good. They tried to turn me into a candle this morning, but other than that, it's been O.K. here. You know, relaxing and quiet and uh . . . listen Harry, there's something I need to talk to you about."

"Go ahead, shoot. I'm all ears."

"It's about the doctor. I was in his office the other day having a look around, and, well, he has a lot of unpaid bills in the files. . . ."

"So?"

"So, that's not all. There's this ID bracelet too—looks like somebody melted down Tiffany's. It says 'To Lover Boy from Lady Bug' on the inscription. . . ."

"So?"

"So stop saying 'So,' will you? Don't you think its a little weird?"

"Well, I wouldn't wear it, but. . . ."

"Don't you think it's a little weird that it was in the doctor's desk?"

"Maybe he keeps it as a souvenir."

"He doesn't strike me as the sentimental type. And, if you had heard the load of crap he laid on me about where he got the money from for this place, you'd think there was something not quite kosher going on here, too. He's trying to cover up something, only I don't know what it is yet."

"So find out."

"I plan to. But that's not all, Harry."

"There's more?"

"When I was in the doctor's office this funny little man appeared out of nowhere looking for the doctor, and well, let's just put it this way: when I first saw him I had an overwhelming urge to say Sieg Heil! But I'll give him the benefit of the doubt and just say he looked a lot like Charlie Chaplin."

"Joyce, are you trying to tell me there are Nazis at the spa?"

"No, I'm not trying to tell you there are Nazis at the spa. I am trying to tell you that there's a funny little man named Mittlehoff running around who looks like someone Eva Braun used to date. He's not a guest, because I checked, and he's not on staff, either."

"Tell me the truth, Joyce, have you been wearing a hat when you go out in the sun?"

"Harry!"

"Alright, I'll run the name past Research and see if they come up with anything. Mittlehoff—how do you spell that?"

"How the hell do I know! I didn't ask to see his American Express card!"

"O.K., O.K., Joyce, take it easy. I'll check it out. Sounds like I was right about the doctor though, doesn't it? There is something fishy going on down there."

"Don't sign yourself up for the Pulitzer just yet, Harry." She paused. "Uh . . . by the way, there's somebody else here that you should know about."

"Oh yeah, who is? Elizabeth Dole? A politico would really round out the story nice, Joyce."

"No, Harry, it's not Elizabeth Dole It's uh. . . ." Her mouth had dried up and she swallowed hard to try and generate some saliva. "It's . . . Maxine Kraft."

"Maxine Kraft? Who the hell is . . . Jesus Christ! *My* Maxine Kraft! So that's where she went. Bradley and I have been worried sick. She's never done anything like this before."

"I know, I mean. . . ."

"What's she doing down there with you, for Christ's sake? I didn't say I'd pay for that."

"Harry, first or all, she doesn't know I'm me. She thinks I'm Joyce Allan and that I'm down here because I'm getting a divorce from my husband and. . . . Oh, Harry, I know it's none of my business, but I really think you ought to come down here and talk to her. You two really have to get some things sorted out."

"Come down there? What the hell for? You tell her to get her ass back to New York, or else."

"Harry, I can't tell her that. Besides, I think she wants a divorce."

"A divorce? From me?"

"You're her only husband, aren't you?"

"Yeah, well, of course. . . . Why does she want a divorce?"

"Harry, I'm already more involved in this than I want to be. Why don't you come down here and the two of you can talk things out."

"What things?"

"Well, look. Oh Harry, this is none of my business, I. . . ."

"What things?"

"Well, uh. She says you're never home. She says she eats dinner with Tom Brokaw every night. She says you're ch. . . ."

"What were you doing, interviewing her, for Christ's sake?"

"No, Harry. It's just that she wanted to talk to someone who would understand how she felt. You know, another woman who's also getting a divorce."

"But Joyce, you've never even been married."

"I know that, but you were the one who told me to make up an identity. Can I help it if the identity I made up is getting a divorce? Anyway, she had to talk to somebody and it's part of my job to be a good listener. But *you* should be the one down here listening to her, not me."

"O.K., O.K. I'll think it over. You just get on with the story." He paused for a minute. "Did she say anything about me, y'know, personal?"

Joyce was torn between truth and loyalty. "Nothing. Just that you were always a good husband and a good provider but that. . . . Oh, never mind."

"What?"

"Nothing. Look, I think there's a plane on Saturday. Think about it, O.K.? And check out that name for me."

"Yeah. O.K." He hung up.

Joyce stood clutching the receiver a moment longer, before settling it back into the cradle.

CHAPTER 24

LATER THAT EVENING, Regina was sitting cross-legged on the floor and Mariette was stretched out full-length on her stomach on the bed. They had finished listening to music, found nothing that they considered worth watching on the hundred-odd channels that the doctor's satellite dish made available, and so were engaging in that other favorite pastime of teenage girls—talking.

"I heard your mother was really pissed off about you going out on the patio with Cliff Eastman."

"'Pissed' isn't the word. You should have seen her. She was turning purple."

"What happened?" Mariette rolled over and slid closer to the end of the bed, letting her head hang backward over the edge.

"Well, she came to my room afterward and . . ."

"Not that. What happened when you were out there with him? Did he, y'know, try anything?"

"No!" said Regina, sounding shocked.

"No? But you wanted him to, didn't you?" Mariette continued to dig. The kernel of an idea was taking root.

"I don't think so. I don't know. Maybe. We just talked. He asked me what it was like, living in New York. That kind of stuff." She shrugged.

"That's ALL?" Mariette sounded incredulous.

"Well he *is* old enough to be my father."

"So? Anyway, I think he's awesome. Totally awesome! Have you seen those eyes? The way he kind of narrows them down and then looks at you from underneath those long black lashes—his eyelashes are even longer than yours! God, I would kill for eyelashes like that— and he didn't try anything?" She was skillfully adding fuel to the fire now.

"No."

"Hmmm. Maybe he's gay." She crossed her legs, resting her right ankle on her left knee.

"He is not!" Regina took the bait and sprang to his defense.

"Maybe you're not his type, then."

"I just don't think he's the grab-and-run kind," countered Regina defensively. "My mother does, though. Boy, that really rattled her cage. You should have seen her, pacing up and down puffing on those dis- gusting cigarettes. Yuck!" She pulled a face to show her distaste. "Any- way, she told me to stay away from him while we're here. Says that being associated with him would ruin my reputation as little goody- two-shoes. Actually, I think she's afraid he's after my bod."

"God, I wish he was after mine. Can you imagine what it would be like to go to bed with him. Wow. Heaven!" Mariette paused, giving the other girl a chance to get caught up in the vision for a moment.

"Have you ever been to bed with anybody?" asked Regina matter-of-factly, as she twirled a piece of hair that hung down from her pony tail.

"Of course I have. I'm seventeen. What do you think? That I'm still a virgin?" Mariette stopped short. Even upside down, she could tell from the expression on Regina's face that she was now on tender turf. "You're not, are you? Still a virgin, I mean."

Regina nodded. "Uh-huh."

Mariette thought for a moment. "I take it that this condition is not exactly voluntary. I mean you're not saving it for Mr. Right or any- thing?"

"No."

"Well, hasn't there ever been anybody you wanted to do it with?"

"Once. When I was sixteen there was this guy I met at a party in Newport. He was tall and had these incredible blue eyes and wavy blond hair. He was in first year at Harvard and he invited me to come up for a weekend and. . . ." Regina was pulling carpet fibers now, still embarrassed at the memory.

"And?"

"And I went. But my mother came with me and we stayed in a hotel and she never let us out of her sight. And I never saw him again. After that, I decided What was the point?"

"Yeah, I can see what you mean. What a drag! Parents just don't understand that their kids have the same biological urges they do. It's like they think they invented sex and so they're the only ones entitled to use it."

Regina nodded in agreement. "That's the way it always is with me. If a guy gets within ten paces of me, Mother's alarm goes off and the drawbridge goes up."

"That's hypocrisy for you. I mean, what do you think your mother and the doctor are probably doing right at this very minute—playing backgammon?"

"Please, the mind boggles." Regina made a face.

"Look, why don't you ask your father to tell 'the warden' to ease up a little. After all, you *are* nineteen and sex *is* normal?"

"I don't have a father," said Regina wistfully.

"Everybody has a father."

"I mean, I never knew him. Mother never talks about him. I think he died before I was born."

"Oh. That's tough. Kinda like me."

"What happened to yours?"

"My father was a Grand Prix racer. You know, like Danny Sullivan. But he got killed in a car accident in Sweden—that's where he met my mother. Some Volvo ran a light, and boom!" She clapped her hands together. "I was only a baby, so I never really knew him. But I'm supposed to look just like him."

"What about your mother?"

"My 'mother' was a boarding school. Oh, it was a very good boarding school. It cost my old lady a mint to keep me there. Keep me out of the way, more like it." Mariette's small, fine features grew hard for a moment, and then she changed the subject. "But that's history. The problem is, what are we going to do about you?"

"Do?"

"You know—about your 'condition'. If you don't find someone to do the dirty deed soon, you're going to die of frustration. I can tell."

"I don't exactly have a lot of alternatives. As soon as we go back to New York, I'm going to Egypt to do a layout for *Vogue*, and then after that to Switzerland to do one for *Elle* and then. . . ."

"Please, spare me the itinerary." Mariette thought for a minute. "Your mother's pretty busy with the doctor, so that will keep her out of your hair for the moment." And vice versa, she thought.

"So it's obvious that it has to be now or never. And that leaves you only one very gorgeous choice."

"You mean Cliff?" Regina shook her head. "I couldn't. I'm too young. He's too experienced. What if I did something really dumb?"

"Don't be silly, youth and experience make a perfect combination. You don't want to do it the first time with someone who knows as little as you do. Some awful, fumbling, spotty undergraduate who wants to get it over with as fast as possible so he can rush back and tell his friends he screwed Regina Taylor."

"You're soooo romantic."

"Just realistic. You want someone who knows what he's doing and can keep his mouth shut. Take it from a girl with experience, if you do it with Cliff Eastman he'll be expecting *you* to do the bragging, not the other way around. And don't worry about doing anything dumb. Just let nature take its course. It's not like learning to ride a bike, you know. It does come naturally, in spite of what you read in all those stupid women's magazines."

"I really don't. . . ."

"Look, if I give you three good reasons why, will you at least think about it?"

"Well. . . ."

"Right. Number one. You are nineteen and you've never done it. If you don't do it soon, whoever finally gets the go-ahead from your mother is going to have to blast his way in."

"Ouch!"

"Exactly. Two. Cliff Eastman is totally gorgeous and is also in the immediate vicinity, and, with the right amount of encouragement on your part, he could be interested."

"O.K., what's the third reason?"

"Your mother told you not to. If you want her to get the message that you're not her little girl anymore, this will do the trick."

Regina started to protest, but Mariette held up her hand.

"Just think it over. That's all. It seems like the perfect solution to both of your problems, to me. You get laid by a pro *and* you get your mother off your back."

She rolled off the edge of the bed and landed on both feet on the floor, like a gymnast coming out of a perfect round. Then she picked up the TV guide and thumbed through the pages.

"You wanna try the TV again? Hey, look, they're showing one of his old movies on Channel 67." She pushed the ON button on the remote, and a younger Cliff flickered onto the screen.

Halfway through the movie, Regina decided that the least she could do was think it over. Mariette *had* made a certain amount of sense and besides, it was true, he really was totally awesome.

After Regina had gone back to her own room, Mariette lay awake in her bed, staring into the darkness. She was waiting for him. She knew he would come. It was just a matter of time.

Suddenly, in the darkness, a muffled knock came at the door, and she reached over and flipped on the bedside lamp.

"It's open." She called out softly.

The door to the hallway eased open and the doctor slipped quietly into the room, closing the door softly behind him.

"I thought you'd never get here." she reprimanded him.

"Sorry I'm so late but, well, you know how these things are."

"That good, was she?" She sounded cross. He knew she was jealous, so he changed the subject.

"How did it go with you?" He crossed the room and sat on the side of her bed.

"Fine. I think I've come up with a way to keep Regina busy for the duration of her stay. And a good thing, too. I'm getting sick and tired of baby-sitting her."

"Good. I knew I could count on you. I need as much time with the mother as possible. The lady's no pushover." He paused.

"Did you know that the sous chef and the three maids all quit today? Not only that, but Gretel the esthetician is talking about leaving, too?"

Mariette nodded. "I know. The kitchen help left yesterday. Adolpho was having a fit. Says he can't cook for the guests with no help *and* no supplies."

"Speaking of supplies, did the shipment come from Barbados today?"

"It came, alright—C.O.D.—I had to send it back."

"Damn!" the doctor clenched his fists. "What is going on?"

"We'll just have to try and manage, that's all," said Mariette soothingly.

"You don't know the worst of it yet. We had a visitor yesterday. I didn't want to tell you, because you'll only get upset. . . ."

She sat up. "A visitor, who?"

"Mittlehoff."

"Mittlehoff! What did the little shit do—fly in on Daniella's broomstick?"

"No, he sailed in on her yacht. She's anchored off the north cove."

Mariette looked shocked. "Oh my god! What did you tell him?"

"I told him to tell her to go fuck herself."

The girl grinned, then. "He'll be lucky if she lets him live, if he gives it to her verbatim."

"That'll be no great loss, believe me. Not that I think it'll do much good, but it might buy us a little more time."

"You can do a lot in a little time, if I remember rightly."

He ruffled her hair. "That's my girl." And then he yawned. "God, I'm tired. That woman has more energy. . . ."

Mariette frowned.

"Well, never mind. You don't need to know *all* the details, just the final result." He walked back to the door.

"By the way, keep your eye on that magazine woman for me. I caught her coming out of my office yesterday. I think she was having herself a good look around. Not that there's anything for her to find, but it won't hurt to know exactly what she's up to."

Mariette nodded.

He opened the door. "Don't worry. Everything'll be alright. I promise."

And then he was gone.

CHAPTER 25

THE NEXT MORNING, Cathy Stewart finally gave up waiting for the maid to arrive with breakfast and went and stood in front of the full-length mirror. It was the moment of truth. With her eyes tightly closed, she slowly pulled her nightgown over her head. Then, still squinching her eyes shut, she dropped it in a flannel heap on the floor.

"I'm going to count to three, and then I'm going to look." She said it out loud, even though she was all alone.

But she had counted to five before she finally opened her eyes and saw herself, naked. Ever since the twins had been born, she had avoided observing the sight of herself undressed whenever possible. "No wonder," she thought, turning sideways. I look like a pink elephant. A pregnant pink elephant—with stretch marks. Oh god!"

Dr. Voight had told her at the counselling session the day before that the first thing she had to do if she wanted to lose weight was to confront herself as she was. Knowing you were fat and seeing you were fat were two different things, according to him. He went on to say that not until she saw what she was doing to herself and stopped hiding the truth behind yards of cloth, could they begin to work on her problems. But, first, she had to accept her condition for what it was. Obesity.

She turned once more in front of the mirror, watching the cellu-lite, which made her thighs look like twin servings of cottage cheese, pucker and de-pucker, as she shifted her weight from one chubby foot to the other. Finally, with a sigh of relief, she reached for the sweat suit that lay over the chair beside the bed.

"Enough truth for one morning," she crabbed to herself, struggling into the pants and letting the cord at the waist out almost as far as it would go. Then she pulled on the top, stretching it way down, and went into the bathroom.

Picking up the toothbrush, she caught sight of her scrubbed moon-face in the mirror. "Fatty-fatty two by four," she chided, blowing out her cheeks until she looked like a squinty-eyed sow. "Pig-face," she said out loud, and stuck her tongue out at the image in the mirror as she spread the toothpaste on the brush. Then she heard the doctor's voice. "The reason why you are so overweight, Mrs. Stewart, is because you do not like yourself very much."

"No kidding," she said, spurting a spray of Crest as she tilted the toothbrush to reach the backs of her front teeth.

"I do not think you eat because you are hungry, only because you have poor self-esteem. You do not think that Cathy Stewart is worth very much. Your weight is not really a problem of appetite."

"But I'm always hungry, doctor," she had complained. "I eat because I *feel* hungry."

"No," he corrected her, "you eat because food alleviates your depression about being fat. Food is a way for you to cope with your life. But, at the same time, it is food that makes your life so difficult to cope with. Do you understand, Mrs. Stewart? It is like a circle where both ends come together, until you cannot decide where it begins." He made a demonstration with the index fingers and thumbs of both huge hands.

She had nodded Yes, but she really didn't understand. She just knew that he thought she should understand, and that she must try to please him, because he was the doctor.

She finished brushing her teeth, held the brush under the running water until all the Crest was gone, took a swig of Listerine, spat it out, and went back into the bedroom to put on her running shoes.

Sitting on the end of the bed and bending over, she grunted with the effort of reaching her feet, wishing, not for the first time, that her arms were longer.

"Do you want to be fat for the rest of your life?" The doctor's question echoed in her mind.

She shook her head. "Of course not. That's why I came here—to lose some weight."

"And you will, Mrs. Stewart. You will. I can guarantee that, if you stay on your diet while you are here, you will lose seven of eight pounds."

"Really?" She mentally calculated her new weight. "Then I'll only have fifty-three pounds to go."

"Ach, but losing weight here is not the answer to your problem, I'm afraid. You will go home again, spend your days with the babies and the hotdogs and the cookies and the soap operas, and in no time, you will be back just as you are now. In order to keep the weight off, we must discover why you gained the weight in the first place, and what is making you so unhappy in your life that the only thing that eases your pain is food. We must find out why Cathy Stewart does not like herself. So, I am going to schedule you two more sessions of counselling with me and we will talk until we find out, Yes?"

"If you say so, doctor, but I really don't think that I have a problem with anything but my appetite. Couldn't you just give me some appetite suppressants so I won't be so hungry all the time?"

He shook his head. "Drugs are not the answer. You are using food the way an alcoholic uses liquor. Experts in the area of obesity call it the three C's of fatness—comfort, control, and coping. Eating gives you comfort and helps you cope. It is the only way you can feel in control of your life. It is the reverse, really, of the state of anorexia—you are familiar with the term?"

Cathy nodded. She had come to envy people who could refuse food, and didn't see why everybody thought it was such a terrible thing *not* to eat.

"Young women with that disease are like you. They often fail to eat because they are frustrated with life, and not eating is the only way they feel some measure of control. You overeat for the same reason."

Control, thought Cathy, doing up her left shoelace, is the key word, and I'm out of it. When it comes to food, I can't help myself. Maybe he's right about my not liking myself, but then, nobody likes being fat. But he's also wrong. I'm not unhappy. What have I got to be unhappy about? I have three lovely children, a successful husband, a beautiful house. I have everything a woman could want."

She tucked her key in the zippered pocket of her top and went down to the pool, ready but unwilling to face yet another two-mile hike.

CHAPTER 26

THEY WERE A SMALL GROUP at dinner that night. Cliff, Belle, and the doctor were all absent.

According to Regina, her mother had been invited to dine "à deux" with the doctor, and no one had seen Cliff since the early part of the afternoon, except Cathy, who reported that she had seen him going upstairs around five o'clock. So it was just the four of them for dinner, plus Mariette, who had elected to act as hostess in the doctor's absence.

Joyce, Maxine, and Regina all chose the A menu, and Mariette relayed their orders to the kitchen, explaining that the maid was feeling a little under the weather. When she returned after what seemed like an unusually long absence, she was carrying three orders of mushroom salad, lamb chops dijonnaise, and what looked like diced, frozen carrots. Total, 260 calories.

Cathy, who hadn't had anything to do with mushrooms since she was eight years old and found out that they were a fungus, and who would have been even less inclined to order them if she had known that only an hour before these particular ones had been growing in a field behind the kitchen, ended up with Navajo stew and bulgur, followed by fresh fruit, for five calories more.

Cathy looked glumly at her bulgur and stew when Mariette placed it in front of her, and poked it gingerly with her fork.

"What's this?"

"Bulgur," said Joyce, popping a sliver of mustardy lamb chop into her mouth and savoring the taste. It was amazing how good everything tasted when you didn't get much of it.

"I know it's bulgur. It said that on the menu. But what *is* it?" She sounded peevish.

She must be in the throes of chocolate withdrawal, decided Joyce, offering an explanation.

"Wheat. Ground and cooked. Kind of like grits, I think."

"Grits. Yuck, I hate grits." She poked it again. "This looks like lumpy glue." Reluctantly she took a forkful. She was starving after all the exercise, and any food was better than no food—almost.

"Well?" Joyce stopped chewing long enough to swallow and to carve off another sliver of chop.

"It tastes like lumpy glue, too." Cathy pouted. She was faced with a dilemma. Eat something you don't like, or go hungry.

After a few minutes of pushing the bulgur around the plate, trying to hide it under the stew, she gave up, took a forkful and swallowed, grimacing. Then she eyed Joyce's second tiny lamb chop.

"Oh no. I need *all* these calories. You choose your menu, you have to live with it." Joyce thought she could easily see how food could become one's primary interest. Only good manners kept her from moving her dish further away, to protect her chop from the covetous Cathy.

While they were waiting for the minted pears and fresh fruit to arrive, Cathy, uncomfortable at being thrust into a situation where there was no male authority figure, launched another attack on the doctor's interest in Belle.

"I don't think it's right for your mother to monopolize Dr. Voight so much. After all, we are guests here, too," she said to Regina.

"Actually, I think it's the other way around. He's the one who's so hot to trot. He practically insisted that Mother have dinner *alone* with him tonight." She raised her thick, glossy brows for emphasis. "I think he wants to jump on her bones."

Maxine gave a startled gasp. Why did children have to talk like that?

Cathy, who was taking the doctor's absence from the table as a personal rejection, refused to be put off. "I still don't think it's fair. Anyway, does he have to be so obvious about it?"

But Regina just shrugged. She had other thoughts on her mind at the moment.

All through the meal, Joyce had been stealing covert glances at Maxine. There was no doubt that their little talk at lunch had had some effect. She seemed much brighter than she had the previous afternoon, chatting on about how she had met Adolpho, the chef, the day before, and what a nice man he was. She seemed to be very impressed by the fact that he was cordon bleu and that "he was a man who knew his food."

After dinner, Maxine said she was going to pay another visit to the kitchen, and Cathy, who said she was exhausted after the day's efforts, announced that she was going to bed early. Mariette and Regina went off somewhere together, and Joyce was left to her own devices.

She knew she had two choices. Either she could go up to her room and start to work on the article—which is what she *should* do, or she could go up to Cliff's room and find out why he was avoiding her—which is what she definitely should *not* do. The choice was obvious. Sometimes you have to do something you know you shouldn't do.

A few minutes later, she tapped lightly on his door. If he was asleep, she didn't want to wake him. And, if he didn't really want company, he could just pretend he hadn't heard the knock. And if. . . .

A voice responded from within saying what could have either been "Come in" or "Go away." It was hard to tell. Joyce decided to accentuate the positive and turned the crystal door knob and went in.

Cliff was lying on the bed, ankles crossed, arms folded behind his head, naked from the waist up or fully dressed from the waist down, depending on your point of view. From Joyce's point of view, it was the former. She had a strong urge to run her fingers through the black mat of chest hair which spread itself from one powerful shoulder to the other before tapering down into a long V that disappeared beneath the waistband of his slacks.

He raised his eyebrows when he saw that it was her. "Well, well. Don't tell me its monsoon season already."

"Why have you been avoiding me?" She demanded tersely, ignoring the sarcasm and the chest hair, and getting straight to the point.

"Avoiding you?"

"I haven't seen you for three days."

"And three nights," he added.

Joyce nodded. "Oh, so that's it. Can't take a little rejection, eh?"

He rolled over onto one elbow so that he was facing her. "A *little* rejection? You are the first woman who has ever turned me down. That is not a *little* rejection."

"I am?" Joyce couldn't help the grin that was spreading across her face. "Really?"

He rolled back onto his back, putting his hands behind his head again. "I don't believe it. I just told you that I was crushed by your rejection, and all you can think of is how terrific that is for your ego."

"Were you?"

"Was I what?" he asked grumpily.

"Crushed by my rejection?"

He thought for a minute. "Well, maybe 'crushed' was too strong a word. 'Dented' a little is more like it."

"You could have tried again."

"Would you have said Yes?" His voice echoed the hope which leapt into his eyes.

"No. Maybe. . . . Oh, I don't know," she replied, with the irritation of the undecided. Cliff sighed. "Look, Joyce, I'm glad you find this all so ego-gratifying, but could we discuss your evident need to destroy what's left of my confidence some other time. I've had a rough day." He closed his eyes.

Joyce debated with herself for a minute, and then sat down in the chair beside the bed.

Cliff opened his eyes again. "You're still here."

"You look like you could use someone to talk to. Besides, I think I owe you one. Tell me what was so rough about today."

He thought for a moment. "You're right. You do." And then he sat up and scrunched a pillow behind his magnificent shoulders. "I had a call from my agent today."

Joyce nodded. So that was it.

Cliff continued. "He's got a part for me but. . . ." He shook his head. "He actually thinks that *I* should consider playing an extraterrestrial rabbit. Can you believe it?"

"An extraterrestrial rabbi?" Joyce drew a long beard on her mental picture of Cliff.

"Rabb-i*ttt*." He bit off the "t" and shrugged, as though the word itself revealed the entire truth of his dilemma.

Joyce was struggling with the idea. Erasing her previous picture, she tried to form a new one of Cliff Eastman, eighteen-carat dream-boat, dressed up like an outer-space Easter bunny.

"Incredible, isn't it? After all these years of sweeping women off their feet, I am supposed to play a furry second fiddle to one of the Brat Pack."

"Oh Cliff, I am sorry." She was trying to suppress a giggle. The mental picture she had been searching for had just formed. "I mean that's, that's not good, is it?"

"It's a long way from being the romantic lead, unless you're into 'Watership Downs.'"

She had managed to force the giggle back down, hoping that he hadn't noticed. Obviously, it was not funny to him.

"You think it's funny, don't you?"

"No, I . . . well, you have to admit there's a certain amount of humor in it." He didn't look like he was about to admit any such thing. She composed her face and tried to change the subject.

"Rabbits can be very uh . . . uh . . . appealing." She was desperately trying to sound encouraging, but when she said the word "rabbit," the giggle started to rise again. She cleared her throat.

"Only to other rabbits. I'm a lover, for Christ's sake, not a pet!" He sat up, swinging his legs over the side of the bed, and reached for the bottle of aspirin on the night table. He shook three out into his hand, threw them into the back of his throat and then swallowed them without any water, pulling a face as one got stuck part way down and began to melt.

"Do you have a headache?" Now there was an insightful question, thought Joyce, desperately trying to find something else to say to take her mind off rabbits.

"In a manner of speaking." He lay back on the bed and resumed his earlier position. "God, I could use a drink."

"That's not the answer, you know." Great, she thought, Joyce the temperance leader was just what he needed.

"No, it isn't, but it'll do until one comes along." He paused and rolled over on his side again.

"Do you know how old I am?"

"Well, not exactly. But I'd guess you were somewhere around forty-five?" She hoped he wasn't younger.

"Close. Actually, I'm forty-seven. And, in spite of myself and all the years in Hollywood, I seem to have managed to hold onto most of my looks and all of my talent. I really am a good actor, you know."

"I know. I mean, I've always thought so."

He sighed. "The reason I came here was because I got turned down for a part. It really was a great part, too. Right up my alley. Could have had me back up there on top before you could do this." He snapped his fingers. "And do you know who they picked for it instead?"

Joyce shook her head.

"Pierce Brosnan." He spit out the name as though it were poison on his tongue.

"Oh, Pierce Brosnan? He's very good. He. . . ." His glare stopped her in mid-sentence.

"I *know* he's good. He's too bloody good. He's also a lot younger than me. That's why he got the part. They're trying to tell me that I'm over the hill, a has-been at forty-seven because I can't draw the youth market any more. And now this idiot agent of mine wants me to play a seven-foot rabbit in a silver suit!" He was almost shouting now.

Joyce was quiet. Let him get it all out of his system, she thought. It'll make him feel better. At least it always did with Harry. He ranted on for another minute and then was silent for a while before speaking again.

"So, that's it. That's my story. And I guess part of yours, too, now that I've spilled my guts." He crossed his arms over his chest. "'Aging Star Seeks Solace at Spa'. I can see it now."

"Don't worry. I wouldn't do that. What was said here tonight is off the record. Totally off the record. Just one friend to another. O.K.?"

He sat up and leaned forward. She caught the scent of his after-shave. "You know shhweetheart, you're a dame with a lotta class." Screwing up his eyes and talking over his bottom lip, he did a passable Bogart.

Joyce knew instinctively that it was time for her to go. She stood up. "Well, time for me to go to bed. I'm exhausted."

The tension in the room suddenly shot up like mercury on a hot day. He patted the bed beside him.

"Why go all the way down the hall when I have plenty of room right here?" He looked incredibly seductive, and she felt her pulse racing. It would be so easy to say Yes. She moved over to the bedside table and picked up the aspirin bottle. Her hands were shaking as she pretended to read the instructions on the label.

"Nope, nowhere does it say 'take Joyce, and if pain continues consult your doctor.'" She put the bottle down. "Cliff, I don't want to be a palliative for your ego-ache. It wouldn't do either one of us any good if I went to bed with you under these circumstances." She walked over to the door.

"Joyce?" he called after her, the husky tone of his voice sent ripples of desire pulsating across the room like a magnet.

"What?" She didn't turn around. If she turned around now, she knew that she would be there until morning—at least.

"Come here," he commanded her softly.

"I . . . I can't. Cliff please don't do this. It's not. . . ."

But before she could finish she sensed that he was standing behind her. And then, a moment later, she felt the warm insistent pressure of his hands on her bare shoulders. Turning her slowly around to face him, he captured her eyes with his own and she felt her knees grow suddenly weaker. Then as he held her there, imprisoned in his gaze, she felt a hot flush begin to suffuse her skin, emanating outward from where his hands caressed her shoulders until it traversed her entire body. In spite of the heat, she shivered.

"Stay with me tonight," he whispered against her hair.

"Oh Cliff, I can't. . . ." she said, her voice quavering with the effort of refusing him.

"Stay with me," he murmured, through a flurry of kisses against her throat.

"Oh Cliff. . . ."

"Stay. . . ." he pleaded softly, as his mouth found hers and she responded to him, drawing his kiss into the very depths of her being.

He held her there in the kiss for what seemed like a long, long time, coaxing, commanding, beseeching, and still part of her fought to regain control. She was afraid of what lay on the other side of surrender. Not from him but from herself. But she was losing the battle. And, like drowning, after the first short, frantic struggle, the peace of the deep water is welcomed with acceptance and relief. And Joyce Redmond was just about to sink into the deepest water she had ever been in.

Unfortunately, Cliff, the consummate master of seduction, had failed to perceive that his conquest was at hand. Instead of gently easing her toward the bed, he decided that to clinch the deal he would play his ace card. The one that never failed. He whispered something in her left ear.

The unexpected presence of words in the realm of sensation shocked her almost as much as what she thought she had heard him say, and instantly her mind became alert and her body was put on hold.

"What did you say?" she whispered against the pulse of his throat.

He repeated the offer. "I said, if you'll stay, I can be any man you like. You name it. It's your fantasy. You can go to bed with any character I've ever played, or if there's some one else you'd prefer, I could wing it."

"What!" She broke away from him. "That's so sick! I don't want to go to bed with them. I want to go to bed with you. No, wait. I didn't mean that. I meant. Oh, I don't know what I meant." She ran over to the door. "I don't want to go to bed with anybody but Fredo!" And she slammed the door shut behind her.

Cliff stood dumbfounded in the middle of the room. "Fredo? I don't get it. If she likes Italians, why didn't she just say so? I was great as Marc Antony."

CHAPTER 27

THE FOLLOWING MORNING, Belle Taylor went in search of the doctor. The past few days had been very interesting, not to say enjoyable. But even while she had been basking in all the attention, she had also been racking her brains to figure out just what it was that he was really after. Not for one moment had she considered the possibility that his motive was simple passion. All her instincts told her that there was something more going here than just great sex. Men didn't come on like that to women like her because they were overcome with desire. They saved that for young twinkies like Mariette.

But, if passion was not the motive, then what was? She thought she had a pretty good idea. And now she wanted him to either confirm it or deny it. Belle Taylor was a woman who always liked to know where she stood, even when she was lying down.

After he had left her the previous evening, she had gotten up and smoked a couple of cigarettes, trying to think it through. But no matter how she looked at it, it only came up one way. She was not the self-deluding type, and she knew that, without a doubt, the most attractive thing about her was her bank account.

"You're a cynic, Belle," she had said to herself, watching the tip of her cigarette glowing orange in the dark.

"Not a cynic, just a realist," she had answered back. But then, after she got back into bed, she found herself nuzzling against the pillow where his head had been, breathing in the slightly animal scent he had left behind. "There's no fool like an old fool," she mumbled to herself, as she drifted off into the best night's sleep she had had in ages.

Now, as she was walking across the patio on the way to his office, she began to examine the situation with the same cool head that she brought to any business transaction. Why did he want money from her? He seemed to have more than enough of his own. Although, God knows, looks could be deceiving. How many times had she had to pretend to be flush when she was really flat broke?

Of course, this place must have cost a bundle, maybe a bigger bundle than the doctor could conveniently lay his hands on, she reasoned. Could that be why he had gone to so much trouble to seduce her? He needed more money for the spa? Well, if money was the issue here, she was determined to find out what he wanted it for. Aside from the fact that she liked to know exactly where she stood, her business curiosity was piqued. From little deficits grow big opportunities.

She turned into the pathway that led to his office, pushing aside a bough of syringa which blocked her way. Whatever he was trying to sell her on, last night, he certainly had given a terrific presentation. All that was missing was the slide show and the graphs. She smiled to herself, remembering.

The trouble was, though, that it was just a performance. And even though he had attempted to be an enthusiastic and creative lover, somehow she had got the feeling that he was trying *too* hard. He fucks like someone who does it for a living, she thought as she knocked on the door, plenty of show, but not much substance.

"Come!" came the muffled invitation from inside.

Belle opened the door and went in. He smiled and stood up and came around from behind his desk, when he saw that it was her. Unexpectedly, she felt a little rush of excitement at being near him again. "Stupid old broad," she said, under her breath.

"Liebchen. What a lovely surprise!" He held out his two hands but she waved them aside.

"Hans, I want to talk to you about last night."

"Ach, last night, last night was. . . ." He was searching for a word. "Wunderbar!"

"I won't argue with that."

A beam of self-satisfaction spread across his handsome face.

"However. . . ."

"However? There is a problem, liebling?" He looked puzzled.

"You might say that." She walked casually around behind his desk, surveying the papers scattered across the top. Desks were always a mine of information.

He watched nervously as she scanned the desk, and then tried to distract her.

"Kommen Sie. Sit over here by the window and I will put you to sleep and try to hypnotize you out of your nasty little habit." He gestured to a chair on the opposite side of the room to the desk. "Come?"

His lips were still smiling, but his voice was tinged with apprehension. What was she doing here?

"No thanks. I had enough sleep last night." Suddenly spotting the corner of a purple cover, Belle moved aside a sheaf of papers. "Well, what have we here?"

"Bitte?"

She held up a folder.

He came toward her, reaching for the folder. "But liebchen, I. . . ."

"What a coincidence that you should just happen to have a copy of this when my daughter and I were visiting your spa."

"But Belle, what is wrong with that? I was only curious about you. I am curious about all my guests. It is the policy of the spa to know as much as we can about our guests so that we may give them the best service possible. I. . . ." His voice trailed off.

"Know as much as you can, eh? Does that include studying the most recent copy of the financial report for The Bellissima Corporation? How did you think that reading this would enable you to give me better service. Or was that what was going on last night?"

"Liebchen, you don't understand. . . ."

"Oh, now *I'm* the one who doesn't understand. Well, you're wrong again. I think I understand very well. I am not a stupid woman, Hans. I know that the reason you've been screwing your brains out for the last few days is because you read this," she shook the folder at him again, "not because you were overcome by uncontrollable lust. You had something more in mind than a simple roll in the hay, didn't you?"

She advanced toward him and unconsciously he took a step backward. He had never met a woman like this before. Well, only one.

"Let me tell you something, Hans-baby. I don't know exactly how much you expected to gain from cosying up to me, but, just because you got into my pants, don't think for one minute that you're going to get into my portfolio."

She threw the report back onto his desk, sending a pile of papers skidding off the other side onto the floor. "If you're looking for the bottom line, this is it. . . ." She moved over to the door and yanked it open, "I'm going to find out exactly what you're after, Hans, because nobody is going to think they can play me for a fool. Especially not you." And she slammed the door shut behind her with such force that the glass rattled.

If she had turned around she would have seen the smile melting from his face like ice cream on a hot day.

After she left the office, Belle went straight back to her room and placed a call to New York.

"Hello, Mildred? It's me. No, everything is fine. Everything O.K. there? . . . Good. Look, I want you to get some information for me. O.K., got a pen? Right. See what you can find out about a Dr. Hans Voight. He says he owns this place. Better check with Europe, too. He's got an accent, German, I think. See what you can find out about him for me. Oh, and Mildred, put special emphasis on the financial stuff, then call me as soon as you get it."

She hung up and lit a cigarette. She didn't mind being fucked, but she wasn't about to be fucked over. Maybe Mildred's investigations would throw some light on just what it was that Hans-baby really wanted. And then, maybe she could turn the situation around to her advantage.

* * *

While Belle was plotting her next move, Maxine was up to her elbows in hot, sudsy water.

"Is this the last pot?" She called over her shoulder to Adolpho, who was busy peeling some rather moldy-looking yams.

"The last pot, the first pot, what difference does it make?" He sighed in despair. "It is impossible to run a kitchen with only one person."

"So what am I—chopped liver?" She pushed a strand of hair out of her eyes with her elbow.

"Maxine, you are a guest. You shouldn't even be in here. If the doctor found out. . . ." Adolpho shook his head.

"What? He'll fire you. What?"

Adolpho grinned at her then. "You're right. What would I have done if you hadn't come along?"

"What would I have done if I had to spend one more day with nothing to do but change the color of my nail polish?" Maxine wiped her hands on a dish towel and came and sat beside him. "So what's for lunch?"

"This is." He gestured at the bowl of peeled yams.

Maxine shook her head. "It's not enough."

"You're telling me. But the suppliers won't deliver unless its C.O.D." He shrugged. "I told the doctor. He said he's dealing with it. Thank god most of the staff has left. At least I don't have to worry about feeding them and the guests." He dropped another yam into the bowl. "Do you think we could try the mushroom salad again?"

"It's a little soon. Besides, I don't think there's enough left in the field." Maxine thought for a moment. "On the way in from the airport—you should excuse the expression—I saw some chickens at the side of the road. . . ."

Adolpho stopped peeling and looked up. "Chickens?"

"Chickens." Maxine nodded her head and stood up.

A half-hour later Maxine and Adolpho had three good-sized hens cornered in a small canyon on the lee side of the island.

The chickens, cluck-clucking in alarm, were nervously pecking at the gravel and scratching up dust with their powerful legs.

"Nice drumsticks?" whispered Maxine, pointing to the largest hen. "Did you bring the pillow case?"

Adolpho whipped a case embroidered with the spa logo out from under his jacket. "Here it is."

"Well, go on then." Maxine pointed to the chickens.

"Me?" said the startled Adolpho. "I am Adolpho. I trained under some of the greatest chefs in Paris. I do not catch chickens, I sauté them." He shook his head and thrust the pillow case at Maxine.

"And I am Maxine. I trained under Mrs. Morris from Brooklyn, and I say you have to catch it before you can cook it. Here, give me that." And she took the pillow case.

A few minutes later she returned, carrying a squawking, fluttering pillow-case-full of chickens. "One got away, but there's two in here. Should be enough for lunch and dinner." She handed him the bag.

"But they're still alive!"

"You have to wring their necks if you want them any other way."

"But Maxine," said Adolpho helplessly, "I do not have a wringer."

Maxine regarded him with suspicion for a moment, and then relented. "Come on, I'll do it."

Adolpho was obviously impressed and relieved. "You are an amazing woman, Maxine. Truly amazing."

Maxine smiled at him. "You know, that's the first time anyone ever said that to me. Now let's go. I'll pluck. You cook."

CHAPTER 28

WHILE MAXINE WAS PULLING PIN FEATHERS and Adolpho was pulling a face as he watched her, Joyce was up to her newly-arched eyebrows in spa activities. So far today there had been the hike, then a Jazzercize session, followed by a manicure, a pedicure, and now, a session of aromatherapy, whatever that was. She looked at her card. An hour and a half. That seemed like a long time to do something with your nose.

Curious, she went off to the beauty salon. There was no one at the desk to check her card and so, after waiting a few minutes, she made her way along the hall until she found the aromatherapy room.

It held a long table draped with a padded pink terry towel cover and three glass shelves with tiny bottles full of what Joyce deduced correctly must be aromas. A moment later a tiny, doll-like, Oriental woman appeared and instructed Joyce to get undressed.

"I've spent so much time taking my clothes off this week, I feel like I should be working in Times Square," quipped Joyce, as she folded her clothes and placed them on the chair.

"Hai," said the little woman, giving an abbreviated bow.

"Times Square? You get it. No?" Joyce shook her head.

The woman stood smiling, waiting for her to finish, her eyes unreadable.

"Please to lay on the table and we will begin." She waved a graceful hand.

Maybe she doesn't know what goes on in Times Square, thought Joyce, as she hopped up on the table and lay face up—the better to smell things.

"No, please to turn over." Her voice tinkled like wind chimes.

"Over?"

The woman bobbed her head. "Hai. We always begin with the back."

Begin what with the back, thought Joyce, but she obediently turned over. The next thing she knew, little flutter-touches were racing up and down her spine.

"You must relax, and enjoy," whispered the chimes and then she felt icy droplets of liquid being scattered across her shoulders. The hands began to massage, then, but so lightly that Joyce was not always sure that she was being touched. It was a marvelous 'almost' feeling.

"This is lavender," explained the chimes. "It is an essential oil that is good for tension. The scent of the lavender affects the right side of the brain and relieves stress."

She continued to rub in the oil in microscopic circles all over Joyce's back and buttocks, working down to the backs of her thighs and then to the calves, until the whole room was suffused with the scent of lavender. Joyce breathed deeply. She was beginning to relax.

An hour later, she awoke with a start to find the woman still massaging, this time with oil of tangerine, to invigorate.

"Was I asleep?"

The woman nodded and smiled. "Hai, I give very good massage, yes?"

"You can say that again. I mean yes, very good." Joyce lay back on the table. I could really get used to this, she decided, as the tiny, powerful fingers rubbed the last of the spicy scented oil into her wrists and forearms.

On her way back to her room, fifteen minutes later, so relaxed that she was practically staggering, Joyce literally ran into Cliff by the hibiscus hedge that separated the changing rooms from the pool.

She smiled a silly smile. "I've just been aromatherapied."

"I can smell it." He moved closer and took another sniff. "You smell like Happy Hour in a gay bar."

"I don't care. I feel won-der-ful." She tried to throw up her arms, but her muscles still felt like jelly and she swayed against him. He reached out an arm to support her.

"Listen, Joyce," he lowered his voice and looked around to make sure nobody would overhear. "I've been thinking, I could use a little R&R."

"Oh not again, Cliff. We went through all that last night. I'm not the cure for what ails you." She pulled away, still unsteady on her feet.

"Take it easy, I didn't mean that kind of R&R. It's Saturday night. I want to go out. I'm bored."

"Out? Where is there to go? We're in the middle of the Caribbean, or hadn't you noticed?"

"Apparently there's a little town at the north end of the island. It's called Cotton. Alfred, the guy who gives the massages, said there's a bar there, and that they have dancing."

Joyce was unconvinced. Drinking and dancing, either way, it could get complicated. "I don't know, Cliff. Besides, it's a long walk to the other end of the island, and. . . ."

"No problem. Mariette said I can have the keys to the Rolls."

"She did, did she?" Joyce still looked doubtful. Leaving the spa was supposed to be against the rules. It was like going AWOL.

"What about the doctor?"

"What about him?"

"Well he won't be too pleased when he finds out the two of us have decided to go over the wall."

"Joyce, we're guests, not prisoners of war."

She thought for a moment. Why did he want her to go with him?

"I don't want to go, if you're going just so you can get drunk." He started to protest, but she held up her hand. "And I don't want to go if you're going just to try to get me drunk." And then she added, "I'm not the kind of woman who drops her drawers after a couple of drinks."

"Joyce. How could you think that I would . . . ?" He looked offended.

Joyce shrugged. "Don't tell me the thought hadn't occurred to you."

He looked sheepish. "Well maybe just briefly, but I dismissed it right away."

"Because you know I'm not that kind of a girl?"

"No, because I never met a journalist who couldn't drink me under the table. But seriously, if I promise to behave myself, will you come with me? It won't be any fun going alone. Besides," he paused and, tracing one tanned finger gently along her forearm, gave her one of his best, deep dark looks, "I do enjoy your company."

"I . . . uh. . . ." Goosebumps ran up that arm and down the other. She shivered, but before she could come up with an appropriate response, he continued.

" . . . and I haven't been able to say that to a woman in a long time."

"Look, about last night, Cliff. . . ."

"Forget it. Last night was last night. This is today. And, anyway, you were right about my motives. I guess I just can't take No for an answer. But, since we're being honest, you came up to *my* room. We were alone. If I *hadn't* asked you to come to bed with me, you would have been insulted."

"Insulted! You've got some nerve." She pulled her arm away.

"Admit it. You did expect me to try something. Every woman I meet expects Cliff Eastman to try and get her into the sack. It's my image, Joyce."

"I don't believe this! You're saying that you asked me to go to bed with you because you felt *obliged* to? I didn't know that fucking was one of your favorite charities, Cliff. But now that I do, I'm removing myself as a possible beneficiary, so you don't have to try to make a donation to my cause anymore. O.K.?" She turned to go and then turned back. "And to think I was feeling so sorry for you. I almost. . . ." He grabbed her arm.

"Aha, so now the charity fuck is on the other foot! You almost said Yes, because you felt sorry for me. Which is worse, doing it for pity or doing it for image?"

But she countered with a question of her own. "You know what your problem is? You think that sex is the answer to everything. You use it for curing your problems, for boosting your ego, for polishing your image. You probably even use it to get over a cold!"

He grinned. "Don't knock it until you've tried it."

"You're impossible!"

"I'm a sex object. What can I say? It's an occupational hazard," said Cliff, easily.

"Well, in that case, I feel sorry for you. I really do." She started to walk away.

But he caught up with her. "Wait, does that mean you won't go out with me tonight?"

She stopped and turned around. "Is this going to be a pity date or an image date?"

"Neither. It's an I-enjoy-your-company date."

She still looked doubtful.

"Look, Joyce, why don't you stop asking questions and just enjoy yourself, for once. Even lady journalists are entitled to time off for good behavior."

She sighed with resignation. "And I suppose even sex objects are entitled to some company every now and then. I'll meet you after dinner, by the garage."

CHAPTER 29

JOYCE WAITED A FEW MINUTES after a dinner of the toughest chicken she had had in a long time, and then made her way past the pool, past the outside cafe, and around behind the various buildings which housed the physical plant of the spa. She only had a vague idea of where the garage was, but even in spite of the gathering darkness, she managed to find it with no problem.

The door was open, and she could see the white gleam of the Rolls reflected in the light of the rising moon. There was no way Cliff could have arrived before her, so she settled herself on the bumper, being careful not to let the skirt of her white Egyptian cotton dress trail in the dust, and waited. He was probably having trouble getting away.

Looking out through the open doors of the garage, she stared up at the sky. Against its damson canopy, the stars showered the night with tiny points of light. It was a beautiful night.

A crunching on the gravel redirected her attention.

"Cliff?" she called out.

No one answered. The crunching moved closer.

"Cliff, is that you?"

A burst of giggles met her inquiry.

"Who's there?" She stood up. What was going on?

Out of the shadows came Mariette and Regina.

"It's us. We want to come with you."

"Come with us? But how did you know? Oh, when Cliff asked you for the keys. I get it." She sighed. Whatever she had expected out of this evening, it had not been this. "Well, it's a free island, I guess. But this is Cliff's idea, so you'd better ask him." So much for romantic, star-crazed nights, she thought, eyeing the two teenagers. More like Mom and Pop take the kids to Disneyland.

"He's not here yet? I wanted to tell him that I couldn't get the keys to the Rolls. The doctor took them. I think he had plans for him and Mrs. Taylor tonight."

"Except that Mother's in her room waiting for a call from Mildred," interrupted Regina, "so I don't think he'll be needing them."

"Well, that's it, then. I'm not walking all the way to the other end of the island." Joyce was ready to call it a night. Next to the two girls in their colourful Jams and T-shirts she was suddenly feeling over-dressed and over-aged.

"We don't have to walk. I couldn't get the keys to the Rolls, but I did manage to get the keys to the truck. The one we use for deliveries. It may not be as luxurious, but it has four wheels and an engine." Mariette held up the keys.

"What has four wheels and an engine? And what are you two doing here?" It was Cliff. Striding out of the darkness into the circle of light cast by the single lamp over the garage door, he made them all jump.

"The truck."

"What truck?" He ran an appraising look over Joyce. "Ve-ry nice."

"The one the *four* of us are taking to town." She ignored his compliment.

"The four of us?" He looked from Joyce to the girls and back again.

"Can't we come, please?" they chorused. "Please?"

He looked questioningly at Joyce. "What do you think? Shall we babysit or not?"

"Babysit!" they cried in unison.

"Sure, I always wanted to be a duenna," replied Joyce with as much sarcasm as she could muster.

Now it was Cliff's turn to ignore the comment. "How can I turn down an evening with three beautiful women?" He smiled, looping his long arms around their shoulders.

I just knew he was going to say that, reflected Joyce, with perverse satisfaction, as she disengaged herself from his left arm.

"It'll just be the five of us, then?" she said, out loud.

"The five of us?" Cliff looked at her questioningly.

"Yes. The girls, you, me, and your image." She flashed him a look that would freeze meat.

"That's what I like, a woman with a sense of humor." He patted her on the shoulder, ignoring the frost warning. "Now where's this truck?"

"It's around behind the garage. I'll show you." Cliff followed Mariette into the darkness. "I hope you can drive a standard," she said, as they disappeared around the side of the building.

"Isn't your mother going to be upset when she finds out you came with us?" Joyce turned to Regina. Maybe there was still time to salvage the evening.

Regina shrugged. "She'll probably have a hairy fit, but that's nothing new. Besides, I don't think she's going to find out. She hasn't said two words to me since lunch, and when I went to see if she was coming down to dinner she said No, she had some work to do, and that she was waiting for a call from Mildred. I wonder why she called Mildred?"

"Who's Mildred?"

"Our secretary in New York."

Before Joyce could pursue the matter any further, the cough of an engine erupted from behind the garage. "Sounds promising."

The grinding and popping of gears announced the arrival of the truck, which lurched into the drive in front of the garage a few seconds later.

"Hop in, ladies." Cliff leaned out the window and gestured to the back of the pick-up, where Mariette was already waiting.

"Sorry there's no room up front, but this thing only has the one seat. I guess they took the other one out to make more room for the supplies. I'll be glad to ride in the back if one of you thinks you can figure out these gears better than me."

The women shook their heads.

"Sorry about this, Joyce." He shrugged apologetically.

But Joyce shook her head. "That's perfectly alright," she replied, in carefully measured tones. "I'll be just fine. I always wanted to ride in the back of a pick-up truck. It's good for my image as a working journalist."

Regina looked up at Mariette, who raised a single eyebrow in response, and then both she and Joyce climbed into the back of the pick-up.

Cliff ground the gears into reverse, turned the truck around, and then coaxed his way into second. This was going to be hard work, but at least it suited his sense of adventure.

He was just about to ease his way into first when a thudding of feet announced the approach of someone heavy running toward the truck. He flicked on the high beams, sure that he would see either the doctor or Belle Taylor illuminated in the swath of light. But to his surprise it was Cathy, hurrying along, waving her arms.

"Wait, wait for me." She ran breathless up to the cabin of the pick-up. "I want to come, too."

Cliff hooked a thumb toward the back: "Hop in." Any more and they'd have enough to play the Lakers.

Cathy, her face beaded with the efforts of her hurried departure, billowed around to the back of the truck.

"Hi. Cliff says I can come too." She hauled herself up and gave a deep sigh. "I almost didn't think I'd make it. If it wasn't for all that hiking this week. . . ."

Joyce asked the obvious question: "Just out of curiosity, how did you find out about tonight? It was *supposed* to be a secret."

"I know. But I was just coming out of the change room this afternoon when I heard you two talking about going to town. I phoned Michael to ask him if he thought I should ask you if I could go with you, but you know what?"

"No, what?" asked Joyce without enthusiasm.

"He was out. And he was out last night, too. Both times the sitter answered. When I'm looking after the children and he's away on business, I stay home. But the minute *I'm* gone, he calls a sitter and out he goes. Well, if it's good enough for him, it's good enough for me.

I'm entitled to go out, too." She folded her arms across her bountiful bosom, as intractable as a Buddha.

Cliff forced the gears into first and, with a spray of gravel and a burst of exhaust, they were off.

Joyce coughed and waved away the cloud of noxious black fumes that belched from the exhaust. The evening was certainly taking a different direction than she had envisioned. She hadn't been on a gang date since high school.

Belle Taylor was lying fully dressed on her bed, her dinner, if that is what you could call the smidgin of chicken curry that lay like a tiny yellow oasis in the sparkling white desert of the Rosenthal dinner plate, rested untouched on the tray beside her. She was daydreaming, a practice she had not let herself engage in in almost twenty years.

Ever since Regina had been born, she had been pushing, pushing, pushing her way up the ladder of success, and it had taken most of her considerable energy and all of her time. She had never taken a moment to stop and consider where she was going or why. She knew only one direction—up, and one reason—because she had to.

In all those years, she had never considered the possibility that there might be something unhealthy, even self-destructive, in her terrible ambition to succeed. Until this morning, that is.

The possibility that the doctor was trying to wangle his way into her wallet had disturbed her, and rightly so. But what had disturbed her even more was that her own motives were no less mercenary. She had known from the beginning that he had been up to something, but she had gone along with it, figuring all the while that she might be able to turn his need for money into an opportunity to make some herself—at his expense if necessary. But it occurred to her now that it had also been at her own expense. The whole business left a bad taste in her mouth.

She was using him using her, which made her no better than he was.

And, on top of that, there was something else. She kept going over the events of the previous evening step by step, trying to understand why the whole business had left such a impression. It was not just that it had been a long time since she had been with a man. God knows she was used to doing without for longer than that—willing and able partners being somewhat of a rarity at her economic level. It was not even that he had been that good—although he had been a definite improvement over the last few men she had shared her bed with. No, it was something else. Something that transcended her anger over the possibility that she was being set up. Something that made her keep wanting to replay the evening over and over in her head as she savored it piece by piece. There was something about him, something she liked.

And that was probably the most disturbing thing of all.

A knock on the door brought her out of her reverie. It was probably Regina, she decided. Dinner must be well over by now. So she stayed where she was, and called out. "The door's open. Come in."

It was not Regina who responded to her invitation, however, but the doctor.

"Oh, it's you." Belle sat up straighter on the bed. Horizontal was *not* a power position. "What do you want?"

"I have come to apologize for this morning. I mean, for last night. You were right. I did send for the financial report to find out all about you. And, when I found out, I decided that you were perfect for what I needed." It was offered in the tone of a confession.

Belle was immediately wary. "Oh, and what was that?"

"Money."

"That's what I thought. And I suppose you assumed I would be some sort of lonely, middle-aged pushover who would be willing to pay for her pleasure."

"Let's just say that I hoped perhaps after you knew me better you might be able to see your way clear to giving me a small loan. . . . But I guess I was wrong." He sounded like a defeated man. "I'm sorry." He shrugged his slumping shoulders and turned to go.

"Just a minute." Belle slid her feet off the bed and came to stand beside him. She looked him right in the eye. "You really are very good, you know that?"

"Bitte?"

"Don't give me that broken-man routine. You think you know exactly which buttons to push, don't you?"

He remained uncomprehending. "I came to apologize. Nothing more."

"Let's cut the crap, shall we?" She got her package of cigarettes from her purse.

"You doubt the sincerity of my apology?"

"Look, Hans. Let's get this straight. I've played this game myself—many times. You want something, and you try to get it one way. If that doesn't work, you try to get it another way. Sometimes you have to come on strong. Sometimes weak works better." She lit a cigarette. "And sometimes it's even necessary to try the truth. The fact remains that you still want money, and if apologizing to me looks like the best angle, then you're willing to give it a whirl. Am I right?"

His face remained blank for a minute and then he broke into a sad grin. "I underestimated you, didn't I?"

"Both times."

He shook his head. "Well, now that we both understand each other a little better, how would you like to go for a little drive?"

"Is this just another angle?"

"Maybe. Maybe not. You'll never know unless you take me up on my offer."

"God, you really are good at this." She smiled slowly. "But not as good as me. Wait while I get my jacket, and we'll see who takes who for a ride."

CHAPTER 30

COTTON WAS THE CARIBBEAN EQUIVALENT of a one-horse town. In this case, though, it was one streetlamp, which happened to be conveniently located in front of the local drinking establishment, a place that called itself—realistically enough—The Bar. Loud music and even louder laughter erupted periodically from inside, and could be heard all the way down the dirt track that served as the main street, not only for human beings, but also for the wild pigs and flocks of shabby chickens who liked to wallow in its dust-filled craters and potholes.

Cliff pulled the truck up next to three of its clones in front of the bar and came round to help the women down. But, just as he was about to help Joyce down, a small brown pig went flying past their heads, squealing with rage and fear, as someone from inside the bar ejected it with more force than was absolutely necessary.

"You're taking us to a place that serves pigs?" observed Joyce caustically, as she waved his offered hand aside and jumped down into the dust.

"No. I'm taking you to a place that evidently *refuses* to serve pigs. And stop complaining, will you. You've been to worse places than this."

Joyce wet her fingers. "How would you know?" She had noticed a spot on her skirt and was trying to rub it off, but it only got bigger. She gave up in disgust.

"You live in New York. Now come on, let's go inside, or rather, outside. The action's supposed to be on the patio at the back." Cliff decided to ignore her grumbling.

The other three were waiting patiently on the veranda that ran the full length of the front of the one-storey wooden building. He led them all in through the front doors and then out onto the patio. The place was jammed, but they were able to squeeze into a table for two by putting three extra chairs around it.

Loud reggae music was being piped outside from the bar and, at one end of the patio, an area had been cleared for dancing—if you could call it that. The dancers were so tightly packed that they moved in unison around the floor, like some kind of large, multi-colored amoeba.

After a few minutes, a waitress who reminded Joyce of the maid who had brought her breakfast on the first morning at the spa, came over to take their order. Cliff suggested that they let him order if they wanted to try a local drink, and that he would pick something different for each of them that he thought they would like.

A short while later, the waitress returned, carrying the tray of drinks. Joyce tried casually to have a closer look as the woman placed a cup of steaming coffee and something golden in a tumbler the size of a juice glass on the table in front of her.

It *was* the maid who had brought her breakfast the first morning. What was she doing working at the local ptomaine palace?

After they all had their drinks, Joyce tried to catch the waitress's eye but, after taking a fleeting look at Mariette, the woman quickly disappeared into the throng.

"What's in here?" Mariette sniffed her drink and pretended that nothing was out of the ordinary.

"Coke."

"Coke! That's all?"

"You are underage." Cliff wagged an admonishing finger at Mariette. "And you," he said to Regina, "have to go home sober or your mother will kill you and then me."

"That's O.K. I don't drink anyway." Regina sipped her Coke. It was enough just to be out without Belle. She didn't need any additional stimulation.

"Well, if we can't drink, we might as well dance. Come on, Regina," said Mariette, heading for the dance floor. She had observed Joyce's interest in their waitress, and was anxious to disappear before she started asking questions.

"What did I get?" asked Cathy, who, oblivious to everything but the maraschino cherry on the end of her swizzle stick, had already sipped her drink and liked it, but couldn't identify the taste.

"You got the Bajan version of a Manhattan. That's two parts rum and one part Falernum, a sweet syrupy stuff that's very popular on the island for making mixed drinks."

"Falernum. Mmmm, it's good." She took another long sip and then pulled the cherry off the stick and chewed it contentedly.

Cliff thought for a moment and then added, "But take it easy, underneath all that sweetness is a rum that really packs a punch."

Cathy giggled, already feeling the warmth of the liquor tingling in her veins. "Rum punch. That's cute."

"What about me? What did I get?" Joyce sipped her coffee. It was strong and aromatic and she savored it. He had certainly picked the right drink for everybody. But then, she reflected, he had had a lot of practice.

"Ah, you got something which ought to take the edge off that mood you're in. That is the best stuff on the island. And believe me, I should know. Sugar cane brandy. Ten years old and smooth as honey. Taste it."

She sipped. It was smooth, all right, but a little trail of flames licked at her throat as she swallowed. She quenched the fire with a chaser of coffee.

"And yours?" She eyed his pint glass with suspicion.

"Mine's a traditional Bajan drink for a man with a big thirst," he caught a flicker of I-told-you-so in her glance, "but a small tolerance. It's called a Tewahdiddle. One pint of local beer, one tablespoon of the brandy for bite, and a teaspoon of sugar with ginger and lemon peel to give it that little touch of the exotic."

"Sounds like a boilermaker to me." Joyce sipped the brandy again. She was beginning to feel more mellow already. "This stuff is powerful."

Cathy interrupted, pushing her glass forward. It was empty. "Can I have another one, please?"

"Already?" They responded in unison.

Cathy looked defensively from one to the other. "Yes. I like that Flamermum. Falerman. Flimerum. Oh whatever. It makes me feel all warm and glowy inside. Please, can I have another?"

Cliff looked over to Joyce who raised her eyebrows as if to say "It's your party". Then he turned to Cathy. "O.K. I'll order you one if you want." He signaled a passing waitress for another drink. "But remember, if you're not used to drinking, this is not the stuff to cut your teeth on."

"Oh boy," said Joyce to herself. "Here we go. It's 'Days of Wine and Roses' all over again."

"What did you say?"

"Nothing. But if she's going to drink that fast we'd better get some food into her first. Spa cuisine is not meant to soak up booze, especially not the ration we've been getting lately. What is there to eat around here?"

She picked up the soiled and spotted handwritten sheet that passed for a menu and which Cliff had been using as a coaster, and read it out loud.

"Cou cou, jug jug, Fish Pash, Twice Laid, Sea Egg Pie, yam balls, Guava Fool, and pickled breadfruits. O.K. Mr. Tour Guide, would you like to translate that, or shall we just order blind and see what we get?"

"Why don't you try the Twice Laid? It's kind of like a quiche with boiled fish, potatoes, onions, and eggs. That should help soak up the rum."

"That sounds about right." She tapped Cathy on the arm to get her attention. "Cathy, do you want to try some Twice Laid?"

"Twice Laid, nurse maid," rhymed Cathy happily to herself, looking around for the next drink.

Cliff knitted his brows together.

"What can you expect?" said Joyce, catching his puzzled look. "The only adult she probably spends any time with is Mother Goose."

It was a different waitress who arrived with the drink, and Joyce was disappointed. She wanted a chance to talk to the maid/waitress. It couldn't be an accepted practice for spa staff to moonlight, could it? Come to think of it, though, breakfast had been served buffet style for the last two days, so maybe she wasn't spa staff anymore.

While Joyce was pondering this possibility, Cliff ordered the food and Cathy attacked the cherry.

"You think she'll be alright?" asked Joyce, after a few minutes. "I've never seen alcohol hit anybody so fast."

"Sure, she's fine. Once she gets something solid in her stomach she'll be O.K. No more booze, though. I don't want to have to carry her back to the truck, for obvious reasons."

CHAPTER 31

CLIFF SIPPED HIS DRINK. The beer tasted good, but not as good as he had expected. He looked over at Joyce. She was watching the two girls up on the dance floor trying to learn the limbo, and he followed her gaze.

Regina was just going under the bamboo stick, her long legs bent almost horizontal at the knee, her blue-black hair swaying down, touching the ground and gleaming in the light of the colorful paper lanterns that were strung around the dance floor. She was so young, so "juicy" was the word that came to mind. He wondered for a moment what it would be like to have those long, long legs wrapped around his waist, and then reprimanded himself for being a dirty old man, and turned his attention back to Joyce.

He watched her swirl the brandy, warming it with her hand, and then sip it, arching her throat as she swallowed, longing for the heat but trying to avoid it at the same time.

"Penny for your thoughts," he said softly.

His question startled her out of her reverie. She put the glass back on the table. "You know, Cliff, there's something very peculiar going on here."

He looked around, wondering what she was referring to. "Where?"

"Not *here* here. At the spa. I'm sure that the waitress who took our order was the maid who used to bring breakfast."

"Now that you mention it, she did look kind of familiar." He took a sip of his drink. "And you know something else, this morning I went to get a massage. Alfred was gone. The place was all locked up. And there was a note on the door that said 'Gone sailing.' What do you suppose that meant?"

"That's exactly what I mean. Mariette is serving the meals, I've been making my own bed, the food's getting pretty repetitive. I mean, lately it looks more like the menu for the annual convention of the Poultry Growers Association of America."

He nodded. "You can say that again. I had no idea there was so many ways you could serve chicken. I wonder what's going on."

"I don't know, but I think I'll have a word with Mariette. If anybody knows, she does." Joyce nodded toward the two girls who were working their way through the crowd, back to the table.

"It's like sardines out there!" exclaimed Regina, throwing herself gratefully into a chair.

"Only without the oil," added Mariette, rubbing a bruise on her shin.

Joyce didn't wait for the two to get comfortable. She turned immediately to Mariette. "Who's Mittlehoff?"

"What?" Startled, the girl looked up from rubbing her leg.

Joyce repeated the question. "Who is Mittlehoff?"

"You know about Mittlehoff?" asked Mariette guardedly.

"Let's just say we've met. Who is he?"

Mariette turned her attention back to her leg. "Nobody, nobody," she mumbled from beneath the table.

But Joyce persisted. "If he's nobody, then how come we both know about him?"

She sat up. "Look Joyce, I . . . I can't tell you. The doctor wouldn't like it if I said anything."

Joyce decided to keep up the pressure. "Mariette, there's something going on at the spa, and I want to know what it is, or there isn't going to be any story."

Mariette looked shocked, and Cliff, who had been listening to all this, decided to fulfill his role of romantic hero-in-residence and intervene. "Oh come on, Joyce, give the kid a break."

Joyce turned on him. "Give the journalist a break and butt out, will you?"

He looked offended. "Come on, Regina, let's go trip a light fantastic or two, and leave Margaret Bourke-White here to get on with her career."

Regina looked confused. "Trip over a what?"

He sighed. "Let's dance." And he took her by the arm.

Cathy, who was tucking into her Twice Laid and making little sounds of pleasure as she chewed and swallowed, looked up as the two left the table. "What are they going to do?"

"They're butting out," replied Joyce pointedly.

"Oh." Cathy took the hint and went back to her food.

Joyce leaned forward and put both elbows on the table. "Look, Mariette, something is wrong at the spa. You can't hide it any longer. The staff is leaving, the food is lousy, strange little Nazis are hanging around, and you know what it's all about. Tell me, and I promise that I'll make the story as sympathetic as possible."

Mariette chewed on her lower lip for a moment. Her plan to get Cliff together with Regina had developed complications. "Joyce, nothing is going on. And anyway, the doctor is handling it. Please don't ask me anymore, O.K.? Just enjoy what's left of your stay and then write a nice article about the spa." Her voice was even, but her eyes were pleading.

"You're a smart girl, Mariette. You know I can't write a glowing recommendation about this place under the circumstances." She paused, letting it sink in. "Of course, if I knew what was going on, maybe I could soft-pedal it, but . . ." and she shook her head.

But before Mariette could say anything else, Cliff and Regina returned to the table.

"I hope you two have finished your little tête-à-tête. We had to dance so close out there, her mother will probably insist I marry her, now." Cliff gave a lascivious grin at Regina. "Not that I'm complaining, of course."

Regina blushed to the roots of her hair.

"Marriage stinks." It was Cathy, who had finished her food and her second drink and had become very reflective.

"What?" Joyce had almost forgotten she was there.

"I said, 'Marriage stinks and Michael Aloysius Stewart is a prick.'" Then she hiccuped. "Pardon me. Must have eaten too fast."

"Look . . . ah . . . Cathy, don't say anything you'll be embarrassed about if you remember it in the morning." Cliff put a cautioning hand on hers.

"Embarrassed? Why should I be embarrassed because he's a prick?"

Cliff started to say something else, but Joyce interrupted him. "Let her talk. It might be just what she needs."

"Jus' what I need. . . . I need. . . . Nobody cares what I need." said Cathy, her eyes filling with tears. "You're right to get a divorce, Joyce." She dabbed at the corner of each flooding eye with her paper napkin.

Cliff looked questioningly at Joyce. "She still doesn't know who I am," she whispered back. He nodded. "She must be the only one who doesn't."

"Otherwise, you could have ended up like me." Cathy was talking to herself more than anybody else.

Regina, feeling uncomfortable at this sudden display of adult ennui, decided to go powder her nose and take the suddenly subdued Mariette with her.

Cathy was on a roll, now. "Do you know why I married Michael?"

Cliff and Joyce both shook their heads.

"Neither do I. That's the awful part. I never really stopped to think about it. He asked me. My parents liked him. My friends liked him. So I married him." She thought for a minute. "I married him for everybody else as much as for me. But it was the normal thing to do. Everybody I knew was getting married." She gave a deep sigh.

"And then, after we were married, he didn't want me to work, so I stopped working. Then he wanted babies, so I had babies. And now, when he wants dinner I give him dinner, when he wants clean laundry I do his laundry, and when he wants to make love I let him. I wait all day in that house for him to tell me what he wants me to do-oooo."

Her voice trembled and she took a minute to compose herself before continuing.

"Did you ever see 'The Stepford Wives'? Well, that is what it's like, believe me. I exist to serve everybody else, and of course nobody ever asks me what I need, because if they did, I might tell them." She took a deep breath, trying to stop a rising hiccup, but it popped out anyway.

"Do you know what it's like, spending all day every day with small children? They want this. They want that. And I have to give it to them, because I'm their mother. But who gives to me? Who even talks to me? Every time I go for a checkup I'm afraid they're going to declare me brain-dead." She hiccuped the last of the word and a big wet tear slid down her face and onto the traces of the Twice Laid.

"Oh Cathy." Joyce was filled with empathy, and she covered Cathy's hand with her own. No wonder she ate so much, if she was this unhappy with her life.

Cliff cleared his throat. "Well, you two sure are a fun pair. I think I'll go and dance with the girls while you solve the crisis," he said to Joyce as he got up from the table.

"Thanks a lot," she called after him, but he couldn't hear her for the music.

She patted Cathy's hand. "Look, Cathy, it's just the rum talking. You love your husband and you love your children. You'll feel better about all this in the morning."

Cathy shook her head. "No I won't. When I go back, everything will be just the same, and the doctor was right. I may lose a few pounds but I'll put it all back on, because eating is the only thing in my life that *I* can decide to do. It's the only control I have." She was sobbing into the napkin now, shredding it into soggy wads of paper.

Joyce drank the last of her brandy and tried to remember the last time she had been this depressed. What with Maxine and her marriage and now Cathy and hers, she was beginning to despair for the whole institution.

She watched the dance floor and, in a few moments, Cliff danced into view holding a willowy Regina loosely in his arms as they swayed to the soft beat of the music. Typical, she thought. Just like Harry. He sets up the play and then leaves me to run with the ball.

* * *

When they got back to the spa, it was after midnight. Joyce was dead tired, and all she wanted to do was crawl between the cool blue sheets and go to sleep.

She went straight up to her room, kicked off her shoes, and headed for the bathroom. But, as she passed the telephone, she noticed the red light blinking on and off. A message? Who would call her here? Who else, she thought, picking up the phone and pushing the button for the operator on the front desk. Harry.

The operator confirmed her suspicions and said that Mr. Kraft had left an urgent message that she call him right away no matter what time she got in.

"How many exclamation points after the 'urgent'?" Joyce yawned into the receiver.

"Pardon me?"

"Never mind. Thank you." She placed a finger over the plungers and cut the operator off. Next she dialed the number of Harry's private line at *Destiny*. After five rings, a bleary voice came on the other end.

"Hello."

"Harry, it's Joyce."

"Joyce? What time is it?" He sounded like he had been in a deep sleep.

"After twelve."

"After twelve! Where've you been?"

"Why, do I have a curfew?"

"I've been trying to get hold of you all evening." He was awake now, and sounding more like his old self.

"I was out."

"Out? Out! You're at a spa in the middle of the Caribbean, for Christ's sake. How can you go out?"

"Believe me, it wasn't easy." She changed the phone to her other ear and picked up a pencil. "Now, what's so urgent?"

"Urgent? Oh yeah, just a minute while I get my notes." The receiver on Harry's end thunked on the desk top, and Joyce could hear the distant whisper of rustling papers.

He came back on the line. "Right. Listen to this . . . uh. . . . Research came up with a Norbick Mittlehoff who used to work for the Banco Internationale de Suisse." She could tell he was reading from somebody else's notes, because he kept stumbling over the words. "Uh . . . it says he left there about eighteen months ago and went to work for a Baroness Von Hasselberg." He stopped reading. "Of course we don't know if this is your Mittlehoff."

"He's not *my* Mittlehoff. He's the doctor's Mittlehoff. And even if it is the same person, what you've told me makes it all about as clear as mud, anyway," she said, irritably. "Was this what your urgent message was all about?"

"I thought it might be important."

"Harry at . . ." she looked at her watch "12:47 in the morning, *nothing* is important but sleep."

"It wouldn't be 12:47 in the morning if you had been in when I called you earlier." He sounded annoyed.

"What is that supposed to mean?"

"It means I want to make sure that story is ready on time, and how can it be when you're out gallivanting all over the Caribbean?" He paused for a breath. "Who did you go with, anyway?"

"With? What makes you think I was 'with' anybody? Besides, it's none of your business."

"As long as you're on an assignment for me, *everything* is my business." His voice was getting louder and louder.

"Is that right? Well you can just. . . ." And she was just about to tell him about how she felt about that, when the phone went dead.

"Men!" And she slammed the phone back into its cradle, and strode off into the bathroom.

CHAPTER 32

RELUCTANTLY, Harry hailed a cab and headed for 77th and Madison. He was reluctant because, for those who like their corn pancakes blue, their asparagus white, and their redfish black, the Upper East Side is epicurean heaven. For those who care less about the esthetics and more about appetite, however, it was another destination entirely. The only appetite these bistros, eateries, and grills were dedicated to satisfying was the appetite to be seen in the right places with the right people, eating the right food. Therefore, the food was almost guaranteed to be an exercise in bizarre chic, with chefs up and down the avenues trying to outdo each other with a variety of incompatible comestibles forced into combinations and styles that would cause a grandmother to faint dead away.

But, as everyone who was anyone, knew, it was not really the eating of the food but the creation of the "culinary experience" which was the ultimate goal. This phrase was tacitly understood by those who frequented such establishments to mean that eating the food was of less importance than observing it, discussing it, remembering when you had something just like it in Portofino last summer, and generally letting it go cold on the plate.

Harry thought it was all bull. He therefore approached the acid-etched doors of The American Grill with what can only be described as a certain lack of enthusiasm.

Inside it was steamy, with peculiar-smelling vapors erupting from the kitchen every time a waiter scurried through the swinging doors, spray from the glass-washer stinging the bar patrons with its hot, chemical effluvium, and sixty-odd people sweating from the excessive heat caused by cramming that many of them into only a few-hundred square feet.

Harry paused by the door and was momentarily crushed against the cigarette machine by the rollicking exit of a table of four who were either terribly anxious to get back to work or terribly anxious to get out of The American Grill. When they had gone, he stepped out into the aisle that divided the long, narrow room in half, and looked around.

It was a cross between a laundromat and a hospital waiting room. Anonymous grey carpet covered the floor, cane-back chairs held up, not by legs but by a length of bent chrome tubing, rested under white-clothed tables that nestled beside stark white walls. The only break in the searing austerity of the décor was a thick grey stripe that ran around the room about four feet off the floor.

Harry scrunched up his eyes, trying to see if his son was seated somewhere in the depths of the restaurant. But it was hard to make out anyone more than a few feet away, because the only illumination came from a scattering of light fixtures which consisted of inverted, V-shaped strips of aluminum masking one sorry bulb. As such, it was not bright enough to get even the most desperate of moths excited. Emphasizing the paucity of fixtures was the circumstance that the lights were on dimmers and the dimmers were on "low."

Why, asked Harry of himself, had he let Bradley pick the restaurant? He was in the mood for a steak sandwich and fries, not bark soup and duck liver soufflé.

He slid onto the one empty seat at the bar and ordered a scotch. The bartender, who had three blenders all whirring away at once, looked disappointed. He asked Harry if he preferred single malt or blended, Scottish, English, or Canadian. And when Harry shrugged his indifference and stated "just scotch," he thought the bartender was going to burst into tears.

Harry tried to appease him by asking for a dish of bar snacks. But when it arrived, he decided that the pieces of shredded coconut and dried banana chips wouldn't go with his drink, and pushed the dish outside.

"Haven't you got anything with salt on it?"

The bartender shook his head. "Salt is very bad for the blood pressure," he said didactically, and walked away to serve the "real" customers at the other end of the bar.

Harry was in no mood for a lecture on the evils of salt. He was starving, and he was still ticked off that Joyce had been out running around the night before, probably with that actor, instead of getting on with her story. It hadn't occurred to him yet that it might not be the editor who was ticked off, but the man.

A cold gust of wind announced the arrival of more customers, and Harry turned to see if one of them was Bradley. But he couldn't see his son among the crowd of five or six expensively dressed young people who had just come through the door, so he turned back to the bar and resignedly sipped his scotch.

"Dad?"

Harry felt a tap on his left shoulder and turned around. There stood a young man who had been part of the crowd at the door. He looked a little like John Kennedy, Jr. Nice grey sports jacket, black slacks, white button-down shirt.

"Bradley?"

The young face broke into a smile. "Didn't recognize me, eh?"

"No. . . . Of course I. . . . Weil. . . ." Harry had a closer look. "Didn't you used to have blue hair?"

"Nor for the last couple of weeks, Dad. I guess you haven't been around enough lately to keep up with me. Besides, that stuff is all past tense now. Conservative is in." He leaned against the bar next to Harry and nibbled at the banana chips.

"Conservative, eh? Well, I can't argue with that. At least you look like a human being now. Want a drink?"

"Yeah, that'd be fine."

Harry signaled the bartender. "I'll have another scotch and my son will have. . . .?" he turned to Bradley.

"I'll have a peach schnapps and orange juice. Thank you."

The bartender broke into a smile. Peach schnapps was *the* drink. He looked smugly at Harry and hurried away to fulfill his mission.

For a few minutes, silence settled awkwardly between them while they waited for the drinks. Then Harry spoke.

"So, how've you been?"

"Fine, Dad. Fine. And you?"

"Good. Good. Busy." Harry took a long pull on the scotch. "How's school?"

"I graduated last semester, Dad."

"Right, right. History, wasn't it?"

"Philosophy."

"Right, Philosophy." Harry nodded and stared ahead, thinking how out of touch he had become with his son. "So what are you going to do now?"

"Well, Dad, that's one of the things I wanted to talk to you about this afternoon. I was glad when you called. I didn't want to do it without telling you, and I haven't been able to talk to Mom about it. She's kind of off on her own cloud lately, you know?"

"Yeah, I know. That's what I wanted to talk to you about, Bradley. But you go ahead and tell me your news first."

Harry wasn't looking forward to telling his son that his mother wanted to divorce his father. Especially when the two of them had always been so close. Bradley had always been his mother's kid. He even looked more like her.

"O.K." Bradley cleared his throat. "I don't know how you're going to feel about this, Dad, but here goes. You remember Janie?"

"Janie?"

"The girl I've been going out with for the last year or so."

"Oh, that Janie. Sure, I remember her. Tall girl. Nice ti . . . , I mean, good figure."

"Well, I'm going to move in with her."

"You're going to live together!" Harry raised his voice above the thrumming of the glass-washer. "How can you live with a girl when you haven't even got a job? You haven't got a job, have you?"

Bradley shook his head. "No, Dad, but let me finish. Janie has her own company. She graduated in business administration from Columbia last year. After she got out, she could see that the opportunities for women weren't what they should be, and she's got this entrepreneurial thing, so she started her own company."

"Just like that? Her own company? That's a pretty big step. What does she do, design clothes, make jewellery? What?"

"She gives parties." Bradley began to fidget. He knew his father would find this amusing.

"Parties? What kind of parties? Nobody gives parties for a living, unless you mean she's a caterer. She a caterer, that it?"

Bradley hedged a little. "Well that's part of it. Certainly part of it." He took a long sip of the drink. "Actually Dad, the name of her company is Pet Parties Inc. She gives parties for pets." There, it was out. He waited for the older man's reaction.

"Parties for pets. You mean like cats, dogs. . . ." Harry spoke slowly, trying to digest the idea.

"Yeah, cats, dogs, gerbils, birds, snakes . . . whatever."

Harry grinned. "You're pulling my leg, right?"

Bradley shook his head.

Harry's grin faded. "You mean you are actually planning to go and live with a girl who makes a living helping animals to socialize?"

"Dad, don't put it down. Janie says that pets are an eight-billion-dollar-a-year business in this country. All she's doing is carving out a share of that. You know how people feel about their pets? Pet Parties Inc. is already booked solid until August. This is big business, believe me."

"Booked until August, you say?" Harry was thinking about the demented little turd of a cat that Joyce had, Fredo—the refrigerated kitty. He wouldn't mind giving a party for old Fredo alright—a bon voyage party. He wondered if Joyce would go for it. Then his mind skipped a few spaces and he was thinking about what she might have been doing last night with the actor. Would she do that? Well they weren't playing tiddly winks, that was for sure.

"Dad?"

"Huh?" he muttered glumly, still thinking about Joyce and the actor.

"Well, what do you think?"

"I think the whole world's going to hell in a handcart, that's what I think." He pushed the thought of Joyce aside, it was only making him miserable, and tried to concentrate on Bradley's announcement. "But, if you want to be with this girl, then I guess you should be with her. Life's too short to waste on being with people you don't care about." He made a parental hesitation. "No point in my asking if you're going to marry her, is there?"

Bradley shook his head. "Marriage isn't part of the scenario at the moment, Dad. We're still trying to sort out the dynamics of our relationship. Find out if we're compatible."

"Compatible? What's compatible? You both like sushi? What?"

"You sound just like Mom. We just want to see if we like living with each other first, before we go for the big "M." A lot of couples are doing that, these days. Marriage isn't something to be taken lightly."

"Tell me about it," said Harry flatly. "Anyway, what is your part in all this pet stuff? She gonna make you a partner or something?"

"No, Dad, I'm not exactly going to be part of the business. Although I will be helping out when she needs a hand." Bradley squirmed uncomfortably. "I'm going to be staying at home, basically looking after Janie and the apartment. You know, like Mom does."

"Bradley, Bradley," Harry shook his head and gave a deep sigh, "just answer me one question. Yes or no, and I promise that I won't ask it ever again."

"Go ahead."

"Are you a fairy?"

"What?"

"Do you like guys?"

"No, of course not! Just because I'm going to be a househusband doesn't mean I don't have perfectly normal sexual feelings. Anymore than Janie's running her own business means that she is less of a woman. Dad, times have changed. You have a lot of catching up to do."

"Catching up? I'm forty-nine years old. I'm not sure I can catch up. I'm not sure I even want to."

"Come on Dad, life is full of change. Your problem is that you're stuck in a rut. You and Mom should get a divorce. Start over. Find new lives. Open yourselves up to new experiences." He finished off his drink and picked a piece of orange pulp off his upper lip. "By the way, what did you want to talk to me about anyway?"

"Funny you should mention it. I've been having a hell of a time trying to decide how to tell you this. I didn't want it to color your view of getting married. I had a whole speech worked out about how sometimes marriages just wear out and how just because a marriage doesn't last forever doesn't mean it wasn't a good marriage. And a whole bunch of other stuff." He shook his head wearily from side to side. "But it looks like you just beat me to it. Your mother's gone off to "open herself up to new experiences," and I'm going down to see her tomorrow. I think she wants a divorce."

"A divorce? That's great, Dad. You guys should have done it years ago. You'll have a great time."

"Bradley, I'm talking about divorcing your mother, not spending a week at Club Med."

"I know that, Dad. What I meant was, a man your age, you'll have a great time with the ladies. There's a lot of women out there who really dig grey hair. Really. And there's no point in being miserable all your life, that's what I say. Wait till I tell Janie. Her mother's been divorced three times!" He looked at his watch.

"Wow! it's already two thirty! I gotta go, Dad. Promised I'd help Janie with this baby shower she's giving for a pregnant persian this afternoon."

"No lunch?" Harry didn't know whether to be relieved or disappointed. He had seen some of the food being delivered to nearby tables. He didn't recognize any of it.

"No time." Bradley slapped his father on the back. "Thanks anyway, Dad." He moved away from the bar and then came back.

"If you ever need to talk to anybody, you know, man to man, about the divorce, I'll be home most days. Just come over and I'll make us a nice lunch."

"Thanks, son. I might take you up on that."

Harry watched Bradley until he had gone out the front door and then turned back to finish his scotch.

"My son the househusband is gonna make me a nice lunch." He said softly under his breath, trying to decipher his reaction to the news. "I guess that was something else he inherited from his mother."

He reached for a handful of banana chips, paid the bill, and went outside to flag a cab.

CHAPTER 33

AFTER LUNCH—if you could call it that—Joyce presented herself on the patio by the pool. She eyed the long wooden table in front of her with some misgivings. Ever since the incident with the wax she had been reluctant to offer herself up for possible encasement in any substance which was likely to immobilize her. But now it looked as though she had little choice. Gretel, the esthetician, took her card, ticked off "Mud Pack," and patted the table with one gigantic hand.

"Up ve jump," she boomed, and Joyce obediently hopped onto the table.

"Ze bathing zuit vill haf to go."

Joyce shook her head. "Uh uh. The suit stays. It's a two-piece, there's plenty of flesh for you to work on. Don't think for one minute that I'm going to lay here in public, in the nude." Joyce lay back and Gretel shook her massive head.

"Ach! You American vimmen are zo . . ." she was searching for a word, "zo tied up."

"You mean uptight?" said Joyce, pulling up the straps of her bathing suit.

"Yah. Das is it. Uptight. You spend a vortune on your botties to make them beautiful. Zen you are afraid that zomeone vill look at you." She shook her head again, puzzled by it all. "Zere is notink wrong with ze human botty. It is a vork of art, not zomezing to be hidden away behind ze bathing zuit."

"You may have something there, Gretel," said Joyce, adjusting herself more comfortably on the table. "But I'm not about to be a pioneer on the nudity frontier, so could we get on with this, please."

"Yah, yah. Ve get on with it. Maybe ven you are all coveret up you vill feel betta. Nobotty vill be able to zee your botty for the mud."

Gretel gave a laugh that was somewhere between a cackle and a guffaw, and slapped a handful of warm stickiness onto Joyce's bare stomach. She smeared it around and around until it covered the exposed skin, and then scooped up another handful and began slathering it down her legs and thighs. Joyce lay there, thinking of lobster being drizzled with drawn butter, and then moved onto visions of cakes being iced, as Gretel's strong hands massaged the goo into every inch of the exposed skin. Lately, food was everything.

After a few minutes, she was finished. "Zere, you are all coveret up. Now ve vait for the zun to do its vork." Gretel looked at her watch. "Half an hour, maybe forty minutes. I vill come back, undt you vill be nice undt hard. Your botty vill be cleansed of all the garbage."

Gretel departed, and Joyce turned her head slightly to see if anybody else was around the pool, but the patio was empty. She closed her eyes and concentrated on feeling the sun baking the mud onto her skin, pulling it tighter and tighter, squeezing all the "garbage" out. It felt like her skin was shrinking. At this rate, she wouldn't have a toxin left in her whole body. There wouldn't be room for one. She began to feel sleepy.

After a few minutes, the sound of approaching footsteps roused her. She opened her eyes. It was Cliff.

"You look like a giant gingerbread man. Good enough to eat."

Ignoring the implication, she waved a rapidly crusting hand at him. "Could you move over a bit? You're blocking my rays, and I'm supposed to be hardening. The sooner I harden, the sooner I can get out of this earthenware overcoat."

He moved to the side, shading his eyes with the back of his hand, now that the sun was right in front of him.

"About last night. . . ."

"Ah yes. Last night." She cut him off. "We must do it again, sometime. Perhaps we could hold a yearly reunion. Every year on the same day we could all get together and you could have a good time while I get stuck playing Sigmund Freud."

"My, we are testy today, aren't we?"

"You really put me on the spot last night with Cathy. You could have stuck around and helped me out. It's tough when somebody pours out their heart to you. I mean, what was I supposed to say to her? Divorce the prick, or stay with him and let him browbeat you for the rest of your life 'cause that's all there is, baby? What do I know about marriage, except how to avoid it?"

"Was she O.K.?"

"She was fine. I'm the basket case."

"You can't help it if you have a kind face."

"Right, the kind that says "O.K., dump on me.""

"I think you should be flattered that she trusted you enough to let it all out. It's a big gift to be able to make people feel that they can trust you, be secure with you, confide in you. Don't knock it."

"A gift, you say? Well, in that case, can I return it for something else? Have you any idea how depressed I felt when I finished with Cathy?"

He smiled and the sunlight glinted off his caps. "Look, Joyce, there's something I wanted. . . ."

"Unless it's topsoil, forget it."

" . . . to ask you. Would you like to have a little picnic supper down on the beach? I still owe you a date for last night, you know."

"*On* the beach? I *am* the beach." She tried to blow a flake of mud from the end of her nose. "How many people are coming along this time?"

"Just us. I'll try and scrounge up some food. You just be there at five o'clock. O.K.? We'll have a little swim, and, uh, see what comes up, as they say." He moved out of her line of vision. "Oh, and Joyce, don't bother to shower. I've always had this thing about gingerbread."

"Very funny. Have you ever thought about guest-hosting for Carson?" she called after him.

She heard him walk away and closed her eyes, thinking. What was going on here? Why did he keep trying? Why did she keep letting him? Was all this just so he could have a perfect score—a hundred pitches, a hundred hits? Did she really want to go to bed with him, or was it just the game she was enjoying? Or was that his motive? Men were so complicated. Even worse than cats.

After a few minutes, another set of approaching feet stirred her out of her reverie.

"Joyce, are you sleeping?" whispered Cathy.

"No, I'm detoxifying." Joyce didn't open her eyes.

"Can I talk to you for a minute?"

"Do I look like I'm going anywhere?" She sighed and blinked against the strong sunlight.

"No, I guess not." Cathy took a deep breath. "O.K. about last night. I just wanted you to know that I really, really, really, appreciate what you did for me. You know, letting me get it all off my chest. I've never had anybody I could say all those things to before. You don't know what it meant to me. And I . . . I wanted to say that I am really sorry if I spoiled your evening. I didn't mean to."

"I know you didn't, Cathy. And I'm glad that you feel better. I hope you can get things sorted out." And Joyce realized that, in spite of what she had said to Cliff, she meant it.

"Oh, I will. I know I will. I have another session with the doctor this afternoon. But you know something? Half the battle was admitting to myself how I feel. Always before, when I would start feeling like that, I would think how disloyal and ungrateful I was being to Michael, and I would push those feelings back down inside me and go and get something to eat. But last night, I let them all out, and now I know that all I have to do is deal with them. You made me realize that. You also made me realize that there's nothing wrong with putting what you want first. There's nothing wrong with working on your own needs as well as everybody else's."

"Cathy, look, I. . . ." Joyce tried to sit up. She wanted to say something important and insightful. Something that would encourage

Cathy, but at the same time discourage her from going too far. She didn't want to contribute to another divorce. But the mud was like a shell of cement around her. She was literally stuck to the table.

"That's O.K. Don't get up. I'll see you later," said Cathy, and she left.

Get up, thought Joyce, listening to the receding footsteps. I'll crack like a broken vase if I move an eyelid. . . .

"You look like a *rogelach*." The chirruping of Maxine's voice filled the momentary void of silence left by the departing Cathy.

"Why does everybody keep talking about food?" came a muffled query from the mound of clay where Joyce's face should have been.

"Harry said I should tell you he's coming down tomorrow."

"Me?"

"Don't worry, he told me all about you. I know who you are. I spoke to him on the phone last night and he told me."

"He never said anyth. . . . Ah, Maxine, about the other day. I wasn't trying to deceive you about my getting a divorce. I would have told you the truth right then, but you were in a hurry and I *was* supposed to be here incognito. . . ." Joyce was struggling to talk without moving her lips, but Maxine interrupted her.

"So what's the problem? What you said was perfectly true; the fact that it wasn't you who was saying it doesn't change a thing."

Joyce thought about that for a moment and then decided that it made sense after all.

Maxine patted Joyce on the head and the sound echoed eerily inside the mud helmet. "Harry says you've got a real head on your shoulders. Anyway it wasn't what *you* said that was so important. It was what you let *me* say to you. Talking to you and Adolpho has given me the courage to do some serious thinking. Now Harry and I can sit down and discuss what's going on, like two adults instead of husband and wife."

Maxine departed with one more echoing pat, and Joyce wished that her forty minutes had been up ten minutes ago.

"Hi, Joyce. How do you like playing 'living statues'? I had this one yesterday. It's a real drag, just lying there. Kind of boring isn't it?"

"Mummmmm!" replied Joyce, whose lips had apparently hardened in the shut position.

Regina continued. "Have you seen my mother? Mildred's on the phone. Says she's got to talk to her and I haven't seen her since this morning."

"Mmmmmmm!" complained Joyce rolling her eyes.

"I guess not. Sorry I disturbed you. Bye."

Joyce tried to call after her. "Mmmmmmmmmm!" she cried. "Mmmm-Mmmmmmmm!" She tried to lift herself off the table again but she was stuck fast.

She lay still for a minute, trying to reason away the rising tide of panic which was welling up inside of her. Gretel would be along any minute. All she had to do was stay calm.

Mittlehoff hurried along the corridor that led to the baroness's private suite. When he got to the door he hesitated, and then knocked twice.

"Come in!"

She was lying face down on the massage table in the middle of the room, a small pink towel laid modestly across her lower hips. Alfred, her new personal masseur, was busy kneading the kinks out of her alabaster shoulders. Mittlehoff came halfway across the room and then stopped.

"Stand where I can see you, for God's sake, man!" ordered the baroness. And Mittlehoff moved closer to the head of the table. He looked nervously at Alfred.

"Uh . . . ?"

"Don't worry about him. Alfred and I have no secrets from each other. Do we, Bunnykins?" She turned her head slightly and looked up at her latest acquisition. Then she turned back to Mittlehoff. "Well, get on with it then."

"Uh . . . Uh. . . ." Mittlehoff stammered. "I . . . I did as you requested. I contacted all the suppliers and made it clear that his credit rating was somewhat questionable. . . ."

"Good."

"So all the deliveries will be C.O.D. until he brings his accounts up to date."

"Excellent. He can't possibly pay them. A little more to the right, Bunnykins. That's it . . . right . . . there." She let out a sigh of exquisite agony.

"And . . . and then I paid the staff their back wages plus a little incentive on the condition that they leave immediately and most of them did, except for the cook, Adolpho, who seemed to have some strange idea about loyalty . . . and Gretel, the esthetician."

"Did you tell her what I wanted her to do?"

"Yes, Baroness. And I believe that Ms. Redmond is scheduled for that treatment this afternoon."

"Marvelous. After Gretel is finished with her, she won't have a kind word to say about the place—in print or out. Harder, please, Alfred, and a little to the left. What else?"

"Well, uh, let me see, the supplies, the staff . . . oh yes. I thought of this one myself." Mittlehoff chuckled maniacally. "Late last night, I cut the wires to the main telephone cable. They are now incommunicado." He showed off his small pointed white teeth and waited for the praise to rain down on his slicked-back head.

"You idiot!" She pushed Alfred's hands away and sat up. "Get me my robe."

The masseur obediently draped the robe around her shoulders and she slipped it on.

"How can I expect him to beg for mercy if the telephones are not working. What did you think he was going to do? Send his notice of surrender by carrier pigeon!"

She stood up and Mittlehoff cowered in the force of her wrath.

"Now I am going to have to go to see *him*. And you, you little worm, are coming with me."

CHAPTER 34

MARIETTE WAS TAKING A LOAD OF SHEETS to the laundry by way of the pool deck, when she came upon the rapidly petrifying presence of Joyce Redmond.

"Oh my God!" She dropped the load of sheets and ran over to the table. "Who's in there?" She knocked on the head of the adobed shape.

"Mmmm-Mmm!" came the muted plea from within the mud.

"Just a minute, I'll get the hose." And she disappeared around the corner and into the gardener's shed. A few moments later she returned, dragging the long green snake of a hose with her. "Hold on. I'm going to turn the water on, now." And she twisted the end of the faucet, releasing a blast of icy cold water.

Quickly she sprayed the area at the top of the table and, in a few seconds, the force of the water began to melt the mud and a face appeared. "Joyce, is that you?" cried Mariette, still spraying frantically. "Are you all right?"

Joyce opened her mouth to reply, but in her enthusiasm to remove the mud, Mariette sprayed a jet of water right down the captive's throat. Joyce coughed, choked and then swallowed. She was dying of thirst after being left out in the sun for over an hour in her ceramic coffin.

Mariette continued to train the hose up and down Joyce's body and, in a few minutes, minus most of the mud, Joyce was able to sit up and then totter to her feet, albeit not without some difficulty.

The girl turned off the hose and offered her a towel. "Joyce, what happened?"

Joyce was busy picking lumps of mud out of her hair. "What happened? What does it look like happened? That sadistic Valkyrie that you call an esthetician just tried to turn me into a human mudpie." Joyce paused while she scooped a handful of sludge from her cleavage and slopped it on to the ground. "This is the last straw, Mariette. The last straw. I am going to see the doctor right now and demand to know what is going on." And with that she snatched the towel and stormed off toward the doctor's office.

When she got there, she knocked once, and then without waiting for a reply opened the door and went in. The doctor and Belle Taylor broke apart, trying to look like they had not just been engaged in a frantic game of tongue hockey.

The doctor cleared his throat and casually wiped a hand across his mouth to remove any trace of Bellissima No. 5. "Ms. Redmond, was ist das? You are all wet."

"*I* am all wet?" said Joyce who now stood dripping puddles of muddy water on the blue and red Bokhara rug. "This place is what is all wet. This . . . this . . . sleep-away camp for celebrity sex maniacs. This . . . this . . . tropical torture chamber. This Caribbean Colonel Saunders franchise! This is not a spa—it's a CIA survival camp!" She was practically shouting now, as she wiped some more mud off her forehead. "If I wanted to join the Whole Earth movement I would have gone to Ca . . . Ca . . . California!" Joyce was so upset she was starting to hyperventilate. She was taking big gulps of air, but none of it seemed to be getting to the right places.

The doctor threw a look of alarm at Belle, and helped Joyce to a chair. "Here, Ms. Redmond, Joyce, sit down and try to calm yourself." He draped the towel around her shoulders and Joyce took a few more deep breaths. After a moment, she started to feel better. The rising panic that had been her only companion for the last half-hour as she lay immobilized and helpless was slowly subsiding. The only problem was that she was beginning to itch—all over.

She ran the nails of her left hand soothingly down her right arm and vice versa. Then she ran both hands down her legs and up again.

"The itching will subside," explained the doctor helpfully, "in a few minutes."

"A few more minutes and I might have subsided." Joyce raked her nails across her throat and tried in vain to reach the center of her back.

"Allow me," said the doctor.

"Don't you touch me!" She pulled away.

"But I can assure you that I. . . ." the doctor looked helplessly at Belle Taylor.

"I think perhaps you should apologize to Ms. Redmond," she said pointedly. "It seems that Gretel must have left the mud pack on too long. I'm sure it was just an accident."

"An accident! She did everything but put the finishing glaze on me. She left me there on purpose," cried Joyce, frantically scratching her stomach.

"I'm sure that is not the case," said the doctor, though he didn't sound too convinced. "And I am sorry that you were discomforted. But I'm sure you can understand that every place occasionally has these little staff problems." He smiled weakly.

"Little staff problems!" Still scratching, Joyce jumped to her feet. "You have more than a 'little' staff problem, doctor. What you have is little staff—very little, no telephone service, and no food. Now I want to know what's going on. What happened to Paradise? Did somebody eat an apple? What?"

The doctor looked over at Belle again. "You'd better tell her," she said resignedly.

"Ms. Redmond can I get you a robe, another towel?"

"No, thank you," said Joyce envisioning little prickles of terry-towel all over her irritated skin. "I'll just drip dry, if you don't mind. What you can get me is an explanation."

"Very well," said the doctor contritely. "I suppose there's no way I can hide the truth any longer. I thought perhaps I could forestall things before they got to this point." He smiled sadly at Belle. "But, there has been some . . . uh . . . interference from another party which has, shall we say, escalated matters somewhat."

He sighed heavily and went to sit behind his desk. Joyce thought he looked older, and shorter. A man pushed to his limits. She almost found herself feeling sorry for him. And then she remembered the mud.

"Before I begin, let me say that I am truly sorry that you and the others should have been inconvenienced during your stay. It was not my intention, not at all." He shook his head from side to side. "If things had worked out differently. . . . But I am getting off-topic.

"Some years ago, after I graduated from medical school. . . ."

"By the way, where *did* you graduate from medical school?" asked Joyce, remembering Harry's file.

"University of Lichtenstein."

"Then why do you tell people you went to St. George's?"

"My dear Ms. Redmond, you come from a country where twenty percent of the population thinks that Los Angeles is the capital of the United States and that Kurt Waldheim is the ABC Evening News anchorman. How many do you suppose have ever heard of Lichtenstein? But, since your country's involvement in Grenada, I thought that at least some of my potential customers would know of St. George's."

Joyce nodded. "I see your point, go on."

"After I graduated, I was still young. I wanted adventure, so I travelled about Europe and, after a time, I met this woman, older, very wealthy." He took a side glance at Belle whose mouth had formed a thin white line beneath her nose. "She was the heiress to the WENCO fortune."

"What's a wenco?" Confused, Joyce looked from the doctor to Belle and back again.

But before he could reply, Belle interrupted. "WENCO is the European equivalent of K-Mart," she sniffed derisively.

The doctor continued. "Daniella—the Baroness von Hasselberg by her marriage to her second husband—and I became close friends."

"He means," scoffed Belle, "that he and the discount duchess were having it off."

"She knows what I mean," he said with irritation. "The baroness and I spent several years together. . . ."

Joyce pointed to the doctor. "Lover Boy and Lady Bug, right?"

He winced, and Belle glowered. "I see you found the bracelet, when you were having a look around my office that day."

Joyce felt a flush rishing in her cheeks.

"I keep it, not for sentimental reasons, but as my little emergency escape fund. It is worth quite a bit." He directed this last at Belle and then turned back to Joyce. "Anyway, after a time I realized that there had to be more to life than just gallivanting around Europe spending Daniella's money. By that time we had visited many spas, and so the idea came to me to open one of my own. Eventually, I managed to get Daniella to agree to put up the money for it, and I came here and opened this place."

"But it didn't take off like he thought it would," added Belle, with a hint of I-could-have-told-you-so in her voice.

"No, it didn't. I began to run low on money. Bills went unpaid. Daniella was breathing down my neck, demanding her money back. Things were tight. And then I heard that you were coming to do the article and I knew that might be just enough to tip the scales, to let the Americans know we were here. And then, of course, when I found out that Belle and her daughter were going to be here, too, I thought it might be an avenue from which I could acquire. . . ."

Belle smiled grimly. "Some interim financing."

The doctor nodded. "But now, of course, it is too late."

"Why is it too late?" asked Joyce, who thought this story a lot more interesting, not to mention entertaining, than the one about the family fortune.

"Because Daniella has done her best to ruin the place. It's obvious that she—and that little scum Mittlehoff—are behind what's going on here. Just after you all arrived, Mittlehoff showed up with an ultima-tum from the baroness, sign over the deed to the place, or else."

"So that's what's been going on. And that's why that she-wolf of the S.S. left me stuck in the mud. I guess she thought that after that experience I'd really crucify you and this place, in the article. Now that I know what happened, of course." Joyce thought for a moment. "But

I don't understand, why destroy the business? If she were to succeed, it would only ensure that you couldn't pay her back, and then she'd be stuck with a place with a terrible reputation. . . ."

"Daniella doesn't really care about the money. She just wants us to have to come crawling back to her."

"Us?" piped Belle and Joyce in unison.

The doctor nodded. "Mariette and I. Mariette is the baroness's daughter. She came with me because she couldn't take her mother any longer. And Daniella can't stand to be left in the lurch. It makes her very angry."

Now it was Belle's turn to interject. "But I thought that you and Mariette. . . ."

The doctor shook his head. "I know what you thought, Belle, but give me some credit, please."

"Well, that puts a different cast on things, I must say." Belle was talking more to herself than to the others, now, but her further comments were interrupted by a knock at the door.

A moment later Mittlehoff appeared briefly in the doorway before stepping aside to allow the woman behind him to move into the room.

Joyce's first thought was that she was stunning—in a lethal sort of way. Tall, svelte, and elegantly dressed, her blond hair twisted into a gleaming golden knot on the back of her head, she swept into the room with all the exquisite grace that accompanies those who know they have the money and the power to destroy whatever lies in their path. Mittlehoff followed on behind her like an obedient daschund.

The doctor regarded her without surprise.

"Hello, Daniella, I've been expecting you."

"Hans." She tilted her head slightly to one side, and then let her eyes wander over the two women in the room.

"You must be the journalist. Redmond, isn't it?" She said to Joyce, pulling off her long, dove-coloured gloves, ". . . . I recognized you by your mud."

Her eyes then shifted to Belle. "Well, well, if it isn't Belle Taylor, the eighties answer to the Avon lady." She looked back to the doctor. "We are becoming downwardly mobile, aren't we, Hans? Next thing I know it'll be waitresses and cleaning ladies." She tut-tutted and handed her gloves to Mittlehoff. "Or perhaps you were hoping for a last minute bail-out? Trying to get a silk purse out of a sow's ear. Well I'm afraid you've been casting your pearls before swine, my dear. She can't possibly come up with enough money to enable you to get rid of me in time. I'm about to call your loan. Mittlehoff, the papers."

Belle bristled and moved a few steps closer to the doctor. "Tell the bargain basement baroness here, that if she says one more word about me, I'll knock the bonding right off her teeth."

"I'm not about to be intimidated by the likes of you," Daniella said to Belle, and then snapped her fingers. "Mittlehoff—where are those papers!"

Mittlehoff moved cautiously between the two women and handed the papers to the doctor and then ducked back behind the baroness.

"Useless worm," she said to the little man and then looked over at the doctor, who was reaching for a pen. "By the way, how is my daughter?"

He hesitated for a moment, "Mariette *is* just fine. Would you like to see her?"

"No, just tell her I'm leaving tomorrow, and if she wants to come with me, fine. Otherwise, I'm cutting off her allowance—permanently. Now please hurry up and sign the papers, Hans; we have to move the yacht into deeper water before the tide goes out."

"Put down that pen, Hans." Everyone in the room turned to look at Belle. "I want to talk to you for a moment—outside." And she took him by the arm and guided him out of the room.

They were back in less than five minutes. Belle was smiling, the doctor was teetering somewhere between apprehension and relief. He started to speak. "I . . . uh . . . That is . . . we . . . uh."

Belle interrupted him. "I'll do the talking, Hans." She looked over at Joyce. "You might want to make a note of this for the article you're going to be doing." Joyce scrambled to the desk for a pen and some paper. She had a feeling something major was about to happen.

"The Bellissima Corporation has just purchased 51 percent of The Spa at St. Christophe," announced Belle.

"Th-that's impossible!" stammered the baroness. "You couldn't possibly arrange that kind of financing in so short a time. It's Friday afternoon. The banks in New York are already closed."

"I believe that by the time you get back to the yacht, a bank draft for the balance of the loan will have been wired to you," replied Belle coolly. "I arranged for the money yesterday. I always believe in making the most of whatever opportunities present themselves. And, while I am not fond of loaning money, especially to friends—she looked over at the doctor—I am always ready to make a profitable investment. My company will own the controlling interest in the spa and the spa will handle Bellissima products exclusively. It's a very nice little deal."

"But you can't do this," cried the baroness.

"Oh but I can and I did. It's called doing business—something you only get with experience, not inheritance." Belle was being positively smug now, and Joyce waited, her pen poised above the paper, to see what the baroness's reaction would be.

It was surprisingly cool. She picked up her gloves. "Very well. I had not anticipated this turn of events, but let me tell you—both of you— you have not seen the last of me. I am not a gracious loser, as I'm sure Hans has already told you, and I have a long, long memory. Mittlehoff, come!" She moved toward the door but Belle called after her.

"About your daughter. Don't think that by cutting off her allowance you are leaving her destitute. She's welcome to stay on here, or perhaps she would like to go to New York. I'm sure that once I introduce Mariette to the right people she will do very well for herself."

The baroness fixed Belle Taylor with both piercing blue eyes. "Keep an eye on your company, Mrs. Taylor. One of these days you just might find my name on your board of directors." And with that she was gone.

CHAPTER 35

THE SINKING SUN WAS PAINTING the sand cliffs that defined the western tip of St. Christophe in shades of coral and rose. Beneath the cliffs, sheltered from the weather and the view, was a very small, very private little beach, just perfect for picnicking or swimming or whatever.

Cliff spread out two blankets on sand tinged pink from the sediment of scallop shells, and placed beside it a hamper containing a loaf of bread, some barbecued chicken, and a thermos of ice water, which was all he could scrounge from Adolpho.

He sat for a time, letting the fading heat sizzle his skin in the way that only those who do not fear a sunburn can enjoy, watching the waves, dark blue and white-capped, rolling furiously out in the Caribbean, green and smooth as polished jade as they crept across the shore. The water looked inviting. He checked his watch. He had plenty of time for a swim before Joyce was due. Women were never on time anyway.

He stood up and splashed into the trembling surf, going further and further out into the sea until he could no longer touch the bottom. He let the next wave knock him off his feet and then he began stroking, arm over arm, his newly tuned-up muscles pulling his body forcefully through the waves, the salt stinging his eyes as he set his sights on the horizon.

After fifteen minutes, he made his way back to the beach, breathing hard, but exhilarated from the pure physical effort. He was ready for anything.

As he walked out of the surf, blinking the salt water from his eyes, he could see that one of the blankets was now occupied. She's early, he thought, as he drew closer. But then he saw it wasn't Joyce, after all.

There, stretched out full-length and sunning herself like some come-to-life Circe, was Regina. He paused for a minute, debating the situation. He was not ready for this. But she had heard him and, without opening her eyes, she spoke.

"I wondered how long you were going to be out there."

He was aware that she was trying to make her voice sound seductive by lowering the register a point or two, and so he reached down and picked up his towel and began to rub himself down. No way was he about to join her on the blanket. Not until he had put some clothes on, at any rate.

"What are you doing here?" he asked casually.

She sat up, resting on her elbows, lavender eyes like two pools in the bright sunlight. "I wanted to see you—alone."

"What for?" She was making him nervous. He knew what for, alright, and it wasn't to sell him Girl Scout cookies. But he was stalling, trying to get his bearings.

She didn't answer him, only stood up and moved closer. Taking the towel from his hands, she infiltrated her body next to his so that their arms and legs were touching. He caught a whiff of young heat, and something else. Baby powder?

"Regina, look, I. . . ." He started to brush the hair out of his eyes. But he didn't quite make it. She curved herself closer to him, letting her silky dark hair cover them both like a drawn curtain, and, raising her lips to his, she kissed him.

It was a young kiss, full of inexperience and nervous passion. And it excited him far more than he had imagined was still possible. Without thinking, his blood still pulsing from the exercise, he responded, pulling her close to him.

Then suddenly, as her tongue was tentatively introducing itself to his, he thought of Joyce. If she walked in on this she would mistake it for . . . mistake it for what it was, he thought ruefully. Pushing Regina gently away, he turned around to conceal the rising bulge in his swim trunks and retrieved his pants.

"What's the matter? Wasn't I doing it right?" She sounded disappointed.

"No, you were doing it just fine. Too fine." He pulled on the pants. He was just doing up the zipper when she came up behind him and circled her slender young arms around his waist. It startled him and he caught the zipper in the fabric and it stuck halfway up. "Damn!"

"What's the matter?" She came around in front of him.

"The zipper, it won't budge." He tried again. But it remained steadfast and unmmovable.

"Here, let me try." Regina took hold of the zipper. But the warmth and pressure of her fumbling hands in that area did not ease the situation one bit.

Cliff pushed her hand away. "Look let's . . . uh . . . sit down. Maybe I can get it to work that way."

Regina stretched out on the blanket again, doing her best to look alluring and seductive. And Cliff sat beside her, careful to keep as much yardage as possible between them. Blankets, young, almost-naked girls, and half-open zippers were a loaded combination.

He tried the zipper again.

"Are you sure you don't want me to help?"

"You're not helping, believe me. And Joyce is going to be here any minute. I don't want her to walk in on a scene from 'From Here to Eternity.'"

"'From Here to Eternity'? Isn't that one of those places that sells clothes for pregnant women?" Regina, who had decided to ignore the possibility that Joyce was due to arrive at any moment, was lightly stroking his chest hair, curling her fingers in the luxuriant mass as she worked her way gradually lower. Cliff had forgotten all about the tell-tale zipper.

"That's Ma-ternity, and please don't even say the word. At your age, that's about all it takes." He sidled a few more inches away from her.

"Don't you like me, Cliff?" She edged closer.

"Sure, sure I like you." He had reached the end of the blanket and was also dangerously close to the end of his rope.

"Well then, why don't you want to make love to me?" She slid the noose around his neck.

"What!"

"I said, I want you to make love to me." The trap door flew open beneath his feet. He struggled for air and control. He needed desperately to regain his footing.

"You're just a kid." He did some quick mental arithmetic. "I'm twenty-eight years older than you, for Christ's sake." Now that was solid ground.

"Well, I'm twenty-eight years younger than you. If it doesn't bother me, why should it bother you?" The ground had less substance than the sand cliffs. It was blown away by logic.

"Look, Regina. You don't understand. You're a lovely girl. A lovely *young* girl. I'm old enough to be your father." Age was his only defense. He pleaded it again.

"I never had a father." She placed long, cool fingers on his thigh.

"Well I'm not applying for the job." He moved her hand away.

"Don't you want me, Cliff?" She reached around and unhooked the top of her bikini, letting it fall slowly forward until her small, pale, perfectly rounded breasts were bared.

"Jesus Christ! That's not fair." His voice was hoarse and he stared longingly at the tempting flesh.

"Touch me," she whispered.

But he didn't move—couldn't move—and she reached out and lifted one of his hands and placed it over her breast. The skin was warm, soft, and quivered slightly with the beat of her heart. The nipple hardened beneath his palm. She regarded him through a forest of glossy black lashes, waiting. Considering she'd never done this before, she thought she was doing pretty good. If only he would take some of the pressure off and react, grab her and pull her into his arms, then they could both get swept away and things would happen naturally, like Mariette had said. She hoped he would do something soon. She was running out of ideas. This was, after all, her first seduction, and she was a bit sketchy about the details.

As he sat there with his hand cupping the small, sweet tit, in the back of his mind a little red light was flashing on and off and a small siren was bleeping "Joyce is coming—Joyce is coming," but it wasn't his mind he was thinking with. That part of him which had taken over the management of the cerebral processes simply asked, "Joyce who?" He leaned forward and kissed Regina hard, and twenty-eight perfectly good reasons—twenty-nine if you counted Belle—flew right out the window.

Matching his tongue thrust for thrust, she pulled him down on top of her, their complete descent to the horizontal blocked only by the picnic basket. He could feel the heat of the sun scorching his back and a different, but equally impelling, heat saturating his crotch. Then, suddenly, the heat went out.

"Excuse me, but I think that's my dinner you're doing it on."

"Joyce!" Cliff sat up and automatically handed Regina her bikini top in the sort of fluid movement that testified to considerable practice at this sort of thing. But Regina smugly refused to put it on and remained lounging on the blanket in all her semi-naked glory.

"You remembered my name." Joyce continued to stand above them. She smiled theatrically, dead from the nose up.

"Uh. I can explain. It's not what you think." Cliff rose to join her.

"How do you know what I think?"

"I mean, things aren't the way they look."

"They aren't? Well let's see, if I said it *looks* like you were trying to resuscitate a drowning victim, then we could rule out that possibility, couldn't we? And if I said it *looks* like you were practising some new kind of exercise routine, then we could rule out that possibility, too."

She pretended to think for a second, tapping the side of her forehead with her index finger. "That would leave only one other alternative, wouldn't it? I mean, to account for the fact that you were lying on top of her with your zipper open."

Cliff looked down at the immovable testament to the obvious conclusion. "It's stuck."

"Going up or going down?"

"Up. No, no. I mean, I was just doing it up when. . . ." Cliff struggled to put the series of events into an appropriate order to convey the correct impression of what had transpired. But, before he could get any further, Joyce turned and walked back up the beach.

"Joyce, wait!"

But Regina reached up and took hold of his hand. Gently but firmly she pulled him down beside her. As he watched Joyce walk away she began to nuzzle his ear. "You know, I think you're just wonderful," she whispered softly.

Cliff heard the magic words and, with one more look at Joyce, he turned to the girl. What choice was there, really, between someone who thought you were full of wonder and someone else who thought you were full of another substance entirely?

Joyce climbed to the top of the cliffs before turning around. When she did, she saw the two of them once again reduced to the horizontal. With a sigh, she continued on her way back to the spa.

"This has not been one of my better days," she said to the little speckled gecko that skittered across the path in front of her. "And that's putting it mildly."

PART THREE

The Outcome

CHAPTER 36

BY THE AFTERNOON OF THE FOLLOWING DAY, Belle had managed to restore the spa to a more or less normal state. With Mildred's help, new staff had been hired and dispatched from New York, the suppliers had been informed that unless they delivered Adolpho's orders immediately, if not sooner, they would no longer find themselves doing business with The Bellissima Corporation for this spa or any future spas, and the telephone service had been restored by a single phone call from Belle to a certain person at AT&T who flew the service man in form Miami on his private helicopter.

The whole place seemed to be suffused with an air of celebration. Adolpho, who was thrilled with the sudden bounty that occupied his kitchen, joyously informed Maxine that he now had *six* different kinds of mushrooms! To which Maxine replied, "Don't talk to me about mushrooms." And when he unpacked a crate and discovered two dozen of the freshest, tiniest Cornish hens he had ever laid eyes on—a little gift from the poultry supplier—he was positively enraptured. Maxine took one look and declared them "A little scrawny, don't you think?"

But it was probably the restoration of the telephone service which had the biggest effect. Harry called to say he was in Barbados and would be over by dinner time, and, shortly after one o'clock, which was a convenient 10 a.m., West Coast time, Cliff got a call from Alvin. He took it out by the pool, partly because he wanted to continue watching Joyce and Regina doing some sort of water exercise with the others that involved large pink and turquoise beach balls and stretching movements that showed off Regina's long, graceful body—and partly because he was just too damn comfortable to move.

He hadn't been expecting to hear from Alvin so soon after their last conversation. Not that he was still pissed off with the offer of the Lucas film. In fact, the idea of playing a rabbit from outer space had long since passed from being insulting to being humorous. It would make for good telling at parties. After all, Joyce had only barely been able to control herself when he had poured out his heart to her about it, and Regina had thought the idea was an absolute riot when he had told the story to her down on the beach. So he was now better able to see the funny side of the situation. Besides, neither of them would have laughed if the idea hadn't been totally incongruous, and that alone made him feel a lot more secure.

The reason he hadn't really been expecting a call from Alvin was simply that Alvin and all he represented had not crossed his mind lately. A wonderful calmness had come over him, blocking out the past and cushioning the future. There was only the present, and he was revelling in it. Nothing could spoil his new-found serenity, not even a call from Alvin Minter.

So he answered the agent's hesitant "Hello" with a warmth and equanimity which surprised the hell out of him.

As a Hollywood agent, it invariably unsettled Alvin when people were suddenly nice to him for no reason. His cousin Morey, who worked for the IRS, had reported the same reaction. So he decided to approach Cliff with caution.

"You alright, Cliff? You sound kind of stoned or something. Been doing a little of the local ganja?" Alvin was a firm believer that every effect had to have an immediate cause. And drugs were always a good excuse for uncharacteristic behavior.

"No, Alvin. I'm just relaxed. 'Mellowed out,' as they used to say. What can I do for you?" Cliff sighed and leaned back in the chaise, contentedly watching as Regina threw the beach ball to Joyce. He smiled to himself. They had both been so good for him in their individual little ways. Of course Joyce was still pissed off, but he was confident he could work round that. Alvin and his world seemed far away.

"It's what I can do you for you, Cliffy old buddy."

"Look, Alvin, do me a favor, tell me what it is, straight up, and don't give me the big sell. If I like it, I'll think about it. If I don't, you are not going to be able to change my mind, O.K.? This is a new Cliff Eastman you are talking to."

"O.K. Cliff. Sure. I can do that." Alvin sounded momentarily discombobulated. Half of his business was selling people things they didn't want. Actors to studios, scripts to actors, deals to producers. So you *had* to dress it up. It was the only way he knew how to do business. Having to tell it like it was was almost as bad as having to tell the truth. It left you very little room to maneuver.

But he cleared his throat and plunged ahead. "Well, here goes. Uh, let me ask you something, Cliff, have you ever considered acting?"

"Are you trying to be funny, Alvin?"

"No, no, no. I mean stage acting. Broadway. The bright lights! It's a chance for you to do something different. Get out of L.A. for a while. Stretch yourself a bit. I thought of you right away when the offer came up."

"Funny you should mention it, Alvin, but that's exactly what I have been thinking about. I want to do some serious acting. Forty-seven isn't over the hill in the theatre." He pronounced it the-a-tah. "I could still have a future there. Besides, I'd like to spend some time in New York. Why do you ask? Have you got something concrete? Something without fur, perhaps?"

Alvin ignored the last comment. "Concrete as Gibraltar, my friend. It's already a hit show, so you're halfway there, right? And they're looking for a replacement for the guy who's playing the romantic lead right now. Apparently he's had enough of treading the boards for a while and NBC has been courting him for a television series, so there's going to be a vacancy. I already put in a good word for you, Cliff. The producer practically shook my hand, he was so excited. Says you'd be perfect for the part, especially with your background, the kind of movies you've done. The whole romantic-lover schtick. He's already talking about how he's going to publicize it if you take the part. I've set up a meeting next week in New York for the three of us to sit down and kick the shit around."

"Sounds interesting, Alvin. You may get back into my good books yet. Now, which show is it? Something Shakespearean? I've always liked the idea of doing 'The Taming of The Shrew.'"

Alvin hedged. "Well, it's not exactly Shakespeare, Cliff. It's a musical. Your part has a lot of singing, but your voice is in pretty good shape and it shouldn't take too long for a good voice coach to get you up to par."

"A musical?" Cliff was trying to think of which musicals were currently on Broadway. "A Chorus Line," of course. But he was definitely too old for that and, besides, there were no romantic male "leads," per se. And "Evita" kept coming back all the time, but he really couldn't see himself as Peron and certainly not Che. Too stuffy and too scruffy, in that order. Maybe it was one of those avant-garde London shows by Webber or Rice. Maybe he could still learn to roller skate.

"Alvin, I don't hear you volunteering any information. You want me to ask the question, 'Which musical?' first, before you tell me?"

"Uh, Cliff, before I tell you, just do me a favor, O.K.?"

"Uh-oh, I smell a rabbit. No guarantees on the favor, Alvin."

"No, no it's nothing like that. Just promise me you won't say No right away. Think it over. It really is a good part, great show, terrific music. You could do a lot worse than say Yes."

"Why do I get the feeling that I'm not going to like this, Alvin?" He sighed into the phone. "Alright, then, let's have it."

"La Cage aux Folles."

Cliff gripped the phone tighter. In his mind it was Alvin's neck.

"La Cage aux Folles!"

"Yeah, and you would be playing the part of Georges. He's the butch one."

"You call that a romantic lead, you asshole!" shouted Cliff across the miles.

"Calm down, calm down. It's a good part, Cliff. Seriously. And they're talking about making an American movie version of the play. You would certainly have a good shot at that. And besides, what do you really care if your leading lady is a man? You've been out with some really ugly broads in the years I've known you, Cliff. If anything, this'll be an improvement." Alvin ran out of steam.

"Look, Alvin, I know you're trying, but I don't want people to think I'm getting heavily into pastels in my declining years, if you get my drift. I mean, if I have to have a reputation, I'd rather be known as a dirty old man."

"What?"

"Never mind."

The agent tried another tack. "Cliff, for Christ's sake. You're a forty-seven year old man who's never been married. What do you think people have been saying about you all these years? That you're just waiting for Ms. Right?"

"It's true."

"True? What's truth got to do with what people think?"

"You have a point there, I guess."

"Sure, Cliff, sure." Alvin could sense, even long-distance, that he was gaining ground. "Look, you've got the name, so why not play the game? And if it really bothers you, we'll make sure that you get fixed up with a lot of good-looking broads so you can get your picture in the *Daily News* and you won't be lonely."

"That's alright. I can handle my own social life."

"Well, then, what's it gonna be? Do I tell Gerry that you'll see him next week in New York, or what?"

Cliff was playing pros and cons. It wasn't a part he would have chosen if he had his druthers. But once you got past the sex thing, it was a good show. He had seen the L.A. version with Gene Barry playing Georges. And nobody thought he was a little light in the loafers. And he did want to spend some time in New York.

"Cliff, I gotta have an answer today," prompted Alvin.

He thought for a moment longer. "O.K., Alvin. Tell Gerry I'll be there."

Then he hung up and sat there considering the possibilities. It could be just what he needed. Besides, Regina lived in New York. And so did Joyce.

CHAPTER 37

CATHY WAS ALSO PLEASED to be in touch with the outside world again. She had made a decision and she wanted to call Michael and tell him about it, with the emphasis on "tell."

So, after the afternoon weigh-in, which confirmed that she had lost another two pounds, for a total of five in all, she went back to her room and placed the call to Tibbermore, Tavitch and Stewart.

A rapid combination of clicks and whirrs signaled that the correct series of electrical pulses was racing madly through the long-distance system, and, in a moment, she got through to the switchboard.

"Good morning, T, T & S," chirruped a too-cheery voice.

"Mr. Stewart's office, please."

"Just one moment, I'll connect you."

But when she got through to Michael's secretary and before she had a chance to identify herself, she was informed, in the somewhat superior tones used by those who occupy the inner sanctums of power at whatever level, that "Mr. Stewart was in conference" and could not possibly be disturbed. Cathy uttered a meek "Thank you," and hung up.

But no sooner was the receiver resting in its cradle than she snatched it up again and redialed T, T & S. The new, improved Cathy was not about to give up that easily.

"Mr. Stewart's office, can I help you?"

"I just called for Mr. Stewart."

"Oh. And I just told you that Mr. Stewart is in conference and cannot be disturbed."

Cathy took a deep breath. "Well, you go and tell *Mr.* Stewart that *Mrs.* Stewart is on the line and that I want to speak to him NOW."

"But, Mrs. Stewart."

"NOW," said Cathy, gripping the receiver tightly, her palms wet with perspiration and anxious audacity.

"Very well," sniffed the secretary, as she put Cathy on hold.

Like good secretaries everywhere, Michael's secretary had long ago learned that orders from the boss were automatically transcended by orders from the boss's wife. It was a typical case of being between a rock and a hard place. Either way, she would get reprimanded for interrupting him. It was only a question of when. Now, because she had, or tomorrow because she hadn't and he had had to listen to an earful over dinner.

A whiny rendition of "Greensleeves" filtered down the polyoptic cable and into Cathy's left ear. She drummed her fingers on the table. It was a gesture that was part impatience and part fear. She knew he would be upset.

In a few moments Michael came on the line. "This had better be important, Cathy. I was right in the middle of a big presentation." His voice was tinged with threat and heavy with hints of husbandly annoyance.

"Where have you been?" She forgot her carefully prepared speech and said the first thing that popped into her mind.

"What do you mean, where have I been?"

"I've called you three times at home and you're never there. All I ever get is the babysitter. Where have you been?" she said, repeating the litany of wives everywhere.

"Look, Cathy, I don't have to give you a blow-by-blow account of my whereabouts every second since you've been gone. I've been out most nights with clients. You should know that. I've been *working.*"

He emphasized the word "working" to delineate what to him were the obvious contrasts in how they had each been spending their time.

"I've been working too, Michael." Cathy refused to be put down, after all her efforts. "You won't believe it, but I've already lost five pounds."

"Five pounds. Great. That's really great, Cathy. You pulled me out of a meeting that could net the company ten million over the next three years to tell me that you have lost five pounds. I'll tell that to Tibbermore. He'll probably make me chairman of the board." He exaggerated the sarcasm to let her see how ridiculously trivial her achievement was, compared to the one on which he was working.

"I thought you would be pleased," she said weakly, disappointed that he didn't see what an important victory it was for her.

"Look, Cathy. I am pleased, really." His voice softened. He wanted to placate her. It would save time, and he wanted to get back to his meeting. "I know you want to lose some weight, but it's no big deal. I already told you, I don't care if you do or not. I like my Big Mama."

"It *is* a big deal . . . to me. And Michael, please, I've asked you not to call me that. I don't want to be anybody's Big Mama. I want to be the way I was." She hesitated. "I want to stay on another week here. I think that by then I will have made real progress, not only with the diet but with how I feel about myself as. . . ."

He cut her off. "Absolutely out of the question." He said it flatly.

"But why? Why is it out of the question? We can afford it. You have someone to look after the children and someone to take care of the house while I'm away. You don't *need* me to be there, Michael."

"Cathy, you are my wife. I want you home. You are the mother of my three children. We all want you to come home."

Cathy felt tears begin to sting her eyes. "But what about what *I* want?"

"Don't be so selfish, Cathy." He sounded exasperated. "The children and I all miss you. Think about how we feel for once." And then he added. "It's not like another week is going to make any difference. So what if you lose another five pounds. You'll only gain it all back. Cathy, you know what you're like with these diets."

"Stop saying that! I've changed. And I'm not being selfish. You are.

It's always what you want. Michael wants this and Michael wants that. When you wanted to trade in the Oldsmobile for a red BMW, did I say anything, even though it's very difficult to fit all of us in the new car? When you work late and go out with clients and don't come home till eleven or later, do I complain?" The tears subsided and she could feel her face burning with years of pent-up anger.

"Cathy, I thought we agreed that my job was very important to the welfare of this family. I work like a dog to make a good life for you and the kids. It isn't easy, you know, being the breadwinner. As for the car, I need that kind of image in this business. To be really successful you have to project a successful image."

"That's a crock, Michael and you know it. You got the car because *you* wanted it. You love your job, and the reason you can spend so much time on *your* career is because I make it possible by doing all the other things, like running your home and raising your children." She was letting it all out now, all the unspoken frustrations of her marriage.

"I work like a dog, too. But you never stop to consider that, do you? You never think that my hard work entitles me to any special treatment. Everything in our whole marriage has been designed around what *you* want, only you. Can't you see that?" She knew she was shouting now, but she didn't care.

"Cathy, I think you've said enough." His voice held the cold, hard edge of disapproval that once would have been enough to silence her.

"Oh you do, do you? Well I don't think I've even started yet. It's time for me to think about what I want for a change, and I want to stay another week."

"Don't raise your voice to me, Catherine," He said coolly, in the carefully measured tones usually employed for talking to hysterical children and disobedient pets. "I expect you to come home at the end of the week and that's my final word on the subject."

Cathy suddenly felt herself growing smaller, losing ground, knuckling under. Her short burst of rage was so uncharacteristic that it had unsettled her, thrown her off her course. She had so little courage to draw on, and she had just about used up her reserve. Then she caught sight of herself in the full-length mirror. For the first time, she saw a noticeable improvement. She smiled at her reflection. "Don't let him bully you," said the Cathy in the mirror. "If you give in to him now, you'll be giving in for the rest of your life."

"Catherine, did you hear what I said? I expect you to come home at the end of the week and that's final." The sudden sound of his voice startled her out of her musing.

"Yes, Michael," she said slowly. "I heard what you said." She was back to her normal decibel rate, but her voice was different, firmer. "And now I have something to say to you." She paused, gathering the remaining shreds of her courage around her. "Don't bother going to the airport on Saturday, because you'll have a long wait!"

She hung up, slowly and carefully laying the receiver into its cradle. There was no need to slam it down. For the first time in a long time, Cathy Stewart was in perfect control.

CHAPTER 38

IT WAS LATE AFTERNOON when Joyce had finally finished the last of the spa activities outlined on her card. It had been an exhausting two weeks, in more ways than one, she thought, remembering the little scene on the beach the day before. But, all things considered, and no one was more surprised at this than she was, she had never felt or looked better. At the back of her mind she was even playing around with the idea of doing a follow-up story on the spa in a few months time. If Harry should go for it.

Feeling relaxed and pleasantly tired now, she decided to go for a last swim before the sun moved off the pool area. God knows how long it would be before she had the opportunity again, sunshine and swimming pools being a rare combination in New York City. So, after changing into her bathing suit and noticing with satisfaction that tan lines had actually begun to delineate the boundaries of the suit across the tops of her breasts and thighs, she grabbed a towel, slipped into her cork-soled mules, and slapped contentedly down to the pool.

Heading straight for the deep end, she threw her towel over the arm of one of the molded white resin chairs that were scattered about in groups of three or four beside their matching tables, and kicked off her shoes.

A moment later, as she balanced on the edge of the pool, dipping a tentative toe into water that was as warm as a tide pool on a hot day, she looked up to see Cliff grinning at her from the other side of the pool.

"Still can't decide whether or not to take the plunge, eh?" He started to walk around the near end of the pool toward her.

She moved away from the edge and slipped back into her sandals. "Go away. I don't want to talk to you."

But he kept on coming, looking even more tanned and more gorgeous in his tennis whites than he had the day she had first seen him at the airport.

"I can't say that I blame you for being upset." He was standing right in front of her now, flashing his teeth and his eyes at the same time. "You and I do seem to have a hard time getting together, don't we?"

"You've got a lot of nerve. You were the one who was . . . who was. . . ." She sought for an appropriate turn of phrase. "Thrashing around like a grunion."

He laughed. "I wasn't thrashing. And what's a grunion?" He was taking this all far too lightly as far as Joyce was concerned, and his attitude infuriated her all the more.

"Maybe you can get Annette Funicello to look it up for you in one of her school books, next time you're playing Beach Blanket Bingo," she said acidly.

"Joyce, I think in all fairness you should know that what happened yesterday was not my idea."

"No, I could see that the thought never crossed your mind. Next thing you'll be telling me that she raped you."

"Look, she was there when I came out of the water and. . . ."

"Don't tell me . . . she forced herself on you."

"In a manner of speaking. She took off her top and. . . ."

"And you lost all control."

"You don't know what it's like to be a man. Sex is not always a matter for logical debate. A rising. . . ."

"Don't give me that bullshit about 'a rising prick has no conscience.'

That's just an excuse to avoid responsibility. Now, if you don't mind, I'd like to go for a swim." She kicked off her shoes once more and moved past him toward the water.

"Joyce?"

Balancing on the edge of the pool, she looked over her shoulder. "Maybe if I translate this into Californese you'll get the message better. 'Call me sometime. We'll do lunch.' Or, as we say in New York, 'Get lost, buster.'" And she dove into the deep end.

After swimming a few laps she climbed out and returned to her chair. Cliff was sitting on her towel, absently twirling his tennis racket.

"Why are you still here?" she asked, pushing a handful of wet hair out of her eyes.

"I wanted to tell you—after I apologized—that I'm going to be in New York for a while. There's this Broadway show and. . . ."

"You mean I'm not going to have the comfort of a continent between us? Can I have my towel, please?"

He got up and gave her the towel. "Can I have your phone number?"

She was furiously rubbing her hair with the towel. "Cliff, I really don't know how to make this any clearer. I don't want to see you. I don't want to hear from you. I don't want to know what city you're in."

"But you do want to go to bed with me."

"What!" She stopped rubbing, the towel half-covering her face.

"You're jealous about what happened yesterday. That means you still feel a certain attraction to me. Besides, you said it yourself. If I may quote, 'I don't want to go to bed with them, I want to go to bed with you.' You haven't changed your mind about that. It's obvious." He nodded toward the top of her bathing suit.

From beneath the veil of towel she looked down and saw immediately what he was referring to. "The water was cold. And I wouldn't go to bed with you . . . if. . . ." She tried to come up with a suitably remote set of circumstances.

Cliff looked at his watch. "Whoa! I've got a game in five minutes. Gonna try out the new pro." He picked up the tennis racket. "I'll give you a call at the magazine as soon as I get settled in. You can show me around New York." He started to walk away and then turned back. "Oh Joyce, by the way, after you left yesterday . . . we ate the chicken."

Joyce pulled the towel from her head and stared after him. Did that mean that he hadn't . . . ? That they didn't . . . ?

"Joyce! Hey, Joyce!" She spun around at the sound of her name being called. Harry and Maxine were walking, arms around waists, toward her.

While she watched, stunned both by Cliff's last comment and this overt and unexpected display of affection between two people who she had assumed could not be trusted in the same room together, Maxine looked up at Harry, eyes glittering, lips smiling and parted, and he looked down at her and gave her waist a little extra squeeze. They were acting just like lovers.

Joyce put the wet towel down and then picked it up again, suddenly very conscious of the skimpiness of the bathing suit. She held the towel bunched up in front of her, trying to conceal what was so obviously unconcealed. Salome and the dance of the seven beach towels, she thought, wishing she had six more.

"Joyce. We've been looking for you," called Maxine cheerfully. Her arm was still draped possessively around Harry's waist, and she leaned her weight full against him and flashed a triumphant smile as they came to a stop in front of Joyce.

Harry, suddenly uncomfortable with maintaining this cosy little domestic arrangement in front of Joyce, relaxed his grip on Maxine and moved half a step to the right, stuffing both hands into the pockets of his grey slacks. They were, thought Joyce, noting this change of attitude with a small pang of satisfaction, part of the suit that he usually wore to the office. He still had on the white dress shirt, too. But the sleeves had been rolled up to accommodate the climate. Only the tie and the jacket were missing, and they were probably lying on the bed in Maxine's room.

"Joycee. How's it going?" Harry gave the greeting matter-of-factly to a point somewhere over her left shoulder. She recognized with surprise that the sight of her in a bathing suit was making him uncomfortable. To counteract this, he was making an effort to talk to her without actually looking at her.

Sensing his discomfort gave her more confidence. She threw the towel casually over the arm of the chair.

"You look uh . . . really uh well, Joyce." Now that was a good neutral word. Well. It could be applied with equanimity to aging relatives, people you hadn't seen since high school, or half-naked employees. And Harry embraced it with the relief with which a drowning man clasps a life preserver.

"Thanks. I've had a very healthy couple of weeks." She paused. "You two look pretty happy. Everything must be O.K."

"O.K. isn't the word," replied Maxine. "Harry and I have had a long talk. We made an important decision today, and we owe it all to you." Maxine glowed up at Harry, who smiled down and slipped a tentative arm around her shoulders.

"I owe you one for this Joycee. I mean it," said Harry, with gruff good humor.

"Well, it certainly is a relief to know that you didn't let my advice on the subject of marriage interfere with yours," said Joyce, slipping back into her mules once more and retrieving the towel. "I'm not sure I could handle the responsibility of breaking up a marriage, especially the marriage of someone who signs my paychecks. Anyway, what do I know about relationships . . . or marriage." She laughed self-consciously and looked around, wondering how to escape gracefully from this tableau before she ran out of mea culpas.

"Oh, but you were absolutely right about us, Joyce." Maxine put a restraining hand on her arm. "Wasn't she, Harry?"

"Of course she was right. I don't pay her to be wrong."

"But I thought you two had made up."

"We did." Maxine gave Harry a conspiratorial smile. "We made up our minds to get a divorce." She laughed then. "And it's all thanks to you."

"You mean you're going to get a divorce and you're both happy about it?" Joyce looked at Harry for confirmation.

He nodded. We both decided that we like each other too much to stay married. After all, why bury a good relationship under a bad marriage?" He said with a grin.

"But, it's not supposed to be like this. I mean, you're supposed to hate each other and fight and get lawyers and. . . ."

"You've been reading too many magazine articles," replied Maxine. "Harry and I had a good marriage, and now that it's over, we're going to have a good divorce. Bradley was right; it's time we both got on with our lives." She slipped her arm from around his waist. "I have to go. I've got an appointment at the hairdresser. I was thinking about having some streaks put in. It was Adolpho's idea. What do you think, Joyce?"

"Streaks would be nice." Joyce felt that this was all too urbane for her. One minute they were talking about divorce and the next, the issue was hair-coloring.

"I think you're right. Besides I'm going to have to look my best if I'm about to be 'available' again." She gave Harry a nudge. "You might just change your mind about this divorce when you see the new me," she added teasingly.

"No way. I'm not about to go through another of Bradley's 'lunches,' and I'd have to do that if he heard I was dating his mother."

Maxine laughed. Private joke, thought Joyce, who was beginning to feel she had just been transported into the second act of a Noel Coward play.

"See you both at dinner." Maxine started off toward the beauty salon and then turned and spoke to Harry. "Don't forget to ask her about you know what, Harry."

"Don't worry. I won't."

They both watched until she disappeared behind one of the ubiquitous hedges. And then Joyce sank down on the chair. She had run through so many emotions in the last few minutes that she was starting to feel a little weak.

"Maxine's a fine woman. But I'm glad it's over," said Harry, turning around. "You O.K. Joyce?" He sat in the chair opposite her.

"Just getting my bearings. I'll be alright in a minute."

Harry crossed his legs. "Sure is a nice place here." He looked around to give her time to sort out her bearings, whatever they were.

"You look really good, Joycee. Different. Younger. Must be all that sunshine and salt air.

"You look like you could do with a little of that yourself, Harry."

"Yeah, you're right. I plan to take better care of myself from now on. I've got to. There's nobody else to do it for me anymore."

"How's everything at work?" Joyce desperately wanted to talk about something she understood. Something normal.

Harry sat back with a sigh and stretched his legs out in front of him. "O.K. I guess, except for Naomi."

"What's up with Naomi? She should be back any day now. Her fifteen weeks' maternity leave is about up."

"Yeah well, it is and it isn't."

"What does that mean?"

"She got pregnant again."

"Again? You're kidding? I didn't think that's what they had in mind when they coined the phrase 'maternity leave.'"

"Tell that to Naomi. With the new baby and another one in the oven, she's decided to stay home and play wifey for a while."

"Sounds like she already played that game once too often," said Joyce marveling at the how and why of it all. "Is she planning to come back to work later on, or not?"

"It doesn't look like it."

"So who's going to write the food section and the cooking column?" asked Joyce, mentally crossing her fingers and praying, "Not me, please not me."

"Well, Joycee, I was going to talk to you about that when we got back, but since you brought it up. . . ."

"Oh Harry, please not me. Please don't ask me to write the food stuff as well. Writing food stuff is boring. Harry, really boring."

He sat forward in his chair. "Ask you? Who's asking you?"

"Isn't that what you were just going to say?"

"No, it isn't. So just shut up and listen for a minute. I know you don't want to take over for Naomi. You can't boil water, as I remember, so you'd be lousy at the job anyway."

"Thanks a lot. And I can, too, boil water. I just choose not to."

"Alright, don't get on your high horse. I'm letting you off the hook, remember? As it happens, I already have somebody else in mind to do Naomi's job. She's a great cook. Lots of experience. Needs the job."

"Can she write?"

"I don't think she is going to be up for a Pulitzer next year, but she knows what a verb is."

"Well, who is it? Somebody already on staff?"

He was hedging. "Not exactly."

"Well what, exactly?"

"Maxine."

"Maxine? You want your soon-to-be-ex-wife to come to work for *Destiny?*"

"I know it sounds a little strange, but she knows her stuff when it comes to food, and she's going to need a job. I can't afford to support the two of us living apart in the style to which she has been accustomed. Not in Manhattan, anyway. So, when you think about it, this is the perfect solution, right?"

But Joyce was shaking her head. "Harry, this solution is a long way from perfect. I'll admit we need somebody and right away, but think about the down side for a minute, the way you two used to fight. . . ."

He held up his hand. "*Used* to fight is right. That's when we were married. Now we're getting divorced, we won't have anything to fight about anymore. And it'll be good for her. She needs to get out in the world, have a life of her own, meet people. You even said that."

"Did I?"

"That's what she said."

"O.K. O.K." What did she do, memorize every word? thought Joyce. "But when I said it, I didn't think that she was going to be working for me. Cooking *is* one of my departments, you know."

"So what's the problem? If you can work for me, then why can't my ex-wife work for you?"

"Oh Harry, sometimes you amaze me, you really do." She stood up and walked to the edge of the pool, trying to see all the way to the bottom. Too bad drowning was out of the question. She was too good a swimmer.

"Joyce, what's the matter?" He came up behind her.

"Life is just too complicated, Harry. I keep trying to make it simple, but it just gets more and more complex." She shook her head.

"Are you talking about that guy I saw you talking to? The one with the tan."

"Partly."

"He's that actor, right?" Harry stumbled around trying to find the right words to ask the question which had been bugging him for the last few days. "Are you and him. . . . That is . . . are you two. . . . Jeez, Joycee, you know what I mean."

"I know what you mean. What I don't know is why you're so interested."

"Interested. Who said I was interested? It's just that . . . well, now that I'm gonna be a single man again, I thought maybe you and I could have dinner one night. You know, I'll pick up a pizza and a bottle of wine and come over to your place and. . . ."

"We did that already, remember, when you were still a married man."

"Oh yeah, right." Harry was at a loss for words. It had been a quarter of a century since he last asked a girl out for a date, and he was trying to remember how it went.

But Joyce stepped in and filled the void. "Harry, if you want to have dinner one night, we could always go out."

"Out? You mean sort of like a date?"

"Sort of."

Harry smiled. It was easier than he remembered.

Joyce continued. "You know, there's this terrific new place up in the East Seventies, supposed to be the be-all and end-all of the new restaurants. . . ."

The smile faded from Harry's face. "You don't mean The American Grill?"

"How did you know?"

"Somehow I just had a feeling being single wasn't going to be as easy as it looked."

EPILOGUE

"YOU LOOK HAPPY," said Trixie, putting one caller on hold and banishing another into telephone limbo as she accidentally pushed the wrong button on the console phone. "God, I hate this new telephone system," she complained miserably.

Joyce waited for her to finish grumbling. "Is he in?"

Trixie nodded. "Mmmm-hmmm." Then she took a quick look around and lowered her voice to a more conspiratorial level. "Gee, things sure are a lot quieter around here since he and Mrs. Kraft, I mean Ms. Morris, decided to get a you-know-what."

"The word is 'divorce,' Trixie, and I don't think it's really any of your business." And with that Joyce walked over and knocked on Harry's door, and then, not bothering to wait for an answer, she opened it and went into the office.

"What's with her?" sniffed the receptionist, who had been hoping for a tidbit or two from Joyce to spice up her update on the report about Maxine and Harry getting a you-know-what.

"Hi," said Joyce softly. "You busy?"

He looked up from his desk and grinned like a schoolboy with a crush on the teacher when he saw that it was her. "So-so. Can you stay a minute?" He stood up. "Here, sit down." He gestured to the chair on the opposite side of his desk.

But, as usual, Joyce ignored the gesture and sat on the couch instead. Harry, sighing with the resignation of a man who knows he cannot win, came around in front of the desk and half-stood, half-leaned against the corner of it. A new set of protocols was being established here, and he was still unsure of just how to mix his new role as lover with his old role as boss. So he folded his arms across his chest and thought about how good she looked in blue. After a moment he broke the silence. "That was a great dinner you cooked last night."

Joyce raised her eyebrows. "Not bad for someone who can't boil water."

"Look, I already apologized for that, didn't I? And how did you know braised beef was my favorite, anyway?"

"I asked Maxine."

"You asked my *wife* what to cook me for dinner?"

"Of course. Who else would know? I suppose I could have asked your mother, but it's hard to get a medium on such short notice," she said, teasing him.

"Was she upset? You know, about me and you. You and me." He unfolded his arms and stuffed his hands into his pockets. He didn't know if Maxine might be inclined to make things difficult.

"Harry, we only had dinner. We didn't elope. And anyway, she's really very happy being the almost-ex-Mrs. Kraft."

He relaxed a little. There were times he had to keep reminding himself that his marriage to Maxine was just a technicality now, waiting only for the legal decree to reduce it to the realm of memory. It was O.K. for him to go out with Joyce. It was O.K. for him to stay home with her, too, for that matter. It really was."

Oh, I almost forgot." Joyce reached into her pocket and pulled out a small brown paper bag. "Here."

"What is it?" He reached for the proffered sack.

"Your tie. You left it behind this morning."

"Oh. I wondered what I did with it. Thanks." He spoke a little too casually as he leaned back and opened the top drawer of the desk and then flipped the incriminating piece of evidence inside. Then he slid the drawer shut and fidgeted against the desk, changing his weight from one leg to the other. "Uh, Joyce, about last night. . . ."

"What about it, Harry?" She gave him a long, slow smile that said volumes of things he had never been able to say to Maxine.

"I just wanted to say one thing . . . uh . . . Jesus, I'm so out of practice with all this morning-after stuff."

"That's O.K., you don't have to say anything. We both know how it was. No editorial comment needed."

Harry let out a sigh of relief. "Boy, that was easier than I thought. I didn't know if I should send flowers or. . . ."

"Just relax, alright?" She stood up and came over to the desk, surprised at now effortlessly they could fit their new relationship into their old circumstances. "You can save the flowers for next time. Now, before you ask where the hell is it, I finished the piece on the spa." She tossed the file folder on top of the pile of papers that already occupied Harry's desk and the floor in the immediate vicinity.

"There shouldn't be any trouble getting it typeset in time for the May issue. Wanna read it now?"

"You mean you *want* me to read it now. Which means that you think it's pretty good."

"You got it."

He picked up the folder and opened it to the first page. "O.K. Sit down." But Joyce remained standing. Harry sighed and began to read. "They call it spa-ing. It's the eighties answer to whatever ails you. Whether you want to shake off some stress or shape up some muscles; work on your attitude or your amplitude; tune up your body or tune out your life for a while, the spa is the place for you . . ."

He paused. "The opening's good."

"So's the rest."

He read on silently then, except for hmmm-hmmming and uhhuhing occasionally. He had picked up a pencil, and every now and then made a slash or a squiggle in the curious language that only editors and typesetters understand.

Joyce shifted her weight from one foot to the other. She could tell he liked the piece. He hadn't looked up yet. Nor had he uttered even one incredulous epithet. Finally, he closed the folder, scribbled something across the front and set it aside. Then he looked up.

"Not bad. Nice balance of information and human interest. You did O.K., Joyce, and now you can congratulate me."

"Congratulate *you?* What for?"

"For thinking up this idea in the first place, and for picking you to do it, in the second place. I am a terrific editor."

"Congratulations," said Joyce flatly.

Harry let out a rumbling, good-natured laugh. "Come on, I was only kidding. You did a good job. A real good job. Now, how about we have a little lunch to celebrate?"

"Sorry, Harry, lunch is booked."

"Dinner?"

Joyce shook her head.

Harry thought for a minute. "Joyce, this is probably none of my business but. . . ."

"You're right, Harry. It *is* none of your business."

He looked hurt. Joyce relented. "Look, you've been married almost all your adult life. You're used to having one woman around. It's cosy, comfortable, secure. I understand that. But I've been single all my life. I'm not used to having one man around all the time. I'm not sure I'm ready for the responsibility of that kind of relationship. Do you understand what I'm saying?"

Harry hunched his shoulders. "Sure, I get your drift. You want to see other guys. No big deal." But his voice gave his feelings away.

Joyce went and stood beside him and, placing her hand on his forearm, gave him a gentle kiss on the cheek. "Harry, we have something very nice going on here. It might develop into something more. It might not. Let's give it some time. O.K.? See how it goes." And then she smiled up at him urging him to agree. She knew that he was still mentally married and that it would be very easy for him to just switch "wives," but becoming a stand-in for Maxine was not the way she envisioned herself. Let him get used to being single for a while. It would give them both the time they needed to adjust.

After a moment or two, he made an attempt at a grin. "Yeah, I suppose you're right. You're always damn right. Now how about getting outta here so I can get on with some work."

"I'm gone." Joyce headed toward the door and then turned around. "Brunch on Sunday?"

"Brunch?" Harry said the word as though it were part of a foreign language.

"If you're going to learn to be single, you have to learn brunch. It's required." She opened the door. "Well?"

"O.K. brunch it is. But no weird food, alright?"

"No weird food, I promise."

When Joyce got back to her office, Michelle was firing off rounds of sneezes like an unrestrained Uzi.

"Look at these! Aaaaa-chooo! What am I going to do? Aaaa-choo! Where am I going to put them? Aaaa-chooo, Aaa-Aaaaa-choo! Woses make me sneeze." She finished with a plaintive snuffle, and fished a Kleenex out of her purse.

"A vase in my office would be nice," suggested Joyce, picking a little white card from atop one of the several bunches of long-stemmed red roses that occupied Michelle's desk.

"Easy for you to say. Aaaa-choo! We're a magazine, not a florist. Where am I going to find enough vases for all these?"

"You'll figure it out. And look at it this way, the sooner they're out of your office, the sooner you'll stop sneezing." Joyce started to go into her office. She wanted to be alone when she read the card. She guessed who it was from. But Michelle stopped her.

"Wait. That's not all. This came just before you got back." She reached under the desk and handed Joyce a large box wrapped in white tissue paper and tied with a white satin ribbon.

"What's this?" asked Joyce.

"You could open it and see," coaxed the curious Michelle.

"You mean I could open it and *you* could see." But she began to tear at the wrapping paper while Michelle hovered behind her, trying to stifle the urge to sneeze.

"Well, what is it? It's too big for jewellery. Too small for a fur. Ooooo, I can't stand it. Hurry up!" she pleaded. "Aa-Aa-aa-choo!"

"Just let me get the lid off and we'll both know," said Joyce, lifting the lid off the box. Inside, lying on a bed of tissue paper, were a diving mask and a pair of flippers.

Michelle looked disappointed. "I don't get it."

"But I do," replied Joyce and, smiling to herself, she took the card and the box into her office and closed the door.

Carefully, as though she were dealing with potentially volatile objects, she placed the card and the box on her desk and then, sliding into her chair, she sat staring at them for a few moments. If she opened the card, wouldn't she be putting herself in the position of having to make a choice? Cliff or Harry. On the other hand, if she threw it into the garbage pail, her life would go on in much the same fashion as it always had—except perhaps for the peripheral addition of her new relationship with Harry and whatever it might develop into. This, she reflected, was one of life's turning points. She took a deep breath and picked up the card. But before she could open it, Michelle came in bearing two vases thick with roses.

"I'm dying to know what this is all about," she said pointedly. "But I won't ask . . . unless you want me to."

"You're not sneezing." replied Joyce.

"I took an anti-histamine, and I can take a hint. So where do you want me to put these?"

"Wherever," answered Joyce absently, fondling the little white envelope in her right hand.

Michelle placed one vase on the desk and one on top of the filing cabinet and, with a parting look at her bemused boss, she left the room.

The minute she was gone, Joyce tore open the card and read the inscription.

"Just in case you decide to take the plunge," it read.

And it was signed. "Cliff," with a P.S. "My number is 555-7492."

Well, I was right, thought Joyce. This has all the earmarks of a definite turning point. All I have to do is pick up that phone and dial . . . or toss this into the trash.

"Well mother," she said to the empty room "you usually have an opinion at times like this. What do you think? What should I do? Who should I choose?

"Choose? What's to choose? Harry is a nice man, a decent man. He has a job. The other one has a life that reads like the *National Enquirer*. His résumé is *People* magazine!"

Joyce looked at the card again and then at the contents of the box. And then she thought about Harry.

"It doesn't bother you that Harry's been married to someone else?" she asked the voice.

"Pssssh!" said her mother's voice. "So he's second-hand. Look at it this way—at least he's house-trained. You won't have to break him in. You could have a future with a man like Harry."

"A future," mused Joyce. "It might be nice. But still. . . ."

"Take it from me, you're thirty-eight. If you don't start making a future soon, it'll be too late. Believe me, a man who can give you a future is just what you need. This other one, this actor, is just a passing fancy, a little excitement, a few fireworks. And you can't live on fireworks. Six months, a year, and what'll you have? A few memories, that's all."

Joyce put the phone back into the cradle. "Maybe you're right." If she wanted to, she could make this thing with Harry into something more. Something permanent, maybe. It would be so easy. So comfortable. . . .

"Of course I'm right. I'm your mother."

So predictable . . . so secure. So completely different from whatever she might have with Cliff. So, what was the problem? And what was wrong with a few fireworks while you're waiting for the future to unfold? She picked up the phone again.

"What're you doing?" demanded her mother's voice.

"Take it easy, mother. Harry may be the man to make a future with but, until then, Cliff is the man to make one terrific memory." And she began to dial.

A few minutes later she dragged her purse out of the bottom drawer, put the lid on the box, tucked it under her arm, and left the office.

"Cancel my lunch," she called over her shoulder to Michelle as she started through the double glass doors. "If anybody calls, tell them I'll be back later."

"Where are you going?" asked Michelle, eyeing the box.

"Swimming," replied Joyce, as the doors swung shut behind her.